The Resistance

"The fight against enslavement and death, the resistance to brutality and annihilation, had to be conducted separately by the resources of each underground organization, and without any kind of assurance that a trace of the deeds or even the existence of any particular resistance group would be left on this earth."

—Meyer Barkai

The narratives, in diaries, memoirs and other documents, that had been concealed by their authors in secret places, were found after the war and collected at the Ghetto Fighters' House in Israel. Writer and lecturer Barkai made several trips there and translated these courageous and inspiring narratives for this volume.

THE GHETTO FIGHTERS

Translated and edited
by Meyer Barkai

This is an authorized abridgement.

BELMONT TOWER BOOKS ● NEW YORK CITY

A BELMONT TOWER BOOK

Published by
Tower Publications, Inc.
Two Park Avenue
New York, New York 10016

Library of Congress Catalog Card Number 62-11331

Printed in U.S.A.

Published by special arrangement with
J. B. Lippincott Company

The Ghetto Fighters is an edited and translated version of
Seifer Milchamot Hagetaot, edited by Izhak Zuckerman and
Moshe Basak, published in Hebrew in Tel Aviv, Israel, by the
Ghetto Fighters' House and Kibbutz Hameuchad.

EDITOR'S NOTE

All the material in this volume is based on authentic documents written by eyewitnesses and participants in the Jewish resistance movement during the period of Nazi occupation in the lands of Eastern Europe. Most of those who recorded their observations and experiences in those tragic days were either killed outright or tortured to death by the German invaders and their local collaborators; some managed to survive the holocaust and are now living in the United States, in Israel, and in other countries of the free world.

The voluminous diaries, memoirs and other documents from which selections were made for this book were written by members of the Jewish resistance movement in the hope that the world would thus have a reminder for all time of the resistance of the Jews to the extermination plans of the Nazis.

The documents were concealed by their authors in cellars, garrets, and other secret places, or were buried in backyards, in order to prevent their falling into the hands of the Germans. In some cases clues to their whereabouts were left with trusted friends or relatives; in other instances, documents were discovered entirely through fortuitous chance.

An intensive search for documents was begun immediately after the Second World War and is still going on. The thousands of documents retrieved in the past fifteen years have been gathered in the Ghetto Fighters House—the House of the History of Jewish Resistance, near Haifa in Israel. This great repository of the history of the Jewish resistance movement was established in Israel with the support of the Government and the co-operation of prominent Israeli personalities, among them the nation's second president, Mr. Ben Zvi.

CONTENTS

FOREWORD

THE FIGHTING GHETTOS
A SAGA OF THE GHETTO UPRISINGS

Though it flourished heroically throughout the Second World War, the Jewish resistance movement in Europe was overshadowed for many years by other events. But as a shocked and horrified world learned that six million Jews had perished in German gas chambers, crematoria, and experimental hospitals, post-war investigations also began to reveal a record of militant defense concurrent with the period of suffering and destruction. From the records of the Nazis, from the tales of survivors, and, above all, from the diaries, notes and poems of those who lived and died in the Ghettos, concentration camps, and forests, there slowly emerged the history of the Jewish underground.

The story of this resistance movement must be recorded in full, for the decisive spiritual victory won by the thousands of underground fighters, most of whom died in battle, was directly responsible for the temporal victory that established the modern state of Israel.

The battles of 1948 and 1949 in Palestine were the climax of the two thousand year war of liberation that began when the last defenders of Massada, Betar, Mount Moriah, and Mount Zion refused to surrender to their Roman conqueror, preferring death to subjugation. Since then, the battles of the Jews have been many and varied. When conditions made active battle impossible, the Jews resisted passively. They learned the art of group preservation—of living, and then dying when they could no longer live with honor. They engaged in mass self-destruction when the only alternatives were slavery or conversion, destroying their bodies to safeguard their souls. And the enemy, who often thought he had won the battle, discovered that that which he had sought to destroy had been revitalized through trial by blood.

These were the battles the Jews won in the flames of the Auto da Fé of the Inquisition, in encounters with the Crusaders, in the sufferings imposed by the Marauders of the Chmelnitzky era, and during the pogroms of Czarist Russia. This was the battle won by the Jew when parents slaughtered children in the name of God and Israel.

Some of the enemies of the Jews could not understand this miracle of survival. The truth lay in the words of the Prophet Ezekiel: "And when I passed by thee and saw thee wallowing in thy blood, I said unto thee: In thy blood live; Yea, I said unto thee in thy blood live!" (Ezek. xvi:6)

With this heritage, the underground fighters of World War II actively resisted the Nazis. They fought not only for their lives but for the honor and future of their people. For centuries, the Jews had been persecuted, driven from country to country in search of a home, herded into Ghettos and denied the rights of citizens. They had been forced to fight for their very existence. In their fight against Nazis, they fought against everything that galut (exile) meant, and only a few survived the battle. But they won the victory. With the dead fell the Ghetto walls, and in their place today stands the State of Israel.

In retrospect, Jewish resistance during World War II is seen as one great, cohesive fight against extermination; as one courageous movement against the enemy. But while the spirit of the underground fighters was just such a united whole, the battles they fought were not. Isolated from other Jewish communities by the same walls that separated the Jew from the non-Jew, each Jewish group was conscious that it acted on its own responsibility, that there was no hope of help from the outside. The fight against enslavement and death, the resistance to brutality and annihilation, had to be conducted separately by the resources of each underground organization, and without any kind of assurance that a trace of the deeds or even the existence of any particular resistance group would be left on this earth.

Until now, books pertaining to the resistance movement have been episodic in content, relating the details of specific uprisings. But these uprisings would not have been possible without the unifying influence and excellent organization of the underground movement. This anthology records the panoramic sweep of the entire Jewish resistance movement in Poland, in the words of the people who fought and died for the honor of their people.

It is remarkable that a people, isolated in bestial squalor and marked for extermination, should have risen above humiliation and death to capture its terrible present in diaries, social and historical treatises, and poetry for the benefit of future generations. Many of what undoubtedly would have been the most revealing works were lost in the Ghettos, the forests, and the death furnaces with their authors. But some were buried in the ground or smuggled to the free world through the underground, and so survived.

The documentary sources from which this book was compiled number more than two thousand. They include the records of the Nazis, who carefully itemized their own atrocities; the chronicles of Jewish historians, who have constructed a whole literature of the period; the simple stories of the untutored, and the more comprehensive works of well-educated men and women; and the reports of those who survived the debacle.

The natural division of the documentary material follows the three realities of Jewish existence during the tragic period recorded: the Ghetto, the concentration camp and the forest. The world of the Polish Jew was convulsed in horror; like a volcano, it spewed its burning fury over the entire country.

When the Nazis marched into Poland, the Jews regarded the conquest as a national catastrophe that had befallen their homeland, rather than as an event involving them as a religious group. Having lived in Poland in relative peace and comparative safety for many years, they considered themselves a part of an oppressed Europe. If the Jews were persecuted, the same could be said for the Polish gentiles. When the pressure on the Jews seemed more severe than the pressure on their countrymen, they considered it their fate as members of a minority group with no one to intervene for them. They thought of rebellion in

11

terms of a united Europe rising *en masse* to fight the Nazi oppressor.

Along with the rest of the world, the Jews were unable to associate the enormity of Hitler's intent with the reality. They could not realize their isolated position under the swastika. For Hitler intended to dominate the world, and the Jews and their heritage were making the fulfillment of his ambition impossible.

Hitler knew that the Nazi doctrine could not co-exist with the moral and ethical code of the Jews. The ideology of the Thousand Year Reich could not be imposed on a world that carried in its heart the three-thousand-year-old doctrines, "Thou shalt love thy neighbor as thy self" and "Ye shall have one statute both for the stranger and for them that is born in the land." Therefore, Hitler undertook to accomplish in ten years what the whole world had not been able to manage in two hundred decades—the total destruction of the Jewish people.

But Hitler was not in a position to launch his program of extermination when he first arrived in Poland; for at that point he still had to account to a major part of the world for his behavior. Therefore, during the first phase of his campaign, he limited his persecution of the Jews. He began by taking away their rights as citizens—he ordered them to wear arm bands, to forfeit their property, and to relocate in the narrow confines of the Ghettos. Many Jews were sent to labor camps during this period of relocation. To deceive the world, Hitler promised the Jews an autonomous governing body in each Ghetto; but once these groups were established, their autonomy extended only so far as was necessary for them to carry out the orders of the Nazis. Having centralized the Jews in the several Ghettos, Hitler forbade them contact with the outside world, and communications even within the confines of the wall were limited. During this phase, the campaign against the Jews amounted to an extremely methodical attempt to break spirit and body through humiliation and military terror. The area of the Ghetto was decreased to worsen the over-crowded conditions. Starvation and deprivation became deliberate weapons; looting and pillaging depleted the last material resources of the people. As more slave labor was needed, as more concentration camps were built, the Ghettos became deportation centers.

The second phase of the Nazis' extermination program was initiated outside the Ghetto walls. To forestall possible opposition to his extermination program, Hitler began an international propaganda campaign designed to make the Jew an object of derision and contempt. Through wild rumors of Jewish practices and habits, the Jew was made to appear subhuman, beneath the pity of his fellow-citizens. The Poles, Latvians, Lithuanians, Ukrainians, and Rumanians were invited to join actively in the persecution of the Jews. These peoples, either to improve their own captive conditions or to satisfy their anti-Semitic prejudices, accepted the invitation with alacrity and zest. In such an atmosphere, it was not difficult for the Nazis to launch their final extermination program. When the Nazis opened their gas furnaces and crematoria a year and a half after they had entered Poland, they did so with the full approval, and often co-operation, of the vanquished non-Jews.

Within the Ghetto walls, the Jews were deciding to establish their own patterns of resistance. Violent discussions of policy were held in each of the isolated Ghettos.

Most Jews still could not recognize the situation for what it was. The Ghetto dwellers still believed that an uprising of the conquered nations against the Nazis was inevitable. Therefore, they supported a policy of passive resistance until such time as they could join a general revolt against the oppressor. As they had very little knowledge of the happenings outside their own Ghettos, they feared that a premature uprising in one Ghetto might precipitate a senseless massacre of Jews throughout the country.

There were dissenters, however, who urged flight into the forests, where it would be impossible for the enemy to find and persecute the Jews—where one might become hunter instead of quarry. Some Jews did escape to the Eastern border regions adjacent to open spaces and marshes, the most notable sectors of the Jewish anti-German front.

But all who left the Ghettos did not leave for the relative freedom of the forests and swamps. Many were forced into the concentration camps, and there were faced with the incredible cruelty of the Germans, who assembled candidates for the furnaces in hut-towns and barracks. Some dared a last stand, a last defiant act. Just as there is no parallel in history for Hitler's planned cruelty, so there is none for the magnificent courage of these lonely martyrs.

The majority of Jews, however, remained behind the wall—some by necessity, others by choice. The discussions, the decisions and the final heroic rebellions were similar in nature in every Ghetto—though each unit had to think in terms of its own problems. The rallying force, the most active element in each Ghetto, proved to be its underground movement.

The Fighting Ghettos is a record of this underground resistance movement, which came into being in the days following Poland's defeat. Fused from the various political and religious groups that had existed among the Jews in pre-Ghetto days, the underground organized ordinary, peaceful people—tailors, bakers, doctors, lawyers, salesmen—into a bold fighting force. The underground united the people in resistance and in a strong sense of personal dignity.

For the first year of its existence, the underground was primarily engaged in humanitarian and utilitarian activities designed to combat the enemy's attack on the mental and physical health of the Jews. When the Nazis outlawed the education of Jewish children and the operation of the synagogues, the underground organized illegal schools and religious services. To combat the demoralizing influence of isolation and to maintain some kind of contact with the outside world, the underground established a secret system of communications that linked the different sections of the Ghetto and crossed the wall into the territory of the non-Jew. Once this system was in operation, food, medicine, and other necessities could be smuggled into the Ghetto to relieve the terrible starvation, deprivation, and disease that resulted from the short rations and overcrowded conditions imposed by the Nazis.

Those activities of the underground that required work outside the confines of the wall were handled by couriers selected for their Aryan appearance. Working under the constant threat of discovery—either accidental or through betrayal—the couriers secured sources of supply and made necessary arrangements to smuggle needed goods into the Ghetto; they established contact with non-Jewish families who were willing to hide Jews in their homes; they served as a liaison between the Ghetto dwellers and the Jewish Partisans in the forests; and they carried the news of the outside world to those within the wall. Often the couriers had to remain outside the Ghetto for many months at a time, and the longer the period, the more dangerous the mission became.

It was through the couriers that the Ghetto dwellers first learned of the fate Hitler had planned for them. News of the gas chambers, the furnaces, and the experimental hospitals shocked even the most obtuse Jews into a complete understanding of their position.

Even during the darkest periods in Jewish history up to that time, the object of Judaism's enemies had been to break the Jewish people, to subjugate or convert them *en masse*, rather than to kill them as individuals. But the Nazis offered an ultimatum: the "final solution" demanded a Judenrein (Jew-free) world—the extermination of the Jewish people through the death of every individual.

Passive resistance and mass self-destruction—tactics successfully employed by outnumbered Jewish fighters in the past—were not the answer to Hitler's threat; for this was not an attempt to change the religious or social status of the Jews, but an attack on the very seed from which Judaism might once more arise. Only active rebellion could defeat the Nazi aims.

The Ghetto dwellers knew that they would have to fight alone. Many of those who should have been their allies were in treacherous collusion with the enemy; even the Polish underground refused arms and assistance to the Jewish underground. There was absolutely no hope of

help from the outside. The Jew knew that he would probably die in the unequal battle, but he also knew, with the
knowledge of his two thousand year heritage, that in his
death there would be life and honor for his people.

As the policy of active resistance replaced that of passive resistance, the underground became a military organization. Hidden rooms and underground bunkers were
constructed to hold the fighting units. Squad leaders were
selected, and trained in the tactics of war. The people were
educated in the use of arms and were rehearsed in battle
positions. Couriers were sent out to purchase guns, ammunition, and explosives wherever possible. Gun by gun, an
arsenal was collected and then smuggled into the Ghetto.
Children were taught how to steal guns from the enemy
without detection; old and young worked together to store
provisions for the time of battle. These Jews, forced by the
Nazis to work a twelve-hour day at hard labor, worked
through the nights to organize a strong combat force.

Having overcome every humiliation, every kind of persecution, that the enemy could inflict, the Ghetto fighters
were ready to call forth death in their fight for life. They
sold their lives dearly, demanding a heavy toll of enemy
lives in return.

These heroic people wrote another glorious chapter in
the history of the Jews. The modern state of Israel is a tes-
tament to the victory they won for their people throughout
the world. Never again will the Ghetto walls be rebuilt;
never again will Jews permit themselves to be imprisoned
like cattle. Militant defense, not only of beliefs, but of a
homeland, has permanently replaced passive resistance to
oppression.

MEYER BARKAI

New York City

1: WITHIN THE WALLS

THE JEWISH REVOLT

One pervasive, persistent, overpowering feeling had over-
taken us: the devastation . . . the final moment . . . had at
last arrived. But had we seen the full depth of the tragedy?
Did it dawn upon us that this holocaust would engulf millions of our people . . . our Jewish youth and our children?
That it would uproot countless communities whose very
existence was rooted in the soil of Europe—communities
that had been built with toil and sweat and which would
now be reduced to dust and ashes? We had not correctly
measured the abyss. The clouds had obscured the heavens
and we all reasoned: "This is but natural and normal. The
end will come and the storm will pass. And once more will
Jewish life blossom forth in Eastern Europe, in metropoli-
tan Warsaw and also in the Jewish hinterland. There will
be a continuation to Jewish history, a continuation to the
final rebellious generations." We did not understand that
we were standing in the innermost chamber of the tragic
history of our people . . . that we had never known its like.
We did not understand that we were being carried from
rung to rung, and did not feel that we had been singled out
to sink lower and lower.

The white and blue arm bands—we wound them
around our arms. The Ghetto—we complied. The concentration camps—we did not resist. We built Treblinka as if
with our own hands. Herded like cattle in box cars—thus
we traveled. We asked for nothing but a drop of water before death; we struggled to be the first to enter the gas
chambers. And who could have understood in that first
moment that from the white and blue arm band with the
Shield of David—that from the Band of Shame—a
straight line would extend direct to Treblinka?

The incidents began and we grew accustomed to them.
We were humiliated when we were forced to remove our
caps in the presence of the German commanders . . . and
we grew accustomed to that. We wrestled with ourselves

when the Germans seized us for the slave labor battalions
. . . and we grew accustomed to that. We became used to
not eating, to dying of the typhus, to starving. We grew accustomed to all of this. There was a certain force that pre-
vented us from seeing reality as it actually was.

In 1939 we did not understand—we refused to believe
—both out of ignorance and from the desire not to see.
The Jewish community was blind and did not want to
awaken to the facts! If only we had realized; if only we
had understood; if only we had been able to turn the historical tide back to the year 1939 . . . we should have
shouted "Revolt at once!" For then we were at the height
of our strength. Then we were posesssed of vigor and self-
respect. Then we were fortified with so much energy and
emotion. Then we were equipped with so many more
weapons . . . so many more fighting men. Then, alas, we
were sustained by so much more hope. Then, we should
have shouted "Revolt" For there were movements in this
poor Jewish Ghetto, movements that raised the flag of
national and social liberation, movements that instructed
generations of Jewish youth, that could have successfully
opposed the impending danger and doom.

I do not know of any movements except that of the
Pioneers which had the fortitude to see things as they
were, the Jewish reality as it was. This was our education
in exile, in the chapters of Hachalutz (the pioneer movement): to attempt in every possible manner, and with
every intellectual resource, to alter the existing order of
things—both human in general and Jewish in particular.
Such was the inheritance of the individual and the entire
movement. And if it was as yet unable to measure the
depth of the abyss, still it was better prepared to contend
with bad times than to expect the good.

The then-current thinking in Poland negatively affected
politics and quarrels. There was a war on. Europe was entirely destroyed. The foe had reached the gates of Moscow
and Leningrad. Powerful France had fallen. The Balkans
were conquered. The underground forces were isolated,
many kilometers removed from any front, from any hope,
waiting for a future day, believing in victory. Slaughter

continued day after day, the finest people were sent to their deaths; the Polish underground waited.

And there were many in the Ghetto who pressured us to refrain from organizing our own war, many strata and divisions of powerful thought and opposition. There were those who held us back out of evil intent, while others were motivated only by the loftiest and noblest of intentions.

There were groups that co-operated with the Germans: the police, the Judenrat (Jewish Assembly), an organization called the Zinastka and others. I am not of the opinion that all those who took part in these groups were traitors and that all those who participated in these activities were concerned only about their own safety. And neither do I believe that all those who co-operated with these institutions were motivated by malice. But from a strictly objective point of view, all these institutions were converted into instruments of evil, aiding the Germans in rounding up Jews for the concentration camps . . . for death. Leading all was the Judenrat, filling orders, defrauding, accepting the decisions of the Germans. The Jewish police equally defrauded—seizing Jews for the slave labor camps, forcing them into the dreaded trains of destruction, assisting in the wiping out of the Ghetto.

It is not my intention to convey the impression that the police and the Judenrat were similar to the Zinastka—set up by Gantzveich, who, like the other agents of the Gestapo, overt and covert, set out to serve the foe out of a desire for gain.

The Judenrat and the police were opposed to all communal activities and fought all forms of open resistance. After the night of April 18th, Chernikov summoned the leaders of the Jewish underground and argued that underground activities were dangerous to the Jews. He pleaded that they be halted—that we should desist from publishing newspapers; from congregating; from organizing educational activities. The police and Judenrat muzzled any form of Jewish communal activity—and shortly thereafter, were traitors in the "Jewish Affair."

But they were not the only restraining forces in the Ghetto. There were people, idealistic, high-minded people, who opposed a Jewish revolt from other points of view. Some based their opposition on general political considerations; others on historical grounds; while still others were opposed to a Jewish war and Jewish violence because of their religious beliefs.

The chief advocate of restraint—if we are to name names—was Uzech. He did not preach, "Let us not fight," but only "Let us fight when the Poles fight—in the meanwhile, no!" He maintained that the harshness and the oppression of the occupation were not reserved for Jews alone, but were meted out to the entire population. Our war was tenable—according to him—insofar as collaboration with the non-Jewish underground was possible, and if the non-Jewish underground forces were prepared to open a united front together with us. Inasmuch, however, as they did not find it necessary to conform to Jewish needs, the logical conclusion was that we must conform to the imaginary needs of the non-Jewish underground.

There were also those who based their opposition on historical evidence. The man who expressed this point of view with greatest clarity was the Jewish historian, Dr. Izhak Shipper. He was of the opinion that both mainstreams in Jewish history were justifiable: on the one hand, the idea of violence and self-preservation . . . on the other hand, the concept of submission. There are periods when the people are unable to fight and when fighting is unnecessary. Dr. Shipper drew comparisons from chapters in Jewish history, and argued that under existing conditions, if we declared war we would only destroy that which it was possible to save. And when the days of the decimation of the Ghetto drew nigh, he argued that it was better to accept the fate of 70,000 Jews going to Treblinka so that a half-million would be spared. It was necessary to save those whom we were able to save even though we knew that those who went—were condemned to death. This is not to say that he advocated our aiding the Germans in decimating the Ghetto. Heaven forbid! But he did believe that we did not have the right to endanger a half million Jews in Warsaw, and other millions of Jews throughout Poland; for he believed that the scourge would demand, and be satisfied with, 70,000 or 100,000 Jews. These thoughts were expressed by him both in private conversations and also at plenary sessions.

Others based their opposition to resistance on religious considerations. One who expressed this point of view was Rabbi Zishe Friedman. "The Lord giveth and the Lord taketh away," was his motto. We were not permitted to endanger the lives of the Jews in Poland. Inasmuch as the enemy had established collective Jewish responsibility, we could not raise a hand against the Germans, and so bring about the murder of hundreds of thousands of Jews.

But there were not only people who preached restraint; there were also psychological hindrances for every Jew, for the Pioneer movement, for every pioneer. These psychological restraints stemmed primarily from the Nazi doctrine of collective responsibility and collective guilt: this weighed down the decision.

To this psychological hindrance, we may add the lack of proper self-evaluation and self-esteem. The Pioneer Zionist movement did not understand its own strength. There were other political parties in the Ghetto . . . leaders and guides in an active communal life . . . educational activities among the youth. When we argued that the parties did not fulfil their roles—we did not boast that we were the party, the movement and the force . . . that we were the political might, the strength of resistance. Many Jews gave their lives so that our movement would one day take the place of individuals and lesser movements and that it would proclaim: "We!" And this lack of proper self-evaluation was our greatest spiritual shortcoming.

Then there was one other hindrance—an objective and physical one: we were neither armed nor were we trained for armed conflict. Do not think that our first experience at setting up a fighting force (it is not important to recall by what name we called it) was only in 1942 when we received the first news from Vilna and Chelmno. The first Ghetto fighters' organization was established in 1941, on the day the Soviet-German war broke out. We harbored both belief and hope: one day and then another and the Red Army would reach the Polish border and we would have our share in this war. But we were also thoroughly uneasy: what if the Germans drove them back and unleashed a wave of pogroms? Let us defend ourselves!

But days turned into weeks; the German army virtually galloped to Stalingrad and Moscow, and we were not armed. And a fighting force devoid of arms is like a severed limb that wastes away and is gone completely.

At this time, in the spring of 1942, a new strength made itself felt in Poland. The P.P.R. party made its appearance, taking the place of the former Communist Party. This group advocated action after the war had entered into the second stage. Its program was to make constant war on the Germans in every possible place and at every possible opportunity. The friendship between the Allies and the Red Army would be responsible for victory in the Polish affair. The destiny of Poland was dependent upon the future of the Allies and the Red Army. The Jewish members of the P.P.R. undertook the enterprise—and with more luck than the Poles—of setting up an anti-Fascist front. The partners in this undertaking were: Poale Zion Left, Poale Zion, D'ror and Hashomer Hatzair. The Bund and the General Zionists did not take part. We sought a true democratic front with the other parties of the anti-Fascist bloc, and yet we were restricted in our relations with them because we doubted their readiness to join us in actual fighting against the Nazis.

Finally, after a long time, it was decided to establish a restricted fighting force within the block, a force whose base of operations would be in the Ghetto and whose war would be waged in its midst. Mordecai Tennenbaum, who had just come to Warsaw from Vilna, was selected to lead it.

We desired an independent Jewish fighting force, which was not to take orders from the Polish underground. We wanted a Jewish commander and Jewish soldiers fighting in and for the Ghetto, and deciding when to fight.

We were certain that we would not diminish thereby our participation in the general war. And, therefore, it seems to me that the revolt in the Ghettos expressed the Jewish war and accentuated the uniqueness of the Jewish

24

struggle better than Jewish participation in the general Polish underground—even though the Ghetto fighting force was diminutive. For in the Ghetto, the Jewish fighter was alone in his battle for Jewish redemption. We perceived the substance of the Jewish struggle in the Ghetto.

The anti-Fascist bloc was not able to hold its ground and split up prior to the first wave of deportation. On the 28th of July, 1942, the Chalutzic Zionist movements—Freedom (D'ror), Hashomer Hatzair and Akiva decided to set up a fighting force. After the first action, we were able to close ranks with the Bund, the other Zionist parties and members of the P.P.R. We all agreed: War!

And now the problem began. When to fight? And then another question: following the first wave of terror, not more than 50,000 or 55,000 Jews remained out of a Jewish population (of Warsaw) of a half-million persons. And if they continued to take Jews to Treblinka . . . if they continued to remove them from the Ghetto . . . should we fight or not?

And the discussions continued, difficult discussions. We were deeply troubled, and we knew well enough: in this manner had they broken us down, beginning with the deportation of thousands of Jews and continuing on to hundreds of thousands. Therefore did we decide: not one more Jew would we give. They thrust in our faces: "Retribution! You are assuming historical responsibility for the Jewish destiny."

Had the Germans not taken us by surprise and had we been able to call an emergency session of the National Council on the 18th of January, when the Warsaw Ghetto was surrounded by the Army and the S.S.—had we been able to meet with our National Council and Adjustment Board, the revolt of January would never have taken place in Warsaw.

But a miracle took place: the members of Hachalutz were not able to meet with the Council. The fighting divisions of Hachalutz and those of D'ror joined with members of Gordonia and Hashomer Hatzair, who weren't even able to contact one another. Simultaneously and independently, on that day they all decided to fight!

The revolt of January prepared the way for the revolt of April. Had we not made this beginning, had we not taken this responsibility upon ourselves, had we not accustomed ourselves to the fact that it is possible to kill Germans and not die, that it is possible to overcome Germans—we would not have accomplished the April revolt. After the January uprising, all opposition to war ceased. It was necessary to learn from experience; and the troops concluded, with their healthy instincts, with their human dignity: "War, and let the chips fall where they will!"

In the January revolt, the methods of war were tested. Two theories were tried out, and from them we learned for the future: One division fought in the streets of the city; with a resounding echo, it made a deep impression known as the legend of the January Revolt. The people were taken by surprise—not only the Jew and the Pole in Warsaw, but all Poland was excited by legends of Jewish tanks and stories of thousands of Jewish fighters. In reality, all those who took part in this action, face to face with the Germans, except Mordecai Anilewitz, were killed. All the division's arms were also completely lost.

The second division applied a different theory: that of guerrilla warfare. Who knew the hiding-places, the roof-tops, the cellars, all the lanes and alleys that connected the streets, as well as we did?! We were able to pass from street to street in the Warsaw Ghetto without leaving the protection of the houses . . . by going through cellars and over rooftops. We had even prepared escape passages in the houses prior to the revolt. In short: on that first day, for every wounded Jewish fighter, there were many slain Germans; we acquired arms and ammunition as well as experience.

On the second day our fortified division achieved new victories without having even one casualty. We were able, with great determination, to overcome the Germans. By following guerrilla warfare theory, we saved lives, added to our supply of arms and—most important—proved to ourselves that the German was but flesh and blood, as any man.

And prior to this we had not been aware of this amazing truth! If one lone German appeared in the Ghetto the Jews would flee *en masse,* as would Poles on the Aryan side. Now it became apparent that the fortified Jew had the advantage over the German: he had an ideology, something for which to fight. And now the German—once cocky and bent on murder and plunder—felt insecure, knowing that he might not emerge alive from a Jewish house or cellar; and he ceased harassing Jews.

The Germans were not psychologically prepared for the change in attitude that had come over the Jewish community and the Jewish fighters. They were seized with panic. They feared that as the revolt progressed and added strength—they thought we had many more men and arms than we did—it might kindle a rebellion in the Polish quarter. This fear forced them to stop, during January, their program of deporting Jews from the Ghetto by force. They had to try to ship them out by peaceful means.

And at this point we encountered a new situation: the German did not want an open war with the Jews. This was a most serious danger for the rebellion.

At that time, the industrialist Teben came to replace the Gestapo as the head of the Ghetto, and to prove that the Germans did not come to take Jews out to slaughter but to send them to Ponyatov and Trabnik, two concentration camps. They began to deport Jews, not by force but by trickery and treachery on the part of both Jews and Germans. And even though we knew that the Warsaw Ghetto would be decimated before the concentration camps and that the Jews in the camps could survive us by a few months, we knew only too well that the fate of Ponyatov and Trabnik was destruction. We knew the choice was limited. Neither the Ghetto fighters nor the concentration camp inmates could hope to live long. The difference was just a matter of a few months.

The Jews in the Warsaw Ghetto were able to rise and to revolt—but it would be difficult to arrange an uprising in the camps. And one question persisted: was it permitted to cut short Jewish lives by three months . . . five months . . . or half a year? And the answer: a resounding Yes!

As soon as this decision was taken—that we were to be

permitted to place Jewish lives in the balance—we began the war. And the Jewish community, in addition to embracing us and acknowledging our strength, also revealed to us the sympathy of its heart. In the eyes of the average Jew, we were a support in time of trouble. Just as previously he had sought to think, in order to ease his soul, that no danger would befall him . . . now he sought to think, to ease himself, that our strength would save him. And so it was—in the January revolt, we did save him.

Before we began the revolt, before we were able to begin, we made various preparations to assure our success. We knew that in the first action no outside or enemy group had done as much harm as that institution known as the Jewish police. And we also knew that if we did not clear the air in the Ghetto, if we did not eradicate anyone who could do us harm, there would not be an uprising in Warsaw. There was no room for two such opposing forces in the Ghetto. Either the Judenrat and the police, or the Jewish fighting force, would prevail. We therefore passed judgment on the members of the Judenrat and the police.

At midday we attacked the Jewish members of the Gestapo. Those who did not hide were slain, and those who were not slain fled for their lives.

And it became possible for us to force the Judenrat to heed us. We levied a substantial cash contribution on the Judenrat and its auxiliary organizations in behalf of the Jewish Fighting Organization, and we obliged them to raise the funds within three days. At the appointed time the Judenrat submitted the money, and its members pleaded with us to eliminate one of the stated reasons for the request: they asked that it not be recorded that the tax was levied as a fine for services to the Germans. From that day we knew that henceforth the Judenrat would have no decisive voice in the Ghetto.

Once we had cleared the air in the Ghetto we knew that a member of the Jewish Fighting Organization would be able to walk alone on the streets of the Ghetto; and that it would be dangerous for Germans to walk about even in groups. In the period between January and April, one did not see any Germans toward evening. They referred to the

Ghetto as "Mexico." We no longer were under any re-straint—as had seemed unavoidable during the days of Nazi rule. We rebelled in our habits and in our adaptability. We broke through the fence.

We had urgent need of funds to maintain our fighters. We accomplished many feats that brought in millions. In the organization of all of these activities, there was one rule: the fighter did nothing for himself or for any form of personal advantage. All his thoughts were channeled in one direction: to maintain himself and obtain arms. We levied taxes on those of the upper classes who made fortunes during the war in economic collaboration with the Germans. We approached them with the assertion that we had a people's army and that the people must maintain it. They accepted our calls willingly and with the best of wishes.

We had one problem in those days which required immediate solution: in the streets of the city appeared unruly groups of fighters. These groups were mostly made up of men who had not found their way to the Jewish Fighting Organization and who sought—despite this—to fight. But there were some among them who wanted to take advantage of the opportunity of "Mexico" to grow rich by violence: they set up raids on Jewish homes in the name of the Jewish Fighting Organization. We instituted a campaign against these wild groups and eliminated them, adding their good men to our forces.

The Jewish Fighting Organization consisted of 24 regiments. It was our contention that a Jewish fighting force must be composed of strongly-knit military units, and we organized our units accordingly. Men who grew up together during the war, who lived together and who knew each other well, would fight together with greater dignity and strength. Had we been able to train the group over a period of several years, we would have adhered more closely to more sound military principles—but time was short and running out. And we knew that only with the strongest possible ties between regiment and commander could the fighting be properly accomplished.

The revolt of January taught us that those fighters who

were not massed together in one place did not fight—even though they were adequately armed; while those who had been massed at 56 and 58 Zamenhof Street, and at 34 and 63 Mila, had fought well. From that time on all fighters were obliged to serve together in collectives.

Our weapons consisted of revolvers (one revolver for every man), automatic revolvers, home-made bombs with immense explosive force, and German and Polish grenades. We added to this one other substantial weapon: a great ideal and the capacity for self-sacrifice. We saw the ideal of revolt as the central motivating force of our lives. We did not think it permissible to inhabit the lands of the earth and to walk about, after the decimation of 500,000 Jews in Warsaw and hundreds of thousands of Jews in other places, unless we dedicated ourselves to the revolt. And everything—the good and the bad, every thought and every action—was tested from this point of view: did it support rebellion or no? And when the time comes for me to look back and evaluate our errors, I will say: I am almost certain we could have drawn from the Warsaw Ghetto many more fighters than we did; but we feared every backward step. We were concerned lest it occur to someone that he might be able to save his life even without fighting. And it was for this reason that we did not prepare in time either houses in the Aryan quarter, nor automobiles, or men who knew the sewer routes. This may have been a serious error on our part—but it was justifiable under the then prevailing circumstances. We feared many things: that we would delay the moment . . . that perhaps people would begin to doubt, and think: "They are prepared but will not fight" . . . that our fate would be not rebellion but Treblinka. But out of all of this we undertook the historical responsibility, and did not permit Jews to be sent to Ponyatov and Trabnik. We knew there would be no revolt in Warsaw without Jews.

There was a similar spirit throughout the Zionist movements and in our youth movement, reiterating: Revolt! These were our thoughts; this was our life. Revolt! Everything and everyone was prepared for it. We knew that Israel would continue to live and that for the sake of all

Jews everywhere and for Jewish existence and dignity—even for future generations—only one thing would do: Revolt!

Warsaw was a symbol, but Warsaw was not alone in the war of the Jews. Before and after Warsaw there were other rebellions and other experiences: in Czentochow, Bialystok, Bendin, Vilna, Cracow and in all the towns, villages and camps where Jewish youth fought. Not always were they successful, for there were places where the fighting forces did not control the Ghetto, the police, the Judenrat; on the contrary, the Jewish fighters were forced to leave the Ghetto.

And if the Jews of the Diaspora remember the revolt, let there also be a remembrance of those brave young men in the Ghetto of Czentochow who rose up against the Germans and who, when their revolvers did not shoot, fell on their enemies with their teeth . . . and were slain. They produced no echo to match that made by Warsaw, but from the point of view of dedication and self-sacrifice, their accomplishment was no less splendid.

The Warsaw Revolt was an isolated rebellion, but even so it was not the most difficult. There was one far greater in depth and intensity, by which the inmates of Treblinka and Sobivor proved to our satisfaction that a revolt in Hell is possible. The Jews of Treblinka and Sobivor, in the gas chambers, were able to rise up . . . despite the finality of it all and despite the slaughter of millions. They proved to us that it is possible for man to fight even in the depths of destruction.

IZHAK ZUCKERMAN
Commander of the Jewish Fighting Organization, Warsaw

WARSAW: THE JANUARY 1943 UPRISING

The Jewish Fighting Organization was feverishly active in Warsaw and other cities, but before the January revolt, the preparations in Warsaw had resulted in little more than the collection of some ammunition from those in the Aryan section. As a matter of fact, the Germans surprised us.

Two days before the invasion of the Ghetto itself, there had been extensive searches on the Aryan side and people had been seized; but we of the Ghetto felt sure that as long as the Germans were busy there, they would not bother us. As we discovered later, this was exactly what they had hoped we would think. It was merely a diverting of our attention; in fact many Poles who were seized were freed the very same day.

That morning, that is, the morning the action started, our people arose as usual. They felt no special danger, they went peacefully to work. Even those of us in the Organization, who were alert to discover all kinds of tricks, were taken utterly by surprise; the day before we had been discussing how these last days (while the Germans were harassing the Poles) could be used to prepare for whatever they had planned. We thought we had at least several weeks.

That evening a few groups went out on different activities, some to obtain ammunition, one to free two of our boys from the Ghetto police, etc. In our own apartment, we had a visitor, a beloved friend—Izhak Katsenelson. The Ghetto itself had been split into several sections, and Izhak and his son had smuggled themselves across to our section to stop in and talk with us. The father was a shattered and broken man, devastated by the loss of his family. It was over a week since we'd seen him, and we had much news for him; he in turn read to us from his latest work on the catastrophe that had befallen his family. We talked until nearly four in the morning, and then went to bed.

Before we could fall asleep, the watchman rushed in to tell us that there was military activity in the city. We assumed that it had to do with the searches that were going on on the Aryan side, but nevertheless we got up and dressed.

Our apartment, which was headquarters for D'ror, was at 58 Zamenhof Street. We had recently changed apartments for some of us had been involved in the attacks on the restaurants in Cracow and we had been followed by two Gestapo agents. So we were always on the alert.

The people living in the apartment house assembled in the courtyard to decide what to do. Someone went outside to investigate and found the streets surrounded and a military guard stationed at every door; so each house had to make its own plans, since it could not communicate with the others. In our house the only ammunition was four hand-grenades and four revolvers. We decided that with so little there was nothing to do but prepare for a defense from within the house. The Germans would have to break in, for no longer did Jews go to the door to be led off like sheep to slaughter; instead they hid themselves—and we prepared to defend ourselves as best we could.

We had intended that night to hide Izhak Katsenelson in one of the bunkers under the house; but we had not done so, and he insisted upon remaining with us to fight, even though we hadn't enough ammunition. We planned our defense: forty young men and women under the direction of Izhak Zuckerman, and four hand grenades and four revolvers with which to act. Some of us also had clubs and metal sticks and cups filled with acid. If the Germans came, we said, we would burn their abominable faces—even though we knew that there would be retribution, for they would return and storm us and we would all be wiped out. All of us felt the tension, and believed that our hour had come.

Everybody tried to hide. We were very quiet. Sometimes we heard the cries of Jews being led to the Umschlag-Platz and the screams of the Nazis, "Laufen schneller.

33

Laufen." (Run faster. Run.) Our mood varied; sometimes we were all of a tension; then it would ease and a wave of sadness would envelop us. We were waiting for the first shot. It was hard waiting for the first shot. We had lived through months of destruction, yet not one shot had been fired at the murderers. How would it happen? How long must we wait?

Suddenly we heard nailed boots in the entrance hall. At this awful, still moment of decision, Izhak Katsenelson commenced to speak. He spoke with great emotion, a sort of farewell—

"We must be happy for we are about to meet the enemy with ammunition, though it be to die; we will fight with arms, but we will fight not for ourselves but for the future generation. Let us have courage; let us follow the example of our brethren in the Land of Israel—they did not show softness in time of danger, a few stood against many, and their death was not in vain for they inspired all the Jews yet unborn. The Germans could kill a million Jews but they would not overpower us; the Jewish nation lives and it will always live. We will not live to see it, but the murderers will pay for their crimes after we are gone; our deeds will live forever."

His words aroused us, they lit a fire in our hearts. Just as he finished speaking, the door was broken down and a crowd of uniformed Germans swarmed into the house.

They were met by Zachariah Artstein and Chanoch Guttman. Zachariah was sitting in the front room reading, and this diverted their attention from us for a moment. We were in the other rooms, hidden in the corners. The Germans went through the rooms with firm steps, and as they went to the room beyond where Zachariah was, he leaped up and shot them in the back. Two were killed. Guttman at that instant broke into the hall followed by several others; they opened fire, and the bullets found their targets in German scalps.

Everyone fought, some with iron poles, some with sticks, anything. Zachariah Artstein and Chanoch Guttman took ammunition from the dead Germans and ran after those who had escaped.

We were overjoyed; all the suffering seemed worthwhile. With our own eyes we had seen scared Germans, we had seen them turn to run; and we had pursued them. German soldiers who thought they were conquerors of the world were being chased by Jewish boys; with all his ammunition, a German can only use one pistol at a time. We couldn't pursue them into the street, where the other soldiers and S.S. troops were; and soon they had disappeared and we were left to ourselves.

One of our men was wounded; but our spirit was undaunted. It was hard to realize that we had really killed Germans, we had actually made them run. It was confusing, amazing. But we had no time to dwell on this, we must use the few moments we had, for the Germans would surely surround the house and kill us all. Our first thought was how to continue the fight. So there was only one thing for us to do: to leave the house.

We had not planned on a retreat. However, it was quickly decided to go through the attic and over the roofs and thus reach the other side of the street. We climbed up to the attic and crept from one snow-covered roof to another; we followed each other in a long line. It was quite difficult, for one of us might slip and plunge to his death. Finally we started our descent to the fourth floor of 44 Muranovska Street. The minutes seemed like hours, and our progress was slow anyway. We thought we would never reach it, but there was no turning back. But luck was with us and we found ourselves at 44 Muranovska Street.

We sat down to relax and get our breath; but almost immediately we heard the Germans coming, and we were unable even to get the chill out of our bones before the house was surrounded. The Germans would have to come up the stairs after us; so we put armed guards on the stairs where they would have to pass, and as they came into the house we met them with our fire. Two were instantly killed, the rest escaped.

Night was now coming on; evidently the Germans feared fighting us in the dark, so to our astonishment they turned back. All of us came out of that battle alive.

Later on that evening we were able to get to the club house of the Kibbutz D'ror which had been moved from Czerniakow to 34 Mila Street in the Ghetto. There everything was deadly silent, just as it always is after an armed conflict. The house was quite empty of tenants, so we took it over and sat down to plan. We worked out positions for every group and each person in each group was told exactly when and how to attack. Also, this time, we specified a place for us to meet if we had to retreat.

The street was quiet. No more did the Germans shout as they had before. They went by stealthily, one by one, close to the walls of the houses. Before going into a house they sent the Jewish police in as cover, and even then entered only with the greatest care. Their searches were more hurried and less painstaking—they were trembling with fear of our deadly bullets, and they seemed to sense that there were ambushes everywhere.

Our spirits rose. No more did we feel the worry, the anguish of the days that had gone before. We felt redeemed—we felt our lives were again useful. What we were doing would be recompense for the murders, and our own deaths, which seemed inevitable, would not be in vain —would make sense. Beyond that, a spark of hope remained: perhaps we might live.

Tens of thousands of Jews were in hiding that night, trembling with fear. But they lived because a few of us had dared to oppose the invaders. We all lolled around the apartment, tensions fading, talking and even joking. One of us went into the street with the hope of finding matches and some wood for the stove; he found some and the warmth revived us. Someone else found some whiskey. One of us became the brunt of jokes: in the heat of the attack he had become excited, and when he thought everything was lost, he had pulled the pin in a grenade and was ready to throw it in our midst. Our commander had cried, "Stop!" just in time. That one word had saved us from certain death. Embarrassed, he whispered that he had tried to save us from the hands of the Germans.

A second group was listening to a colorful account of the German the narrator had killed, and how he had killed him. He said a German swine had been stretched out ready to leap out on a Jew—now he was in a pool of his own blood which bore witness to the fact that he would no longer be able to murder.

Down in the courtyard, there was a large group of S.S. men all screaming *"Juden heraus"* (Jews outside), but no one listened. We waited, for we knew they would finally break up into groups and try to bring the Jews out by force. Then, split up, their strength would not be so great and we could successfully defend ourselves.

When they reached the apartment we were in, they did not see us. Zachariah stood, put his hands up in a sign of surrender, and walked into the hall. From our corners we leaped forth, attacking. We spilled grenades over German heads, and when they came up the stairs they were met with a rain of bullets. Shocked, they ran back down the stairs in confusion. They were met with another rain of bullets: for Zachariah had gotten outside, and he attacked them from there through the cracks of his hiding place. The stairs were littered with the maimed, wounded and dead; the rest were able to escape into the court. In this battle, again, we ourselves suffered no loss.

Soon the Germans returned in large numbers, with reinforcements, and they advanced with great care, searching for the Jewish fighters. But they were too late, they could not find us, because as soon as the S.S. had left we had taken all the arms from the dead and wounded and run away. As we ran off, we fell into a bunker full of Jews. They gave us what comfort they could, receiving us with open arms. With them was a rabbi, and he turned to us, saying, "If we can know that young fighters like you are left to take revenge, it will be easier for us to die." Just those words took away from our minds all the failures and disappointments of the past.

The January action lasted for only four days. The Germans had planned in that time to finish off every Jew in Warsaw. But they had met opposition, and they stopped. For them, it was not proper that Germans should pay with their own lives for the death of the inhabitants of the Ghetto. So they had to decide on some other system of annihilation—and they knew that time was working in favor of the Ghetto, that a second clash would cost more dearly.

Besides our group from D'ror, several other groups participated in the January reprisal—Hashomer Hatzair and Gordonia, to mention only two. Each separate contingent used different tactics and methods, according to necessity. Hashomer Hatzair was under the command of Mordecai Anilewitz; his group took to street fighting. Of them, Mordecai Anilewitz was miraculously saved, but everyone else was killed.

The January action was the last warning. Until then, some Jews imagined that the Germans would not harm the productive elements among the Jews, because they needed them, and because they would then be able to say that there were still Jews in Europe. But the January action proved that this was not so. The Jews now knew that it was only because of the militant action within the Ghetto that the Germans had been given pause, and that no longer would Jews be able to seek employment on the Aryan side, even in those open workshops where they were ever and always under the watchful eyes of Nazis.

Those Jews who appeared to be Aryan and had money bought documents at fabulous prices, and resettled in the Aryan section; the other Jews hid in bunkers in the Ghetto.

Although not so many Germans were killed in the January uprising, the action was of great importance because these were the first shots of revolt, and by then the Jews discovered that not only could they kill Germans, but they could remain alive afterward. Also, they learned that the show of force had stopped the Germans in their mad plan of massacre. The uprising also caused a sharp psychological turnabout among the Jews. More important than that, the Germans became afraid, and the attitude toward us of the Poles in the Aryan section of the city changed completely. Now, the Poles respected us; they were forced to consider the future now that we had dared, with so little ammunition in our hands, to give the Germans battle.

Now, our supplies of ammunition grew. From the Aryan side we received from the Armia Krajowa (the

Army of the Country) a new transport, fifty revolvers, fifty bombs, and quite a quantity of dynamite. We immediately set to work making mines and setting them in the main streets of the Ghetto and in certain buildings. Where the streets crossed, and German soldiers were constantly marching, many Germans met their death. The Polish underground gave us some instruction and told us how to make other kinds of arms; for instance, we learned how to make a Molotov cocktail. Just at this time there commenced some activity on the Aryan side in the sale of ammunition, and we immediately bought all we could. Meanwhile we did not cease at every opportunity to take the ammunition off the German and Polish police who patrolled our Ghetto streets.

It was a period of great activity for us. No longer did we ask advice of the Judenrat; but ruled ourselves and paid no attention to its orders. Contrariwise, the Judenrat now asked our advice before doing anything. This took unusual turns—for instance, a Jewish person wrote a letter asking the Fighting Organization for permission to form a card club. We had to do some police work of our own—it was necessary to clean out the slanderers in the Ghetto, and some Jews paid with their lives for aiding the Gestapo; the Jews watched what they did in the Ghetto, now. So, we were able to work freely and without hindrance, and to prepare.

To arm five hundred fighters we needed millions of zlotys. At first, we organized committees to collect money from Jews. Then we imposed taxes. We went to banks, to the cashier's office of the Judenrat, and to the bank of the Ghetto, where the watchmen were Polish police. One day, with pistols in our hands, we took all the money from the bank of the Ghetto. Later, finding we hadn't enough money, we taxed the rich Jews. We wrote notes in the name of the Fighting Organization, saying, "We request from you so much," and at first it was paid promptly. Probably they reasoned that non-Jews were requesting the money and they were afraid; but later they found out who was really demanding the money and they quibbled that Jewish "robbers" were asking for it, and Jewish robbers couldn't afford to be as strict as the non-Jews. So some of them refused to give us money, even though they must have known that they'd be killed by the Germans and then all their money would go to the Germans. Still we did not want to go against the high moral standards of our people and actually kill fellow Jews. The holy command was a light tower to us.

In general, supplies were always far short of what the fighting organization needed. Even when we had in our possession millions of zlotys, we had to be most economical and thrifty, even in our living expenses; we even ate little. But to allow Jews to show us disrespect just because they were rich, this we would not do. So prisons were set up, and we arrested the backsliders. Of course we were careful to imprison only those who were dishonest, and did not give of what they had.

Meanwhile, the Germans were not idle. They searched for new avenues of attack. One of these was to send the owners of workshops to the Ghetto seeking labor, and appearing as beneficent persons. We would surround the building where they were holding the Jews, and in the face of this force, the Jews would escape.

We worked frantically and with impatience, our hearts filled with prayer. We longed for the hour of revenge, that it might come soon. And behold, the day came!

ZIVIA LUBETKIN

SMUGGLING WEAPONS INTO THE GHETTO

Along with the many perils and dangers involved in acquiring weapons there was the problem of getting them into the Ghetto.

Illegal entrance into the Ghetto was hard enough, but smuggling parcels into it was ten times more complicated. A man wishing to get into the Ghetto without parcels could do so by joining a Jewish labor group working on the Aryan side and entering with it. If he carried some article with him, he would have to look for other ways. Whatever we received from Fishgrund* was smuggled in by Michael** himself. He got in touch with a Christian smuggler, a railway man who worked at the Umschlag-Platz in the Ghetto. They decided to meet at a certain place.

It was dusk. Michael went to the appointed rendezvous, but did not find the man. So he decided to find a way in by himself. Some Christians who happened to be there told him of a passage through which he could slip into the Ghetto. A gun in his pocket, and ready to defend himself if stopped, he took the risk and passed through a section of the Umschlag-Platz where Germans were patrolling and checking whatever looked suspicious to them. Fortunately for him, no mishap occurred and he passed through the Germans without incident.

Later a different smuggling route was found. The Ghetto wall extended along Okopova and Dzika Streets. In between these streets there was a lane—Parisov Square. A gang of gentile ruffians had managed to bribe the guards in charge of this lane, and it served as a passage for smuggling.

Christian peddlers from the Kerzeliac area would climb over the wall and, at half-price, purchase from the Jews in

* Salo Fishgrund.
** Michael Klepfish.

41

the Ghetto clothing, underwear, shoes, sewing machines etc. These they would transfer to the Aryan side. Some of them dared to break into deserted Jewish houses, take out closets, beds, and other pieces of furniture, and carry them across the wall. This was a combination of secret trade and robbery—open robbery of Jewish property. Eventually almost all the smuggling points were discovered by the Germans, one after another. Many smugglers were shot and passage across the wall grew more difficult from day to day.

Michael Klepfish was the one who showed me this smuggling point—Parisov Square. With Yurek (Aryeh Wilner) he smuggled into the Ghetto the first weapon-shipment—about ten pistols—received from the Polish underground by the representatives of the Jewish Co-ordination Committee on the Aryan side.

The pistols were packed in small boxes and were covered with nails. The boxes were put on a handwagon like ordinary merchandise. Our landlord from 3 Gornocharska Street, Stephen Machai,* served as a porter and pulled the wagon. Behind him at some distance followed Yurek and Michael Klepfish, carrying pistols in their pockets. All the way up to the wall, everything went fine; but in Dzika Street, close to the smuggling point, the handwagon was stopped by a Polish policeman who demanded to see a permit to carry merchandise. A few zlotys quickly satisfied his curiosity and he left. Michael and Yurek sighed in relief. They carried the wagon and placed it close to the wall. On the other side, in the Ghetto, over a dozen members of the Jewish Fighting Organization were waiting for the "merchandise," having been acquainted beforehand with the appointed time for the smuggling. When the agreed password was uttered on the Aryan side, a Ghetto fighter climbed on top of the wall and skillfully caught the "nail" boxes thrown to him by Yurek, Michael and Stephen; he in turn dropped them down into the Ghetto. Had they been caught in the act, they would have replied with gunfire. That is what Michael told me afterwards. They would have refused to let these pistols which they had

* Later found out to be a Gestapo agent.

hoped for for such a long time fall into the hands of the enemy. Fortunately for us everything ended well.

I used this smuggling route frequently later on—first together with Michael, when we had to get steel files for the Fighting Organization. Disguised as poor peddlers, we approached the gate. I was holding the parcel and Michael disappeared into an old half-destroyed building opposite the Ghetto. The "office" of the Christian smugglers was in the gates of this building. There, the fee for passage through the wall had to be paid in advance. We had to wait a long time until a Polish youth gave us the sign. Michael quickly climbed on the wall; I handed him the "merchandise" and he jumped inside the Ghetto. I returned home. This time too everything went well.

On another occasion I went to Parisov Square by myself. My task was to bring over three packages of explosives which had been acquired. The silence of the tomb prevailed near the wall. Not a soul in the street. The known smugglers were gone. Something must have happened. An elderly gentile woman passed by quickly. I stopped her and asked; "What is this silence today?" And the old woman answered: "This morning two smugglers were shot here. A few peddlers were arrested, and now increased patrols are watching the area." Nothing new in that. Frequently there would be casualties in the smuggling, but once peace was resorted the Polish smugglers returned to their business. What should be done? Postponement for a few days would be out of the question. They needed explosives in the Ghetto; my comrades must be waiting already close by the other side of the wall.

Telephoning the Ghetto, I informed the comrades in code that there could be no smuggling today in the agreed place; I would try to pass the parcel through Feiffer's factory.

Feiffer's leather factory was on Okopova Street near Gliniana Street bordering on the Ghetto; through it Jews often infiltrated to the Aryan side. I had to get in touch with the watchman in the factory and bribe him. The trouble was, a German guard was stationed at the factory's gate. His assignment was to check the Jewish cemetery lying along the other side of Okopova Street; he also kept surveillance on the Feiffer factory. Still, I would try. I pressed the doorbell. The watchman opened the gate. There was no one but he in the dark corridor. I tried to persuade him to let me smuggle a small parcel to the Ghetto. At first the old man refused. He was afraid of the workers. I tried to convince him with a gift and with whiskey, and he finally agreed.

I was content. I left the building to call the Ghetto by telephone. I told them to wait for me at six in the evening near the Feiffer factory.

At the appointed time I was hanging around the factory, carrying the dynamite in a parcel. The street was semidark. Traffic was very light. Half-hidden in a gate nearby, I followed the movements of a soldier across from me who was standing on watch. I wished he would move a little! As if to spite me, he seemed to be nailed to the ground. I would have to wait for darkness. I waited a long time for a chance to slip unseen into the building.

Now! The soldier turned aside to light a cigarette. I hurried to the gate and rang the bell quickly. At long last I was inside with my parcel. The watchman told me to follow him. Passing halls and stairs, we reached a small room jam-packed with boxes and packages. I looked around trying to discover the point where I could leave my parcel. The watchman understood me. He pointed to a corner in the room. "Get ready," he said, and switched the electric light off. In the darkness, I heard something being removed. I strained my eyes in the direction he had pointed out before. Gradually I discerned the bars of a small window.

"Hurry up and get your parcel!" commanded the watchman. I approached the window cautiously and peered into the black night. Silence. Nothing stirred. I began thinking, "Perhaps my comrades have turned back . . ." I whispered the password: "Yurek! . . . Yurek!"

"At last you're here," replied someone in a subdued voice.

A shadow appeared in the window. I recognized it in the dark—it was none other than Yanek Bilek, a coura-

44

geous, daring member of the fighting organization belonging to the Zukunft Youth. He had carried out the most dangerous missions of the fighting group in the Brushmakers shop to which he belonged. I picked up the parcel and tried to pass it through the window. There was trouble —the parcel was too big and could not be passed through the openings between the bars. How should I repack it fast? How, without the watchman ferreting out its contents?

"Hurry up! Hurry up!" they were rushing me from the other side.

"One minute . . . I have to repack." I whispered back.

I asked the watchman to leave me alone for a few moments but he answered angrily, "Hurry, let me have it and I'll show you how to do it . . ."

Nothing doing. The old man was already by my side. Nervous fingers manipulated the paper package. The minutes seemed to last forever. I was angry—why hadn't the old man told me to prepare small boxes? He was shaking all over, and from the other side they kept urging us to hurry up.

At long last we finished. I pushed the parcels through the bars. Hands took hold of them. Immediately after the last parcel went across, the window was shut. The watchman put the light on again. His face was red and sweating and he was very nervous. We stood for a minute in silence. I gathered up the packing paper and some dynamite powder which had fallen out, and said, "You see, there was nothing to worry about . . . everything went well."

The Pole panted heavily. "No, I'll never take the risk again! I was frightened to death."

I gave him 300 zlotys and a bottle of whiskey and bade him farewell. His hand was still shaking. Unexpectedly he asked in a muffled voice:

"Tell the truth—what was in those parcels?"

"Nothing special . . . a few paintboxes . . ."

"And nothing more?" He examined me with his eyes.

"Nothing more," I said and turned on my way.

The smuggling succeeded. Such were the ways of the

Jewish fighting Organization. Our "paints," "nails" and "merchandise" kept up our hopes for a day of vengeance and reprisal.

VLADKA PELTEL

APRIL

Beginning of April, 1943

The German scheme to liquidate the remnants of the Ghetto failed. The plan to evacuate the workshops was halted. The date for the final evacuation of Jews to camps has passed, yet the workshops in all sections are still alive with workers. In the central Ghetto as well as in the workshops there are fighting groups, diligently training and preparing themselves for resistance and rebellion. German strategy and the political chicanery, that had managed to enslave the whole of Europe, could not yet finish off the remnants of Jewish Warsaw.

The first spring breezes blew—and brought the odor of slaughter. None of us knew what satanic plot was in the enemy's mind, yet we knew our days were numbered. Rumors that calamity was going to strike kept occurring, stubbornly, and each rumor paralyzed the last live ones left in the Ghetto. Every day, several times a day, the Jews would stop their activities and escape to the shelters. The members of the Judenrat would desert their offices and disappear. Peddlers would shoulder their merchandise. Anyone who was in the street or at someone else's home would hurry in fright to his own home. All these rumors were "based" only on sounds that people associated with actions. Someone would notice that there was an unusual number of Germans at the Ghetto's gate; or someone would notice, on the contrary, that all the Germans had vanished from the gate; or a heavy sound of traffic was heard across the Ghetto walls: such slight occurrences were enough to cause alarm. There were many such occurrences, and each and every one of them would freeze the blood in one's veins. Indeed this incessant alarm was usually based on bitter experience. Yet the action did not begin.

Every day the two terrifying invaders, Blescher and Klostermeier, would walk into the Ghetto. On impulse they would conduct a small action, shooting on all sides without restraint. At first, before they knew the Jews had weapons, they would loiter in courtyards, in houses and attics—looking for hideouts, inspecting every hole. If they caught a Jew they would first torture and then kill him. But of late they had become more cautious: they never went into houses, but contented themselves with firing into the windows and building entrances. When they appeared in the Ghetto, a panic would start as if for a real action. Everybody would run away and the cause of flight would not be clear. Only when things calmed down, and people emerged from their hiding places, would the cause of the danger become known.

We knew that the days were numbered. The state of readiness and preparedness was intensified. Every effort was made to fill gaps, to mend shortages. Day and night groups went out on, and returned from, various missions. Some punished collaborators and some dealt with robber bands. One group released Jewish prisoners or Jewish workmen from the Germans. Others collected food from stubborn Jews who had refused to contribute. The organization functioned properly; everyone was in his place carrying out his assignment.

Several days prior to April 19th, Brandt* came to the Judenrat House bearing good news. He said he was concerned about letting Jewish children have fresh air, and he therefore suggested that the Director fix up the square near the Judenrat House for this purpose. He also promised matzos for Passover. Everyone who was familiar with the German swindle, and who understood Brandt's sadistic nature, was aware of trouble ahead. Such friendly promises always heralded an approaching calamity. Yet many Jews felt differently; they came up with a new assumption, an encouraging one: that now the few thousand who remained in the Ghetto would be left alone. Hitler—they thought—wanted to destroy Judaism and uproot its natural life. This scheme of his he had carried out, whether the few thousand Jews left lived or not. Polish Jewry did

* Brandt was the Gestapo officer in charge of Jewish affairs in the Warsaw Ghetto.

48

not exist any more, and this very fact left a ray of hope. We felt it would be cruel to shake them from this belief; nevertheless, we had to tear down their illusions. But they would not listen to us.

Even many of the pessimists among us believed that we would be allowed to celebrate the Passover holiday period. Great preparations were actually made to celebrate it according to the full traditional customs. Matzos were baked (out of dark flour—with the permission of the rabbis), wine was prepared for the Seder; also there was spring housecleaning, special cleaning of dishes, and everything else, as in natural times. The houses and courtyards looked festive and gay.

The night before the holiday, on the eve of April 19th, a feeling of terror swept the Ghetto Jews. We felt we would not enjoy the fruit of our holiday preparations this time. Persistent rumors were spreading that on the following day the action would begin. Occasionally one could hear reassurances that these were false alarms, as there had been before. People were arriving and reporting conversations that they had had in the workshops, with friends, at Teben's and Schultz's. It was reported that strong military movements were noted around the liquidated "small Ghetto." Someone was told by a Polish policeman that the action would begin on the following day. Jews returning from work on the Aryan side reported an increased guard on the Ghetto gate.

That night all Jews were sleepless. Household items, linens, and food were packed into bundles. There was a mass movement, under the light of a bright moon, the like of which had not been seen in a long time. Some were hobbling out, carrying their parcels on their shoulders; others went to relatives and friends to hear news and report on the situation. There was no more fear of walking the streets. The Ghetto had been cleared of Germans, the authority of the streets was in Jewish hands. This was another bad omen.

That night was a night of vigil for the Jewish Fighting Organization. A state of readiness was ordered for all groups: no movement until midnight and no sleep. But

49

after midnight, no new instructions were given, and the state of readiness was continued. At one in the morning news was received by headquarters and all groups were at once mobilized. We stood in formation and were told that only a few hours separated us from the last battle with the enemy. The men were sent to their positions, and scouts and couriers were appointed.

After the review, the men went to finish their last-minute preparations. Every man received food and bandages. In addition to the usual weapons, every fighter now received grenades and incendiary bottles.

At once feverish work started, with the building of barricades and the bolstering of positions. Every spot that was suitable for an encounter with the enemy was left open. Other passages were especially fortified so as to obstruct the approach of the Germans toward them. Approaches were established between positions so as to maintain contact with them under all conditions.

At three in the morning everything was ready, every man in his proper position. Only small groups remained in the courtyards and the streets, urging the Jews to hurry to the shelters.

At five in the morning only Organization men were out in the open. Everyone else was hidden underground, holding their breath, awaiting developments. The stronghold men were waiting, their fingers on the trigger. The time for action had arrived.

Monday, the day before Passover, April 19th, 1943. A pleasant spring day, pleasant sun rays penetrating every dark corner of the Ghetto of Warsaw. The last day . . . nature arranges in you a strong desire for life. Had the city been dark, if a storm had been raging, if gusts of rain had been pouring down, perhaps it would have been easier to accept death. Yet it seemed that nature had allied itself with the enemy, and had provoked us the more on the threshold of oblivion.

The fighting group of D'ror to which I belonged was stationed at 33 Nalevki Street. With a few other companions I was on the balcony of the first floor house on Nalevki-Gensha Street. We were the first to spot German units marching towards the Ghetto. Two of our other units were in the courtyard, by the windows of the basement apartment. This morning, infantry and cavalry of various military units, S.S. units, and Ukranians, fully armed, were advancing in the direction of the Ghetto as if in battle formation for an encounter with a regular army. Armored cars and tanks, too. They came from the direction of Nalevki and marched in Gensha Street, along the wall, towards the gate on the corner of Gensha-Zamenhof.

I became discouraged at the sight of the enemy forces. We were so weak! What was our strength in comparison to this well-equipped army, armed with armored cars and tanks? We having only pistols and rifles? However, we must hold fast.

At six in the morning, the siege of the Ghetto walls complete, the enemy's first units were marching into the Ghetto in the direction of Nalevki, approaching the triangle of Nalevki-Gensha-Franciskanska. We did not wait for them to shoot but opened fire from our positions. A hail of bullets, grenades and bombs poured down on the enemy. Our homemade ammunition functioned well: Germans fell in the streets, dead and wounded. This was the first clash and the sounds of the explosions conveyed the message to all the groups: the uprising had begun!

The Germans did indeed expect a Jewish uprising, but they did not correctly estimate its force and ferocity. Judging from the events of January 18th, they thought that we had only pistols; now they were surprised by the arms that we had managed to collect—especially the bombs. We attacked first, and the initiative was ours for a long time, while the enemy was on the defensive.

The German units split into small groups, clinging to the walls, afraid to clear their casualties from the streets. "Damn," we heard an S.S. officer yelling at his troops, who were running for cover. He ordered them to clear the dead and the wounded and to disregard the fire, but he himself prudently and consistently remained standing under the balcony.

After the first shock, the Germans' answer came. They

51

were out in the clear, exposed to our bullets, while we had the wall for cover.

Continuous and obstinate fighting was going on in all three sectors of our unit. Jacob Guterman, tall and heavy, a young giant, fired incessantly from a balcony in the front; Feivre Schwartzstein fired an automatic pistol from an upper window; Abraham Drier and Moshe Rubin were in charge of the attack from the two positions in the courtyard, on the rear, by the entrance from Gensha and Kuza; Zachariah Artstein, commander of the D'ror group, was hopping and running from position to position, encouraging and helping his men. Couriers were rushing from position to position bringing news. The noise of enemy bombs and the rattle of German machineguns was deafening. The battle raged for two hours.

Rivka the scout came running with news: the enemy had retreated, not a single German could be seen in the streets. The commander went out to inspect the area and came back radiant: the Germans had left behind several dead and wounded, while we did not have a single casualty. The news spread quickly among the positions, and there was great rejoicing.

True, it was a temporary victory; but even so, it was heartening, and these casualties, inflicted on the Germans by us, raised our spirits, although the end was so near.

The Germans disappeared from the Ghetto for three hours and we had a breathing-spell. Now we were hungry, and we had sufficient food and time to talk about the fighting. Some men rested and seemed to sleep, and others jokingly tried to snatch their weapons away, but were repelled at once by the alert owners. Moshe, who would not part from his concertina, which he always carried with him, played for us to pass the time. Suddenly the observation post reported that tanks and German half-tracks were approaching from the Gensha side. The commandant gave us the alert order, and instructed that, should retreat become inevitable, those of us remaining alive were to go back to our base at 6 Gensha Street.

While he was talking, firing broke out and we were attacked from all sides. At the Nalevki-Gensha corner the Germans brought out the furniture from a Werterfassung nearby and erected a barricade. Under its cover, they fired at us blindly with every kind of weapon, wasting ammunition. We nursed each bullet, firing carefully. During this fight, several Germans were killed, while not one of us was hurt.

At the height of the battle, we threw our incendiary bottles at the German barricade, and it caught fire. Their cover destroyed, many Germans perished. They threw incendiary bombs at our building and it started to burn. We still had time to set fire to the German stores nearby and we started retreating to a new position. We went through attics from one building to another. On our way we were informed that the house on 6 Gensha Street, where we had our base position, was already under enemy fire. On the other hand, we could not turn back; our position in Nalevki Street was on fire. The Germans were in front and the flames were behind us. The floor under our feet began burning too, the smoke rose in smothering clouds, blinding us; burning pieces of the roof tumbled down and set fire to the floor.

We sent out a patrol to find a way out, but our spies took a long time to come back. Every minute was precious. In the meantime we climbed into the attic of 6 Gensha Street and opened fire. Feivre opened fire and killed one German, and took his weapon: the rest of them escaped. This dead German for a moment diverted our attention from the seriousness of the situation. But we quickly remembered that we were in a trap which was closing inexorably. We scurried from corner to corner, looking for even a tiny opening through which we could escape from this hell; but in vain.

It seemed we were beyond hope. And then the patrol came back: there was a way out! We passed through a maze of attics and roofs, through small openings—holes so small that a man could hardly squeeze through. There is no obstacle for dire necessity!

We arrived at 37 Nalevki Street. Looking around in the courtyard, we did not see any suitable place for a stronghold. After a long search we found traces leading to a Jewish bunker.

Unlike the inhabitants of other bunkers, the people in the bunker at 37 Nalevki Street were not glad to see us. When they saw us enter they became very anxious: our fighting, so they thought, would bring them misfortune. Wailing and whining, the women began leaving the shelter, in clear daylight, looking for other hideouts so as not to be with the combatants. How naive they were! They still stupidly believed that non-combatants' lives were safer than fighters' lives. Due to their panic we started to leave their bunker. We knew, of course, that our presence did not involve any special risk for the bunker's inhabitants, but we did this out of consideration for them. We were now without any base or shelter.

The attics of the Ghetto, now and even before the uprising, served as an important traffic artery. Because of the danger in the streets, many of the people in the Ghetto avoided walking there, and there was much traffic through the attics. Passages were established from house to house by holes chopped in the walls. The traffic in the attics increased; the quieter the streets became, the more the communication took place through these passageways. At first we would lose our way in the maze, wondering where the various openings led to; but eventually we learned to use these unique upper streets.

The safety of the attics increased their usefulness: in addition to being just secure passageways from house to house and street to street, they became meeting places. In dark corners people would engage in trade talks—especially weapons' trade.

This communication artery was of special significance during the uprising. Through it combat units were moved from one position to another. Our instructions were that each position was to be held to the utmost limits of endurance and, should withdrawal become inevitable, units were to retreat through the attics. The Germans did not imagine that we had such a transportation network at our disposal. Once they had bombarded a house and set it on fire they were certain that our fighters were lost; but in this re-

54

spect they were very wrong. As long as there were buildings left in the Ghetto we had a secure means of withdrawal through the attics. When houses were captured intact by the Germans, they would search in vain for our fighters, who seemed to vanish into thin air. They did not discover the hidden openings in the attics.

Both observation posts and fortified positions were built in the attics. The attics also served as transportation and communication links between the units, and as passages to the houses where the bunkers of the Fighting Jewish Organization were located.

After leaving 37 Nalevki Street we wandered through the attics, but we were unable to find a suitable stronghold. On our way we passed many refugees who had abandoned their hideouts because of the fires. All of us waited anxiously for the night to come. Occasionally, everything would calm down; the shooting would stop; even the running of the refugees would stop. In a corner of one attic I saw a Jew saying the evening prayers with great devotion, although he was rushing to get through them before the storm should break out again. Suddenly the walls shook, bombs exploded. In the lull between the battles we had advanced a little. Our aim was to leave Nalevki Street, where a strong German force was stationed, and to reach Kuza Street, where we intended to establish our new base. At last we managed to reach 3 Kuza Street, where we at once entered the bunker to take cover until nightfall.

The few hours we spent in this bunker seemed like an eternity. The dark and narrow cellar was so tightly packed with people that the flame of a match or candle would go out at once because of lack of oxygen. The people panted and breathed heavily.

Occasionally the crying of a small child would disrupt the quiet. At once his mother would cover his mouth; his crying might betray us. Hundreds of people could be lost because of this baby's cry. Yet when the crying stopped, many people would be concerned about the child—had he suffocated? That had happened more than once.

At night, coming out of the cellar, we were overwhelmed by the abundant air, even though it was smoke-filled. We established temporary quarters in one of the rooms in the building. Several men went out to make contact with other combat units, to receive information about the fighting in other sections, and also to report about ourselves. A second group went to look for a suitable base for the following day.

Thus, one day of fighting was over. Both the Ghetto residents and the combatants were uncertain of the tactics the Germans had planned for the following day.

Even the fires which had darkened the Ghetto and reddened the sky above it were not taken to be the final German means of attack. Many still believed that only houses from which the Germans had encountered resistance were set on fire. This assumption was based on the fact that the fires set by the Germans broke out at various places in the Ghetto, yet did not spread over whole streets. Every sane person found it hard to believe that whole city blocks could be systematically set on fire and wiped off the face of the earth.

This April night, after the first day of the uprising, was different from the nights of July 1942 and January 1943. On those nights there had been moments of calm and tranquility. But now the shooting did not stop for one minute. True, the action did not continue during the night; but Germans stood at the gates and dropped explosives into the Ghetto, intending to annoy and demoralize the residents and to deprive them of sleep.

Therefore even at night movement in the Ghetto streets was dangerous and we had to wander around through holes and attics. That night the Germans fired from afar and we did not engage in a face to face clash with them. On the following nights, however, their patrols moved inside the Ghetto area, and the shooting came not from the distant gates, but from the ruins nearby.

On the evening of that day, April 19th, I went to the house at 4 Kuza Street to get an electric battery for our group. To my surprise I found myself in Rabbi Meisel's apartment. On the threshold, I remembered that it was Passover, the night of the first Seder.

The apartment was in a state of chaos. Bed linens were

spread all around, chairs were turned upside down, various household items were strewn on the floor, and all the window panes were smashed into little bits. During the daytime, while the members of the family had sought shelter in the bunker, the house had become a mess; only the table in the middle of the room stood: festive, as if a thing apart from the other furniture.

The redness of the wine in the glasses which were on the table was a reminder of the blood of the Jews who had perished on the eve of the holiday. The Hagada was recited while in the background incessant bursts of bombing and shooting, one after the other, pounded throughout the night. The scarlet reflection from the burning houses nearby illuminated the faces of those around the table in the darkened room.

When I departed, the rabbi very warmly wished me success.

"I have lived my life," he said, "but you youngsters— do not flinch, fight on and may God be on your side."

The rabbi walked me to the door and gave me a few packages of matzos for my unit.

"Should we be lucky enough to live till tomorrow," he added, "come over and bring Zivya with you." And so I did. The next day, on the second Seder night, both of us, Zivya and I, visited the rabbi.

Returning to my friends I found myself in a different world. I again enjoyed the warm, comradely atmosphere and the indomitable spirit with which trouble and misfortune were faced head on, tearlessly. In this strong spirit lay the main power of the Organization. It lifted one above the waves of despair, and encouraged one to hold fast and fight the enemy.

The night came to its end. At dawn of April 20th members of our group returned from their various missions inside the Ghetto. Also couriers from our headquarters arrived: Lutek Rotblat (Akiva), Aaron Bruskin (Pavel), and Henrick Zilberberg, the last two from P.P.R. We now had abundant information on the course of the fighting in various sections of the Ghetto, and on the condition of certain strongholds, during the first day of the uprising. The feeling of loneliness eased somewhat. We felt ourselves, once again, an integral part of the Fighting Organization.

In the morning we fortified our new position at 4 Kuza Street. All day long we were expecting the Germans, but they did not come near us. Only from afar did we hear the sounds of battles raging in the Ghetto.

TUVIA BOZIKOVSKY

IN THE TEBEN-SCHULTZ SECTION

At dawn the street looked horrible. The Ghetto walls were surrounded by gendarmes, and the Ghetto guards were reinforced by S.S. men. No one was allowed out of the Ghetto and all the exit permits were cancelled. People scurried in the street like madmen. I tried to get in touch with the Central Ghetto, but the telephone was not functioning. Except for the Ghetto, surrounded by gendarmes with rifles ready to shoot, nothing could be seen. In the distance, we could hear the echoes of shooting and explosions. An action was going on at this time in the Central Ghetto. The German managers of the workshops arrived, our "providers of bread," and claimed that this deportation did not concern the "productive" elements and was directed only against the "savages" in the Ghetto. But no one took their word seriously. Mobilization of the combat units and manning of the positions was our first task. The members of the fighting unit in our workshop, 76 Leshno Street, took positions at the windows of the third floor, under the command of Eliezer Geller. We maintained contact with David Novodvorsky's group at 67 Novolipye Street through the attic, and also with Henyak Kava's group at 74 Leshno Street, at Teben's Works. Lilit (Regina Poden) was the liaison between the two groups. From our positions we could see distinctly the movement of the army marching through Zelazna Street to the Central Ghetto. The area commander's liaison, Meyer Schwartz, received instructions for the rest of the groups. The units assigned to the sections were as follows: Shlomo Vinogron's unit—41 Novolipky Street, Schilling's section; Velvel Rozowski's unit—628 Smotze Street, Rherich's section; Benjamin Wald's unit—36 Leshno Street, Teben's section; Marek Mayrovitch's unit—31 Novolipye Street, Schultz's section; Yulek's unit—66 Novolipye Street, Schultz's section. Schwartz returned after some time to report that he had completed his mission, and to transmit some questions that the unit commanders had asked. One question dealt with two persons we held prisoner who were accused of collaboration with the Gestapo. The verdict of death had not yet been passed on these people. Because of the deteriorating situation the commander ordered their immediate execution. Half an hour later Schwartz returned with the news that the order had been carried out.

At about noon we received the first news of the battle in the Central Ghetto. The source of the information was a German, the owner of the workshop, K. G. Schultz. He said that the Jews were not behaving properly; the gendarmes who had returned from the Ghetto had told him that they had met strong Jewish resistance and that there were two hundred victims of the Jewish aggression. At dusk, after the Germans had left the Central Ghetto, we were able to make telephone contact with our units there. We heard about the great victories in the first battles. The following day at dawn the section commander ordered us to start action, in solidarity with the units fighting in the Central Ghetto. At about ten o'clock we launched our first attack. At that time a company of gendarmes was marching in Leshno Street toward the Ghetto. When they approached the guardhouse in the Leshno-Zelazna section, they were overwhelmed and crushed under the fire of the unit at 76 Leshno Street. Two heavy bombs successfully hurled at them broke their ranks. The Germans escaped, leaving more than ten dead in the street. Several weeks before the deportation, the unit at 67 Novolipye Street had planted a mine under the guardhouse by Smotze Street. Now, when the Germans passed by, the fighters connected the mine to the electric wire but to their desolation the mine failed to explode. The men gritted their teeth, the girls had tears in their eyes—there was no electricity. In their wrath, the unit hurled bombs, the effects of which were beyond expectations. Two bombs killed many Germans. The Germans began moving their army cars, realizing that even from the Aryan, "neutral" side they were in danger from the "productive" Ghetto.

At about four o'clock the situation of the Jews in the

workshop area became clearer. The owners announced that in order to insure calm and undisturbed work for German industry, Jewish workers would be transferred to work camps in Trabnik and Ponyatov. After this announcement was made relatively free movement started again in the street, in preparation for the journey. The local commandant used the opportunity to inspect all groups. In the evening, Germans and Lithuanians appeared in our section and were stationed by every gate to see to it that the deportation the next day would be successful. Since we had only a few guns, a number of combat units went out into the street in order to get weapons from the Lithuanians. Our sorties were successful; we acquired five rifles. The Lithuanians and the Germans did not react, wishing to avoid larger battles. On Wednesday, April 21st, at six in the morning, the combat units manned their positions and waited for the arrival of the Germans. At about seven o'clock the workers who had volunteered to go were already lined up. All the other Jews who remained in the workshop section became illegal. The combat units remained at their posts. Shortly afterwards, the first German company arrived; it was attacked by hand grenades and many Germans were left dead and wounded. The Germans did not react to this attack because they wanted to continue to recruit volunteers for the camps.

At the same time, other combat units attacked small groups of Germans and Lithuanians. Three combat units were stationed near Novolipye and Zelazna Streets to mount a simultaneous attack on the Germans passing through the "neutral" zone. At about ten in the morning, a German unit of considerable size marched toward the Central Ghetto. It was attacked by the three units; our fire was fierce and accurate. The Germans left many dead and wounded behind. Shimon Heller, our best shot, distinguished himself. Later, more than ten Germans who were leading Jews to the Umschlag-Platz were shot. This action was difficult, as we could not use grenades and bombs because we might hurt the Jews, and our stock of bullets was meager.

In the afternoon the Germans laid siege to isolated

houses. The siege of each house was preceded by gunfire at its windows, but the Germans could not avoid a battle: the combat units which had already entrenched themselves in the houses would not let them get close. The fighters were constantly under heavy fire, but they themselves had to use their bullets sparingly. When the Germans broke into several houses and blocked the retreat for the combat units, Shulamit and Shimon Heller jumped from the second floor and were killed instantly. Shimon kept his word that he would not die before killing five Germans. Two fighters managed to pass through the chain of Germans and were seriously wounded.

We couldn't determine the German losses exactly, but they were heavy. The battle lasted for several hours. After the battle the Germans set the whole area on fire. At that time we were ordered to establish our bases and shelters. There were few Germans left in the area, but we knew that the calm wouldn't last long and that the Germans would begin to look in the shelters for Jews, and to liquidate them. Our commanders used the relative calm to establish contact with the other units, especially the Shlomo Vinogron unit which was active in the Schilling workshop area. Meyer Schwartz and Lilit were sent out in the middle of the night. Two days later they returned; they had had some clashes with the Germans on the way.

Since the first day of the action three combat units commanded by Shlomo had been attacking the Germans marching for action. When a German company tried to approach the Schilling workshops, in order forcibly to remove the Jews, it was stopped by the combat units, which inflicted heavy casualties. The German counter-attacks, which were repeated several times, were repulsed. Later on our companions set on fire a large warehouse full of wood, thus hindering the Germans from approaching the shelters of the civilian population. In the days that followed the Germans were afraid to go into the houses. The fighters were delighted when they saw, through their windows, groups of S.S. men performing punishment exercises. Day and night the Ghetto burned. The smoke and flames compelled the fighters to move from place to place, and only very rarely were they able to find a suitable base for their activities.

During these later battles we inflicted casualties on the enemy; but we, too, suffered heavy losses. Hunger and the hopelessness of the situation drove us to find a way to move to the Aryan side. After many days of great effort I succeeded in following our commander's instructions: to pass to the Aryan side, and establish contact with Antek. On that night we sent forty men out through the sewers. This means of transportation, however, was discovered. All the other units that tried to force their way through the chain of German patrols were liquidated in street fighting.

For a long time we listened to the echo of shooting in the Ghetto, knowing that our groups, surrounded by the Germans on every side, were still fighting.

SHALOM GRYEK

THE LAST DAYS
OF THE WARSAW GHETTO

The Ghetto was burning. For days and nights it had been swept by flames, and the fire scorched and consumed house after house. Whole streets were burned at the stake. Columns of fire rose and sparks fell all around and the skies assumed a terrifying scarlet glow.

And nearby, across the wall, life flowed on as usual. The residents of the capital went for walks, relaxed and enjoyed themselves, seeing, nearby, the smoke during the day and the fire at night. Children, innocently enjoying themselves riding a merry-go-round, and peasant girls visiting the capital who also came to the carousel, incidentally saw the flames and knew that the Jews were burning. Occasionally, sparks would ignite a house across the wall; but there the fire was extinguished at once. But here in the Ghetto no one came to help. Everything burned and no one extinguished anything.

Warsaw Ghetto was burning, the Ghetto of the largest Jewish congregation in Europe; and in it the remnants of the Jews, several tens of thousands of them, were writhing in the last throes of death. Only a few days ago, in April, 1943, the Germans had resolved to finish off these remnants and send them to Treblinka in death cars, as they had done unmolested with several thousands in the past. But this time they drew back. Units of the Jewish Fighting Organization, hiding in the ruins, planted mines and hurled grenades at the marching, celebrating army. The Germans were flabbergasted and retreated. They tried one day, they tried the next, and they were repulsed by the astounding Jewish shooting. And after ten days of battle they did not venture to enter the Ghetto. The Germans set the Ghetto on fire from all corners, trusting that this deadly fire would finish by suffocation what they could not finish in face-to-face combat. But apparently it was not so easy to finish off this nation. With their last breath of life the Jews sought refuge among the ruins and flames. The fire drove them out of subterranean hideouts and bunkers. Many were burned alive and smothered by smoke; but many others, men, women and children, rose from the very earth carrying scraps of food, pots, and blankets. Babies and young children were carried in their mother's arms, and the older ones followed their parents. In their eyes were reflected sadness and sorrow, confusion and a crying-out for salvation. All these were moving behind every wall, looking for refuge in hidden ruins that could burn no more, in corners in which the fires weren't yet strong. Who can describe the great sorrow, the intense terror of the Jewish community in flame? I will never forget that night when the whole Ghetto was set on fire from all sides. I emerged from my hideout and around me was *daylight*. The great light was dazzling. Around me was the roar of wild flames, the crashing of tumbling buildings, the din of breaking glass, billows of smoke rising to heaven—and the fire, spreading and consuming.

The first days of May, 1943. Outside, across the wall, everything must have been alive in the spring; while for us the stake was prepared. Multitudes of Jews in great and small caravans were still passing secretly from yard to yard, bypassing the flames. If only one wing of a house was on fire we could move through the rest of it. At first we used to pass through the attics, crawling through the holes, and in this way across streets without being seen by the Germans—who, from across the wall, fired at every Jew seen on the streets. But then the attics were set on fire. We continued our wandering through holes from cellar to cellar. Later on we simply loitered among the ruins, avoiding the fire as much as possible. The heat scorched us from within and our eyes were seared. Again sparks fell, the smoke was smothering; yet we had to pass through.

The block of 7 Mila Street was at an intersection, and in the panic on that night of fire the yard was swarming with Jews. The courtyard was large and capacious and the fire had not touched it yet. Many groups of civilians and fighter units sought refuge there, or accidentally passed by and stayed there. Thus we met and gathered: hundreds of fighters from most of the units arrived from their positions and apartments. Worn out, tense and dazed, we lay on the ground faced with the question, *"What now?"* We didn't have an answer. Around the Ghetto there was the constant murmur of catastrophe. Occasionally groups of Jews would enter the yard, with their meager parcels, their women and children, seeking respite from the fire. They clung to us as to an anchor of salvation, and harkened to our utterances. They would drop in the corners of the yard, exhausted. Some of them raised beseeching hands to us: *"Tiernike, vuhin?"* Dear ones, where to? Tell us, where to?

During our conference, a youth came to us and said that he knew of a possible way out, a passage through the sewers to the Aryan side. The manhole leading to the sewers was near some ruins which could serve as a temporary refuge. We could walk in organized, army groups and maybe we would succeed in breaking through. With hesitation, and after weighing the matter but seeing no other solution, we were resolved: we would go! But what would happen over there on the Aryan side? Certainly extinction and annihilation awaited us there, too. Single people might save their souls, perhaps not all of us would be caught: but all these thousands were ready to go with us—to follow our steps come what may, they said, refusing to separate from us.

It was decided to give it a trial; and five men with Aryan-looking faces were sent out to test the route. They left, and we anxiously awaited their return. New flocks of refugees arrived in the yard. They were confused, they asked questions, they listened; and they, too, remained and waited, joining their lot to the community's fate.

This great human mass was humming. Children's crying and the moans of weakened people were heard. Someone came with a slice of bread in his hand and dozens pounced on it to get a crumb.

The hours were passing. The great crowd became silent. It was immersed in waiting, hunger and prayers for pity;

only an occasional moan was heard. A group of fighters lying supine started a quiet song. The weight of despair was upon us.

One hour after midnight two men came back: the guide, wounded and bleeding, and Tuvia Bozikovsky. They said they had passed through the sewers and reached the manhole without incident. They had lifted the cover with difficulty; one of them had climbed up and stuck his head out. The street was quiet and deserted. They had emerged from the sewer, first the two girls, then the two boys, and one pair had hurried away, their silent steps lost in the quiet of the street. A few minutes later, while Tuvia was still near the opening and the guide was behind him, they had been shot at. They had hurriedly jumped back in the sewer and returned. They didn't know what had happened to the two who got away. That was the situation!

Silence. What was there left to say to the fighters, to the anxious Jews around us? The plan for mass exodus had been cancelled. There was no choice for the time being but to stay in the burning Ghetto and look for a solution inside its boundaries.

A meeting of fighters was held and the units were instructed to entrench in fireproof bunkers and in ruins as yet untouched by the blaze. We told the Jews to look for temporary shelter. But they would not move away from us. Many accompanied the units and joined them on their way. They felt a measure of security in being near the fighters. It was like a man clutching at twigs. The people spread to search for hideouts in bunkers and ruins, and many entered the sewers to hide during the daytime, leaving them only at night.

The end had not yet come! The flames and smoke continued to scorch the houses of the Ghetto, but underground, in the bunkers, not all life was extinguished; and the battle, too, did not cease. At night Jewish life pulsed even stronger amid the flames.

Total darkness prevailed in the subterranean kingdom, in the main bunker of the Jewish Fighting Organization at 18 Mila Street. Outside a pleasant spring day smiled, but in the bunker time was reversed, day was night and night, day.

Anyone passing the shambles during the day would never have believed that beneath the thickness of these ruins, at a depth of five meters, hundreds of people, human beings, were lying, breathing, conversing, awake and asleep, dreaming and perhaps even believing. The ruins were silent. Not a single ray of light came through. There was no cycle of day and night. Only the hands of the clock told us that outside the sun was setting and night descending. And when darkness settled outside, and silence prevailed in the great city beyond the Ghetto walls, and the citizens of Warsaw returned to their homes—the smoldering Ghetto stirred. Those who had been lying cramped would stretch their bodies and emerge from their holes, and the mood would brighten: *another day had passed!*

The yearning for daylight could not be fulfilled. But you could move a little, you could breathe the open air, even though it was the air of the Ghetto, the remains of which were smoldering. . . . One could emerge from the state of hibernation; and soon a bowl of soup, the only portion of food, would be served.

And we, the workers, braced ourselves and got ready for action. There were many preparations for the night. *There was still something to do!* From this place orders had to be sent to all parts of the Ghetto; members of the liaison personnel had to leave for units in other bunkers; and orders had to be sent to the reconnaissance, intelligence and combat units. And perhaps a telephone would be found, so that we could contact our comrades on the Aryan side—before the fire we contacted them every night, but the fire had destroyed almost all telephones—to inform them of the news on our side, to hear something from the other side—and for heaven's sake, would they send the equipment! One person would approach the wall, going to the entrance through a tunnel, to look for the promised sign or signal from the other side. Some would go scavenging in the deserted bunkers for the remains of food and perhaps a little tobacco. Outside the soup would be cooked in a large vat, without fear of the smoke's showing, as during the day. For weeks we had eaten no bread. How could we have gotten it?

Only a few days previously we had still been sending combat units out to ambush Germans, who did not dare to enter the Ghetto in open formation, but secretly infiltrated, one by one. Our men would take up positions amid the rubble, climb on top of a demolished house, observe through a gap, and wait. They would crouch there for hours; all around, complete silence, the skies bright with the beginning of spring. The May sun was caressing, after the chill of winter, and it had been good to lie so, and occasionally feel in one's hand the pleasant sensation of a pistol; to close one's eyes occasionally and dream of a pure world far away, a world uncontaminated by murder, hatred and blood; a distant and beloved land which one might not be fortunate enough ever to see, as one did not know what would happen on this day or whether one would have such a precious hour on the next day to breathe the pure air of God's world. Many of us had been eager to go to these battle positions if only to escape from crouching in the dark, suffocating bunker.

In the ruins close by, shadows moved, shadows of Jews who had also emerged from under the ground, from here and there, to breathe the air, look for food, meet friends and wonder about the future. They stood about the yard in small clusters, their heads together, and whispered to each other. But every night the number of Jews diminished; one felt in the night that the opaque clusters were growing fewer.

Only at dawn did our night begin. We would return to the bunkers and crawl inside. The units of fighters and the messengers would return from their bases. And then, when daylight broke, the German patrols would begin to move in the area. They would sniff like bloodthirsty hounds. Where were those damned Jews hiding, the *last* Jews? As long as there was a single Jew left, still breathing the stale air of the bunkers, this scum of humanity was not still.

At dawn, night would start in the bunkers. Half naked,

the fighters would fall on the rags side by side to get some sleep; but the murmur did not stop. Breathing was hard, the air was impure and stale. One tossed and turned, dozing fitfully. At noon the bunker would begin to wake. The bare bulb would shed its dead light on us. We stayed lying around, but conversations would begin in the corners. Occasionally during the day dry, uncooked grits would be passed around to assuage our hunger. Cooking was forbidden during the day. The hours crawled by in slow agony, the residents of the bunker continued lying on the ground; and there was an agonizing yearning for the evening to come.

One hundred and twenty Hebrew fighters and their command resided in that bunker.

The Ghetto was being razed. We were completely cut off from the world and condemned to death by slow starvation. For weeks people had had no bread and only the portion of meager soup cooked at night somehow maintained their weakening bodies. At night Jews from various bunkers would meet and pass along news of bunkers that had fallen into German hands. Someone who had miraculously escaped from the Germans would tell a horror story of how the predators had descended on the bunkers and caught its residents. The Germans had various methods of discovering the entrances to the bunkers. At times they would remain hiding in the ruins for a whole night, without moving, eavesdropping on conversations and watching to see where the entrances and exits were. After nights of observation they would break in. But mainly they relied on information supplied by Jews themselves, Jews caught, hungry and tortured, who had lost their human dignity. They cajoled them, "Tell us where there is a bunker and we will spare your life. Otherwise . . ." And there were Jews who guided the Germans with terror in their eyes.

More than once people pleaded with us, "End our lives, kill us." And even though we thought that it would be merciful, we didn't have the strength to take a Jewish life. Many went out of their minds from the anxiety, fears and torture. How horrible was our impotence!

One day I went to visit Abraham Gefner's bunker; but

alas, the silence of death pervaded. It was empty, not a soul there. All the residents, among them Gefner, with his warm, merciful Jewish heart, all of them had perished.

Gefner is worth telling about. In the first days of the Ghetto he was one of the richest men in the Warsaw congregation, one of its notables. He had headed the supply institute that was first run by the Judenrat but then became an autonomous unit. Here were concentrated the few supplies furnished by the Germans. Through the institute many other necessities were smuggled in from the Aryan side. Food prices were exorbitant, and the institute collected a fortune. Some of the workers of the institute engaged in black marketeering of necessities, stocked food and made a great deal of money. Gefner was one of the few who took care to give the institution a community character, faithful to its purpose of saving the Jewish masses from starvation. He helped orphanages, public kitchens, and various organizations; our Chalutz movement appreciated him and his work. Not a trace of graft was in his soul. He distributed his large fortune in money and clothing to the poor; and after giving away all his wealth, he still walked the streets of the Ghetto distributing what food he had to hungry urchins. He was the only one of his age and status to display deep understanding and sympathy for the Jewish youth who insisted on defense. At the beginning of the discussions on the formation of the Jewish Fighting Organization he had said, "I'm old, but I'll help you as much as I can. Go right ahead."

The supply institute constructed a spacious bunker loaded with food. When the uprising began, all its members, including Gefner, went underground.

On the seventh day of the uprising I had met Gefner while visiting this bunker. He was squeezed in among the crowd that overflowed the rooms. He had resigned himself to the situation uncomplainingly, trusting to us for help. We were then still walking around feeling victorious; the weapons in our hands raised our self-esteem and our prestige in the eyes of the Ghetto and instilled a measure of confidence in us.

Several combat units were quartered in Gefner's bunk-

71

er. One day it was suddenly attacked by the Germans, who knew that there were Jewish fighters there. They charged from the outside, yelling, "Get out!" The situation was almost hopeless. But Chanoch Guttman kept his wits about him; he ordered Dvora Baran, a member of our movement distinguished for her faithfulness and devotion to duty, to storm out first, assuming that the Germans would not shoot her. And indeed when she emerged the Germans were stunned by her beauty and daring; and immediately she shocked them with a hand grenade and they scattered, frightened. These few minutes were exploited by the fighters, who charged out of the bunker, took positions in the rubble nearby, and poured a hail of bullets on the Germans. Four fighters fell in this battle, and Chanoch Guttman was wounded; but dozens of Germans paid with their lives. And the main thing, the Jews of the bunker escaped death. Among the dead of that day was Abraham Eiger. Lying in a pool of blood he yelled to his friend, "Don't abandon the pistol! Take the pistol!" And he had yelled at the Germans with the last of his strength, "The day of revenge will come!"

The following day we had sought refuge for these comrades of ours; since we were unable to find any, they had remained in this bunker for another day. The delay cost us much. When we returned the next day to transfer them to another shelter, I was told that the Germans had returned and attacked the bunker, tossing grenades inside; and ten fighters, including Dvora Baran, had lost their lives. The wounded Chanoch Guttman was moved to Zachariah Artstein's bunker on a stretcher. There he remained till his last day, when he perished with the rest.

Thus came the end for these bunker residents. After several days we were unable to find a soul there, but sacks of food and sugar were strewn around, and also boxes filled with jewelry and other valuables, apparently collected by the members of the institute in their dealings. Dwellers in the bunkers on nearby streets would come here at night to stock up on food in order to maintain themselves and their starving brethren.

The fighters were lying on their mats or rags, contemplating. Three weeks had passed since the beginning of the battle. The fighting was actually over. Bullets. There were almost no bullets left. The hunger was devastating. A slow, extended death faced us all. What would tomorrow bring? No one knew. And yet there was inner calm. The knowledge that we had done that which we had had to do was comforting. What would happen now did not really matter. The end would come, no one doubted that, but only *how* and *when*.

There was also much clamor and noise in the room in which I was lying. From time to time we quieted each other down, but the noise always increased again. A visitor came by, Alexander (Edward Funduminsky), from P.P.R. He had rushed here for refuge, having barely escaped from other quarters in the last workshop, from which Jews had been taken to their deaths. He told how he had managed to sneak out at the last minute, hiding in the ruins, finally reaching us. We listened to the horrible story and told him of what had happened to us during these weeks in which we had been cut off from each other. I read him a Hebrew letter, Izhak's letter sent from the Aryan side, about the fact that the attempts to assist us had not yet been successful; following which a big argument broke out. We discussed Hebrew and Yiddish, Zionism and Communism; and in the heat of the argument we forgot where we were, raising our voices excitedly, so that the chief rushed, agitated, to our room to calm us down. We might have, God forbid, brought calamity to the whole bunker. After we had calmed down he smilingly suggested that we finish the argument in the afterworld. . . .

We returned to our reality. The question again arose, what should we do? We hadn't imagined that after weeks of battle we would still be alive to discuss our end. We had been certain that the end would come earlier. . . . And now we had been granted life, though a pitiful life; but Jewish fighters remained alive and the load of responsibility was great, not only toward ourselves, but to all those around, cleaning weapons and attentively hanging on our utterances.

Contact with the Aryan side had been completely cut

off. Several days before we had sent groups of fighters through the sewers and a tunnel which was accidentally discovered. But no one knew their fate. How horrible was this necessity to escape to the Aryan side: a person who was lucky and succeeded in getting through without incident would have to walk in fear through the gentile streets, afraid that he might be recognized. He had nowhere to go. When the evening approached and the hour of curfew came, there would be no house that a persecuted, escaping Jew could go to: all doors were closed to him. Up to then our Polish friends had been unable to provide us with places of shelter.

The conversation went on and included more people. Berl Broide suggested that we should go out in the daylight and attack the German guards suddenly, overpower them and leave for the forest. Someone countered him with the argument, "Well, let's assume that we could succeed in overpowering the Nazi guard, how would we pass through the streets of Warsaw on our way to the forest?" Aryeh Wilner thought that all we could do was to go on sending groups of fighters to the Aryan side through the hazardous routes we had been using, even though we had no information about the fate of those who had been sent up to then; whoever got through, would get through. Even if only two out of ten got through, it was better than remaining here, dying of starvation and lack of air.

The choice was difficult.

It was easy to find objections to these suggestions, but it was hard to find alternatives. Mordecai Anilewitz who felt the full burden of responsibility, weighed every proposal; but, in truth, could find no solution. At last Tuvia Bozikovsky said that there was a direct and convenient approach to the sewers from the bunker at 22 Franciskanska Street. We knew that entering the sewer canals was not enough; one had to know the way through them to an exit. The network of subterranean canals was large and complicated; many who had tried to flee through them had wandered around for days and nights and finally perished in fear and from hunger and thirst. "But there is a man in that bunker," added Tuvia, "who knows the way."

74

We were still gnawed by doubt, and the main question was insoluble: how to move to the Aryan streets and where to go from there. Finally we decided, because we had no other choice. It was decided to send a group of ten fighters through the sewers to the Aryan side. They would have to leave at night and hide in demolished houses. Aryan-looking friends would seek our comrades out and see what they could do together. The whole plan was uncertain because we didn't know if this Jew would consent to guide us through the sewers; nevertheless, it was decided that we should go, and I was ordered to leave with the group going to the bunker on Franciskanska Street, to negotiate with the guide, and to see the group off.

Last preparations. We dressed, took up our weapons, and departed. Would we see each other again? Outwardly we were calm, we smiled and cracked jokes, we shook hands firmly and lovingly. Clutching our pistols, we left.

We began to crawl out of the narrow opening of the bunker, which was covered with stones. We slithered on our bellies like snakes; otherwise one could not pass through. We had forgotten that it was night out now; for some reason we had believed that we would see daylight on the outside, our yearning for it was so great after weeks of night. But outside, too, the darkness engulfed us. However, fresh air entered our lungs and we breathed it in with open mouths. We whispered to the watchman to ask whether the Germans were lurking nearby. The guard answered quietly that there was shooting to the left, but that the right was calm and one could pass through there.

We walked silently with rags around our feet to muffle our steps; more than once one of us stopped abruptly, hearing the crunch of glass breaking under his feet. We stepped over the ruins, knowing that here and there beneath us a last spark of Jewish life still flickered. Skeletons of burned-out houses, heaps of rubble. Occasionally the darkness was pierced by a house still burning, not yet consumed. Each time one came outside it was more difficult to recognize the Ghetto. Everything had changed drastically.

Again, calm and tranquility. The quiet was only occasionally disturbed by a window swinging in the wind, by a squeaking iron gate.

As a rule, we didn't walk in the streets. German patrols lurked across the wall, observing the inside; therefore, we picked out paths through the ruins parallel to the streets. We stalked tensely and cautiously in order not to make a sound, our fingers ready on our pistols. Only the day before one of our reconnaissance parties had been surprised by Germans emerging from ambush. Our friends had immediately replied with fire and had killed a few of the Germans; but two of our comrades also had been mortally wounded. Here and there on our way through the yards we met some remaining Jews who were encouraged by the sight of armed Jewish fighters. They asked, *"Vos tut men?"* (What is there to do?) No food was left, everything had burned. Later they told us in whispers how earlier that day a nearby bunker had been discovered and ordinary Jews had defended themselves with arms till the last minute. We felt their burning jealousy. For some reason they believed that we were happy, were certain that we would find salvation. They didn't know how powerless we were. Our impotence loomed large to us because we could offer them no help. We muttered some solace and went on our way. We approached the wall, crawling on our bellies. A German patrol lurked nearby; we sprinted across a street and were again swallowed up by the ruins.

On our way we stopped off at the bunkers of various fighting units, to deliver messages from the command. I uttered the password to the watchman and went in to see Zachariah Artstein. During the first days of the uprising I had been in his unit; I was also well acquainted with the owner of his bunker. At the end of the first day of fighting we had been in the yard of 33 Nalevki Street, shocked, exhausted, hungry and thirsty. A young man whom I had met a few days before, when he came to sell arms, had appeared. A delightful fellow, an ex-Communist. He had invited us to join his bunker. It was rare, indeed, that someone would voluntarily invite additional people to his bunker, crowded as they all were. His large family lived there. He was the actual head of his family, conducting

76

all its affairs. I used to see him distributing food with great care; he never took an extra crumb for himself.

I shall never forget our reception in this bunker that first day, the hearty friendship with which we were overwhelmed. He understood our situation. He gave us some of the cognac he kept for the weak and the sick, to revive us; and then he fed us from their stores. It had been a wonderful feeling to know that we had such backing, that the Jewish heart was pulsing with us.

We had been puzzled to find three dead Germans near this bunker, knowing that it was not our work. Later this young man had told us that while we were conducting the battle and they were lying in the bunker listening to what was going on, three of their young men had gone out, shot the Germans in the rear, and vanished. . . .

We had a happy reunion with our comrades there, discussing the news from the front that we had heard on the radio with them. Then the perennial question arose: Had the Germans suffered their last defeat? And if not, *when? When?*

We also stopped by at the Finkerts' bunker. They were undertakers and gravediggers. The Germans had been "benevolent" to the Ghetto gravediggers; since they needed them for burying the dead and those still being killed, they had left them alive. The Jewish cemetery was outside the Ghetto boundaries, and we used to contact our friends on the Aryan side through the gravediggers. But three days had passed since the gravediggers last left for the cemetery; they hadn't returned and no one knew what had happened to them. We were waiting for a shipment of twenty rifles and for news about help, and there had been no response. Every night we had come to the bunker to inquire, but to no avail. Tonight we were also unable to find them. It was a spacious bunker, with abundant food that they had brought over from the Aryan side. Here one of us could, occasionally, get hold of a piece of bread.

At last we arrived at the bunker in 22 Franciskanska Street. A lively meeting of friends took place. Ten days before, at the beginning of the uprising, the bunker had been discovered by the Germans and many of the people in it had been executed. It had happened in this way: a Jew who worked for the Germans came, accompanied by Germans who had promised to take his family out in safety. He, indeed, took the members of his family with him; and after a few hours the bunker was surrounded by German soldiers. Many had saved themselves only by escaping to the sewers. One hundred sixty of the three hundred had entered the canal and in this way escaped capture. The Germans were unable to imagine that so many Jews had found refuge. After the Germans left, the Jews, having no other shelter, returned to the bunker; but they closed off the old exit, reduced the space inside, and gave themselves into the hands of destiny, hoping that the Germans wouldn't come back since they were sure that they had smoked out all the residents.

We negotiated with the head of the bunker and the man familiar with the maze of sewers, and decided to go on our way that night. The man agreed to go at once, to show the way to one of our men and to return, on the condition that he could join the second group going to the Aryan side.

Last preparations. We took some food; there was a piece of sugar and a handful of dry bread in each person's bag. Who knew where those who left would find themselves, or if they would be able to get food? Instructions on how to behave on the way were given, and the manner of leaving the sewer planned. The intended exit was on Bielanska Street, close to the ruins left by the 1939 bombardment. The ruins would provide the first shelter. If the fighters were to run into a patrol, they were to open fire and break through the ruins. Aaron Bruskin (Pavel) and Hale Shipper, who looked Aryan, left early in the morning to go to our friends across the Ghetto; we pounded the addresses and telephone numbers into their heads. The rest waited for their return. It was decided that a second group would depart the day after tomorrow. They would reach the manhole on the Aryan side at nine o'clock at night and would wait there for a signal—three consecutive knocks—meaning that the first group had arrived safely and the way was clear. The manhole was right in the middle of the street, in plain view, and the danger was great.

Another departure; who knew that it was not forever? The two men and the guide returned two and a half hours later. They said that they had reached the manhole and paused to listen to the noises of the street above. The street had been still. They had lifted the cover and, one after another, had climbed the ladder and left the sewer. The three who were to return had also climbed up and stuck their heads out, breathing the fresh, whole air of the sleeping Aryan street. For a few minutes they had followed our departing friends with their eyes; they had seen no patrols. But after they had re-entered the sewer and closed the manhole they had suddenly heard sounds of shooting. They didn't know whether the shots had been aimed at those who were escaping. But they were worried, they had heard shots! . . .

The night passed. We wanted to return to our base and report on the exit operation, but the people in this bunker held on to us and pleaded with us not to go. Soon daylight would break and one shouldn't be outside. At first I refused to remain there a whole day; but my fatigue was so overwhelming, my body cried out for some rest, and even Marek Edelman, commander of the unit in this bunker, tried to talk us into staying. He, too, was scheduled to leave that night, and would accompany us. Dawn was already upon us.

We stayed in the bunker all that day, waiting for evening. During the day we more than once heard inquiring steps above us and we were quite certain that the Germans had discovered signs of the life going on. It was decided that if we were attacked, the combatants would engage the enemy and the civilians would enter the sewers. Then the guards reported excitedly, "They are coming!" Everyone rushed to the opening of the sewer. Shrieks of terror and panic. The unit actually had to use the threat of arms to restore quiet. But nothing happened. The Germans didn't come. It seemed that they had surveyed the area, heard something, yet did not try to break in.

The day was coming to a close and Chiam Fremer and I went on our way; Marek came with us. Since Marek had a devil-may-care approach to life, we took a candle to light our way, disregarding security regulations. This was strictly forbidden, as a candle might cause disaster; still, it was hard to make our way without it, and we walked secretly through the ruins with it. A gust of wind blew out the candle. We were stuck in a dark ruin. Where were we? Where should we go from there? We started climbing. Suddenly, I don't know how, my foot slipped and I fell into a hole. I knew it was forbidden to cry out. The first thought in my mind was, "Where is the pistol?" My companions were more frightened than I, as they did not know what had happened to me. They found me and managed to pull me out of the hole, though with difficulty; and I walked on, bruised and limping.

We approached 18 Mila Street and our mood lightened. We made plans to play a joke on our friends while entering. But I was shocked when we approached the bunker; for a moment I thought that we had lost our way. Something had changed. The ruins were exposed, the guard wasn't there and the entrance itself—*where was it?* Great terror struck our hearts. I tried to overcome it: perhaps the people in the bunker, in order to improve their entrenchment, had put stones over the entrance in order to conceal it? The bunker had six entrances: we rushed to the second, the third, the fourth entrances. They had vanished without a trace, and their guards were gone, too. One of us gave the password: perhaps the guard was in hiding and would respond to our call. No answer, no signal.

Suddenly we discerned shadows in a nearby yard, walking, sitting. At first we thought that they were members of our groups preparing for action, as they always did, night after night. We approached them happily, recognizing our friends; but we were shocked at their horrible appearance. They were smeared with mud and dirt, trembling and feeble as if creatures of another existence. One person had passed out and a second panted heavily. From Yehuda Vengrover's throat issued a gurgling sound, as if he were choking; and Tusia Altman lay wounded. This human wreckage surrounded us and told us with great emotion what had happened. How the axe had fallen on the shelter

80

of the Jewish fighters at 18 Mila Street, and how a few had managed to survive.

Here we also met three comrades who had left the bunker two days before, and had returned only now. They were Tuvia Bozikovsky, Mordecai Grovas (Merdek), and Israel Kanal. They, too, had been looking for a passage to the Aryan side, had gotten stuck some place and had not been able to return till now. They had met a German patrol, clashed with it, and managed to get away unscathed; they had hidden in the ruins all day. They had arrived here before us and had already heard the account of the horror that had occurred in this bunker.

We managed to piece the following together:

The previous day, at noon, while the fighters were still lying half naked on their mats, the guards had suddenly broken in, saying that the Germans were surrounding the bunker. In such cases the Jewish fighters usually responded in one of two ways: in one way of handling the situation, since the Germans would call to the Jews to leave the bunker, the members of the fighting unit would get out first with their arms concealed. After a few minutes they would stun the Germans with sudden fire, and during the commotion the people would scatter all around and some of them would be able to escape. The second method of dealing with an attack was not to answer the German command, but to remain inside and to resist the enemy with fire should he attempt to get in. During the day it was possible to hold out, since the Germans would not dare to enter a bunker; and an escape could be made at night. We knew that the Germans used poison gas, but we hadn't paid too much attention to that fact; someone had said that if the face were covered with water, gas was ineffective.

So, when the Germans called for the people to come out, the civilians had gone, and the leaders of the *Tshumps* with them; but none of the fighters had left. The Germans had announced that those who came out would be taken away to work and that those who refused would be shot on the spot. Our friends had entrenched themselves near the entrances—waiting, weapons in hand, for the Germans to enter. The Germans had repeated that no harm would come to those who came out; but no one was foolish enough to believe them. Finally they had begun pumping gas into the bunker, and calamity had faced 120 fighters.

The Germans had chosen not to give them a quick death. They had introduced a small quantity of gas and then stopped, in order to torture their prisoners by slow and extended strangulation. Aryeh Wilner had been the first to call out: "Come, let us kill ourselves and not fall into German hands alive." A wave of suicides had begun. Sounds of shots inside . . . Jewish fighters taking their ow lives. One pistol didn't work and its owner had begged his friend to kill him out of mercy; but no one had the stomach to execute his friends. Lutek Rotblat, who was there with his mother and cousin, had shot four bullets at his mother, but she was still writhing and bleeding. Berl Broide, whose hand had been wounded several days before so that he was unable to hold a pistol, had asked his friends to end his life. Mordecai Anilewitz was certain that water rendered the gas impotent and had suggested that they try this method. Suddenly someone came and reported that an exit concealed from German eyes had been discovered. But only a few had left by that means; the rest had slowly choked to death.

So the glory of fighting Jewish Warsaw was felled. A hundred Jewish fighters had met their death there, including the beloved Mordecai Anilewitz, the handsome, valiant commander, who had kept smiling through the darkest hours.

Only a few survived this hell, some wounded from the suicide attempts, some panting heavily because of the gas poisoning their lungs. The condition of Menachem Beigleman and Yehuda Vengrover was particularly critical.

It was a terrible scene. We had all waited for the end, we had known it was nearing but nevertheless. . . . The mourning for the dead comrades, the sorrow for the half-dead tore at our hearts. We had but one wish, to end this dying. We did not know what to do. We scurried around the entrances to the bunker, clawing at the piles of rocks.

Perhaps we would be able to get to the bodies, perhaps we could retrieve the arms; but the Germans had blasted everything with dynamite.

Feeling our deep loss, the handful of us remaining left this horrible place and looked for a shelter for our wounded and exhausted friends, a place where we could think about the next day.

After the shocking experiences of the day it was difficult to fall asleep in spite of our great fatigue. After all, my place was at 18 Mila Street, with my friends. I ought to have shared their lot. Blind fate had taken me away from them, and condemned the best of our young men and women to extinction. Dreams harassed me in my fitful sleep.

All of a sudden I sensed someone standing over me. I opened my eyes and saw the two boys, the guides, who were to have led the group through the sewers. I was momentarily stunned to see them. I did not understand it: what were they doing here? It seemed as if I were still having a nightmare; but I sobered up at once. Disaster must have befallen the group, and only these two had saved their souls. But I was amazed to hear them say, gasping and with excitement, that they had met Simcha Rapheiser (Kazik), in the sewer canals and that they were waiting for all of us.

This turn of events was stupefying. One could hardly grasp the meaning of this news. The joy at leaving the Ghetto didn't penetrate, the horrifying experiences of the day had not yet faded. One was struck by the cruelty of fate: only yesterday the axe had fallen on 100 heroic fighters who could have left with us today. We sat dumb, wordless, frozen to the spot. But the two messengers hurried us on, "The Pole won't wait, and if he goes, we are lost."

But finally, with heavy hearts, we descended into the sewers. Ahead were the guides, behind them the fighters, single file. Marek and I were in the rear.

The caravan of sixty people trudged on through the narrow canal. We plodded through the filthy water, hunched over, each of us holding a lighted candle in one hand. So we made our way, one behind the other, not seeing each other's faces, groping through the dark without food or water. It wasn't a dark tunnel, but a filthy, narrow shaft. The minutes stretched on, every hour seemed like eternity. We walked on for hours and hours. Next day, in the early morning, we reached the section beneath Frosta Street on the Aryan side; and there we stayed.

Kazik and his Polish companion left the canal and disappeared. I didn't have time to give them any messages to convey to the outside. We sat crouched over in the water and waited. We didn't know for what, we didn't know till when. We received no news throughout the whole day. We had no food, no water. I don't remember whether the hunger bothered me, I didn't think of the next day, salvation was not on my mind. Those who had remained, cut off from us, followed me cruelly, not letting go.

We became impatient; and Marek and I, who were at the rear, decided to go forward to find out what there was to be done. We squeezed through among the sitting people and reached the opening. No one knew anything. The first thought that came into our heads, and which was even spoken aloud, was, "Let us return to the Ghetto to get the remaining ones."

When these words were uttered aloud, many volunteered, but only two were sent. The first was Shlamek Shuster, a young boy of about seventeen, fearless and loyal to the extreme. Everyone knew that he would be the best one for a mission of such daring. More than once he had gotten his friends out of perilous situations by his enthusiasm and boldness. Everyone remembered how he had once saved his unit by getting them out of a burning house surrounded by Germans in the Brushmakers' section. It had been necessary for them to break the German line surrounding the Ghetto, and he had been the first to charge them with grenades and battle cries, stunning them. The Germans had been flabbergasted, and by the time they had managed to pull themselves together, Shlamek and his unit had been able to slip through to the larger Ghetto. We sent Yurek Blones with him; he was somewhat older, courageous and sensible, and was able to weigh matters coolly and not lose his wits in trouble. The two left at dusk and we waited both for their return and for a signal from the Aryan side.

Our comrades from the Aryan side didn't come till midnight. Then the cover of the manhole was lifted and we were given some soup and some loaves of bread. We were hardly able to swallow anything, we were so tortured by the pangs of thirst. Yehuda Vengrover, still weak from gas poisoning, could no longer bear the thirst, and he drank of the sewer waters. Who knows if he didn't lose his life because of that? For when we reached the forest the following day, he slumped to the ground and died within a few minutes.

We were told that we would be taken out of the canal the following morning. We replied, however, that two of us had been sent to bring the rest of our friends from the Ghetto, that we didn't know when they would be back, and that we would not move out of here until they had returned. We were afraid that after our exit it would be impossible to take people from this spot again, as the exit was bound to be discovered and guarded by the Germans.

We continued sitting by the manhole; the street life of the capital flowed above us as usual. A few rays of sun, the like of which we had not seen in a long time, penetrated through the narrow cracks. We listened to the noises of the street, the rumble of wagons and the movements of pedestrians. Aryan Warsaw did not know that there, under its feet, dozens of Jews were lying. At times we imagined that passing pedestrians paused at the manhole, and we were frightened; had they heard any noise from underground, were they listening? I heard the laughter of children playing in the streets. Was it coincidence that one of the children was called Monik (a derogatory nickname for Moses)?

In the morning Shlamek and Yurek returned from the Ghetto, distressed. They said that the sewers near the Ghetto had been sealed and it was impossible to pass. The Germans had apparently noticed the exodus and had sealed all canals leading from the Ghetto. The two boys had loitered in the canals looking for other ways to get through, but in vain. They were heartbroken.

Hours passed with agonies of waiting. German sounds came from the street; for half an hour German soldiers stood nearby, talking among themselves. Had they discovered our secret? From our depressed hearts, we prayed for the end to come. The strength of body and soul were dying.

Abruptly, it was at ten o'clock, a clamor broke out on the street right above our heads. The canal was flooded with light the like of which we had not known for many days: the cover was lifted from the outside and the day streamed in. We were certain, for a minute, that the Germans had found us out; and instinctively everyone fled into the darkness of the tunnel. But it turned out to be our friends. They urged us excitedly, "Quick, quick," and began helping to lift the people out. A large truck stood by the manhole. In a very few minutes, forty of us were in the truck, which immediately moved away. A second car was to pick up the rest.

Now, seeing each other in broad daylight, smeared with the slime of the sewers, covered with rags, filthy, our faces skinny and tortured, knees trembling with weakness, we were terrified. We had almost lost the appearance of human beings. Only our burning eyes showed that we were living people. We lay prostrate on the floor of the truck, with our weapons. And so the van, loaded with armed Jewish fighters, traveled through the heart of Nazi Warsaw. (This happened on May 10th, 1943.) Kshatchek, the Pole, our ally, sat near the driver and directed him. In the back of the truck, Kazik stood upright in full sight of everyone on the street, and we, prostrated, saw him and were comforted by the expression on his face. We didn't know where we were going, which streets we were passing; we didn't talk. Around us arose the din of the capital, the noise of automobiles and passing people. I lay there numbed, and my anxiety for those who had remained in the Ghetto was unremitting. The question was pressing, haunting: *"How had it all happened?"*

When we neared the woods some people ran out and

fell on our necks, embracing us. They were members of the combat unit that had left the Teben-Schultz area and escaped in the same way we had; they had reached the forest ten days before. They had been certain that we had been annihilated and that they were the last survivors. We had been cut off from them. Empty streets and walls heavily guarded by the Germans had divided them from us. All our attempts to establish contact with them since the beginning of the uprising had failed. These attempts had cost us three lives, but to no avail.

We appeared subhuman in our rags, with our slimy, unwashed faces, and they almost did not recognize us. They immediately offered us warm milk. Everything was so strange. Our heads spun from the speed with which everything was happening. Around us the forest was green, the day beautiful, spring. Everything that had been locked in our stony hearts for years suddenly broke through, and I wept. More than once in those years I had had the urge to cry, to ease the heavy burden somewhat; but the heart had hardened. It had been forbidden to cry, it was not done. But now, everything was unburdened.

Zivia Lubetkin

THE JEWISH RESISTANCE MOVEMENT IN BRODI

In February, 1943, it was decided to start operations at a certain place. The two members of the Organization who were the most faithful, Steiner and Baumwald, were sent to the forest to choose a good place for a shelter for a large unit. Two revolvers were given to them, and mattocks and provisions. After six days they returned and informed us that they had set up in the forest, about 21 kilometers from the narrow railroad tracks, a bunker for 12 men.

On their way back through the forest our members had met with two Jews from the Jewish Fighting Organization of Cracow, to check the place for the proposed Partisan activities. The fighters of Cracow had Aryan documents and ammunition, also underground literature and a small military first aid kit. The two Jews told them that with them they had had another colleague; but he had disappeared and his whereabouts were not known. They had gone to Lvov, on foot. In Oleshki, the Ukrainian commandant of police stopped them and asked to see their identification certificates. So they shot the police officer and ran away.

After several days Steiner and Baumwald were sent, with two more young men, a second time to the same place. They were directed to dig two more shelters in the forest, to attack the guard they would find on duty, and to take his ammunition. Baumwald returned quickly to the Ghetto and brought a report that the order had been carried out: the shelters were dug and camouflaged, the attack on the guard had gone through nicely, and the group had taken the loot, a rifle.

In March, 1943, the members of the Organization got in touch with the fighting group in Lvov, and set up a combined high command. It was decided to bring underground publications in from Lvov, and to circulate them in Brodi.

Meanwhile, the Germans called up all the young people to report for a medical examination before being taken to camp. The members of the Jewish Fighting Organization were told to report to the forest. Food was brought to them by people who walked from the city to the narrow railroad tracks in the forest; from there, the provisions were loaded in small carts and taken to the bunkers. Deliveries were always made at night. The road passed through swamps and isolated places, past the small villages of Smolna and Zahoduv.

One night, near Smolna, the young men who were carrying the provisions encountered a military guard. A battle started, and two Ukrainian guards were killed; but the supplies reached their destination.

Life in the forest was organized. For instance, from time to time, literary evenings were held. Moshe Shapiro, one evening, read some of his creative works.

About this time the fighters started to gather ammunition. Small fighting groups arranged attacks on the guards in the forest. They also bought ammunition with money. The price of a revolver without bullets was from 1,000 to 1,500 zlotys.

In the forest, they set up a special bunker to take care of the sick. In the Ghetto, the girls were trained as fighters and nurses. They gathered linen, medicine and medical supplies.

A few members of the Judenrat provided the Jewish military with food. Supply points were set up in the forest at different points—17, 18 and 21 kilometers from the narrow railroad in the Leshniov-Panikuvitza Forest.

Communication between the groups was kept up by special contact men, who gave daily reports to the high command in the forest; from there reports were sent to the high command in the city.

On the night of April 28th, at one o'clock in the morning, the guards of the group were attacked as they stood at their positions at a distance of 18 kilometers from the narrow railroad tracks. The attackers were known as the Banderas (a Ukrainian Fascist group, they used the name of the national Ukrainian leader, Bandera). Both sides opened fire. The guards were wounded, and three of the Banderas were killed. In the pockets of the dead were found leaflets of the National Ukrainian Organization, three revolvers and some bullets.

The wounded fighters were brought into the Ghetto. Doctor Koulansky took care of them. He was a member of the Jewish Fighting Organization. After that the Banderas never ceased pursuing the Jewish fighting groups, so that they were forced to watch out for two enemies: the Germans on one side and the Banderas on the other.

Our forest division grew from day to day. Some members came from the Ghetto of Lvov. Jews who had Aryan papers and very good faces and appearances were taken from the Ghetto. Accompanied by a Partisan courier, they would go to the station of Podbortze, near Lvov; and there they would stand, unnoticed, in the row of workmen who were on their way to work. They would get on the train and ride as far as Panikuvitza. A guide would meet them there and bring them to their destination.

From time to time they changed this route. For a short while they traveled to Kamunka-Stromilova, and from there finished the journey on foot. They had a wonderful guide, a fellow we nicknamed "Farmer," because he wore farmers' clothes and acted the part so well in the way he walked and in all his movements.

The main messenger between the high command of the forest and the high command in the city was a girl, Zosia. She also had Aryan papers, and was very good-looking.

The high command worked out a plan to stage a hold-up of the Judenrat treasury and magazines. In the house of the Judenrat there was a special safe where valuables were kept. These had been loaned to the Judenrat for use in bribing the Germans. The location of this safe was known to the Jewish underground. Ten people participated in the hold-up, and it netted about 80,000 zlotys.

This raid had great propaganda value in the Ghetto. From then on the prisoners of the Ghetto knew that the Jewish Fighting Organization was not a myth, and that it was active. The Organization also distributed propaganda leaflets in the Ghetto, calling upon the Jews to fight the conqueror. In one leaflet, they described the destruction going on in the concentration camp in Treblinka. This caused great excitement in the Ghetto, and jolted the Jews and the Judenrat to their senses about the fate of all those who had been taken away.

There were other Jewish underground organizations, one in Toporuv, another in Zlotzuv, and others in the work camps at Lensk, Kozaki, and Sasov. These last-mentioned groups organized systematic escapes from the camps to the Ghettos; from the Ghetto the escapees went to the forests.

So many successfully escaped from the work camps that the commandant of the S.S., the Oberstürmführer Varzog, ordered the members of the Judenrat arrested and held for hostages. He sent troops to pursue the escapees. Two who were caught were shot right where they were found.

As an additional precaution, morning searches were thereafter carried out in all work camps; but the searches revealed nothing of value to the Germans.

In April, 1943, the high command of the forest met with some of the members of the high command of the city in the Ghetto. The place of the meeting was kept a secret, but it was in a room on top of a roof.

Many suggestions were made. One was that the fighters move to the district of Lublin or to the Carpathian mountains, where, according to information we had received, strong Partisan groups were very active.

Another suggestion was to move to the district of Vohlin and Polessia, a place where, according to the underground newspaper *Gvardista,* there were Partisan units.

People were sent out to investigate the best means of transportation to these places. Near Radzivilov, three of our investigators were killed by the border guards. Another group of investigators notified us that near Radzivilov there were large encampments of Banderas, and there was no way of getting past them into the forests.

It was decided that we should start activity in the vicinity of Brodi.

Near the village of Sokolovka a gasoline factory was blown up. An organized attack was made on the Sasov mines to obtain dynamite. There was a labor camp at the mines, and after securing about 50 kilograms of dynamite, the raiding party stopped long enough to wreck that too.

Foyerstein, one of our people, was an engineer; he worked in the machine shop. With the dynamite we obtained he made a mine, which we planted under the railroad tracks between Krasne and Kulkoz, about 40 kilometers from Brodi. A diesel engine and two cars were blown off the tracks, and several Germans were killed.

Along about then, a special messenger came from Lvov with the information that the Jewish Fighting Organization had been accepted into the Armia Lodova. The people became impatient, waiting for the coming of an officer of this new and larger outfit. The Armia Lodova had also promised to send us fighters who were non-Jewish, and equipment.

Our organization money was now completely used up; so it was decided to organize an attack on the government bank at Brodi. May 13th, 1943, was designated as the date of the attack.

At twelve noon, when our fighters stopped to rest on their way to Brodi, they were diverted from their plan by a German military unit which came upon them while on maneuvers. Our fighters started to battle the Germans. Right away Baumwald was wounded in the foot, Iziu Reinholdt in the head. Our fighters retreated to the forest.

Reinholdt reached the swamps and hid himself in the tall bushes. When one of the Germans who pursued him came close, he killed him with one shot. In the swamp Reinholdt lost his revolver, and he didn't come out until he had found it. Luck was with him and he reached the city. He went to a doctor and was taken care of.

Two of our fighters were taken prisoner by the Germans. They were brought to the city and handed over to the gendarmes, who took them to the prison near the city hall. While they were being examined, they succeeded in getting hold of their guns, which were hidden in the folds of their clothes; and with two shots they killed the gendarmes and escaped to the Ghetto, where they were able to hide.

The Fighting Organization put out a proclamation calling for resistance and uprising like that which had taken place in the Warsaw Ghetto. From information in the April issue of *Gvardista,* we knew that little time remained to us, so we urged the people to go to the forests. The girl Zosia who acted as contact for the Partisans led a large group of young people to the forest.

Raids were planned to obtain food for the large number of people now in the forest. At night we attacked the Volk Deutsche rich people, and confiscated meat, cattle, flour, etc.; and always we left behind a document of confiscation, signed with the seal of the Jewish Fighting Organization.

On May 17th, 1943, the guard of the forest told us that the forest was surrounded. We were the first large group to go into battle. There were two German military units, another unit of gendarmes, and some Ukrainian police. The battle went on all day.

After darkness fell, the fighters who remained alive broke through the ring of attackers. Torn, wounded, hungry, and tired, they reached the city.

They hid themselves outside the Ghetto on the roof of an abandoned synagogue. That day a storm tore loose the rest of the tin that had covered the roof. Wet and freezing, the fighters waited for evening. Gusta Stein notified the high command that they were coming. But before the high command had time to get in contact with them, one of the firemen saw them and notified the gendarmes. They caught six fighters, and carried them proudly through the streets of the city to show off that they had hunted down the Jewish Partisans.

It was the morning of May 21st, 1943. The Ghetto was surrounded by units of S.S. troopers from Lvov. Leading them was S.S. Major-General Katzmann. Ukrainian policemen were also participating; in fact all the Ukrainian police in that district had been alerted for duty.

The annihilation of the Ghetto started. The people were taken out of their homes and shelters and gathered in the marketplace. In the center stood a very large box. Every person had to throw into it his belongings and valuables.

When all those who had been caught had handed over everything they possessed, they were forced to sit down with their hands clasped behind their backs.

Soon all the streets were full of sitting people, and they started to bring up the trucks. The people were loaded onto the trucks and the trucks were driven to the railroad station. There they loaded these human beings into cattle cars and open lorries, 100 to 200 people in a car. The cars were sealed with lead seals and locked, and then the locks were wound with wire.

The members of the Jewish Fighting Organization wanted to go to their daily work as usual. But just at the time they were to leave, small groups of Gestapo men, who were in the habit of escorting crews of young people to work camps, came to get them and brought them, all unsuspecting, to the railroad station.

When they reached the station, Varzog notified them that in the beginning there had been no plan to touch the work camps; but when it had been discovered that our young people were helping the Partisans, the Germans had decided to take them away from Brodi, also.

When the young workers learned of this a fear overcame them. In spite of the hundreds of bullets that the Gestapo rained on them, they started to run in all directions. Many fell dead; only few lived. In this action the Germans murdered many of our members, among them the engineer Foyerstein, and Halberstad. Iziu Reinholdt was severely wounded, then killed.

Around two o'clock all who had been caught, about 2,500 men, were gathered into railroad cars; by a whistle, the German and the Ukrainian policemen were notified to stop the work. All those who had participated in the German action were then served their lunch. After eating, the Gestapo men boarded the train, for they were to accompany the Jewish caravan, which, it seemed, was headed for Maidanek.

One of the escapees told us that the train passed through Belsyce. All along the way, as the train passed, they could see dead Jews alongside the tracks and on the roads and in the fields.

People succeeded in breaking open the doors of several of the cars and jumping out, although the train was speeding at 50 kilometers an hour and it seemed impossible to jump and remain alive. The Gestapo men were waiting for this: they sat on the roofs of the cars and opened up with machine-gun fire on those who jumped. Only three people succeeded in escaping from the train.

SHMUEL WEYLER

PREPARATION FOR THE REVOLT

(Having to do with the general meeting of Kibbutz Tel
Chai and active members of the branch in D'ror held in
Bialystok on February 27th, 1943. The minutes of this
meeting were buried in the ground in Bialystok and were
dug up and brought to light after the war.)

MORDECAI: "We are glad at least that everyone's mood is
more or less all right. To our regret, this meeting of ours
will not be a happy one. If you want to think of it that
way, this will be a historical meeting; and if you want to
think of it another way, it will be a most tragic one. Which-
ever way, it's a meeting of mourning.

"The small group of people who are gathered here are
the last of the Chalutzim (Jewish pioneers) of Poland.
Everything around us, everyone but ourselves, is dead. Do
you know what happened in Warsaw? There was not one
person left; and so it is in Bendin and in Czenstochow,
and it seems that the same has happened everywhere else.

"We are the last to survive. Certainly it is not a pleasant
feeling to be the last. It places on us special responsibilities
such as the decisions which we must make today. The first
is, what are we going to do tomorrow? It is foolish to sit
down together and warm ourselves with memories. It
doesn't make sense for us even to sit down together. There
is nothing to wait for; we cannot live in expectation. Just
meeting together may bring death on us all. What should
we do?

"Two ways are open to us—to decide that when the
first Jew is taken out of Bialystok, we will start a counter-
action; that from tomorrow on, nobody would go to the
factory; that when the Nazi operation started, it would be
forbidden that any one of us hide himself. Everyone would
be drafted for action. We would have to see to it that no
German left the Ghetto alive, that not one factory re-

mained undamaged. Further, you may be sure that it is not impossible that after we had carried through these activities not one of us would, by accident, remain alive. But—we would have fought to the last one of us, till the death of that last one. This is one way.

"The second way is to go to the forest. Today two went out to check and find a place for us there.

"Those are the two ways, and it is only right that we should take them up and deal with them in a realistic and practical way. Anyway, before this meeting ends, we will set up military discipline; upon us is the burden of deciding.

"Our ancestors will not take care of us. This is the ultimum. This is the last minute before the final deed. The approach must be, nevertheless, idealistic; the idea of the movement shall guide us. Everyone who thinks he has a chance to remain alive, and wants to, and who we think can exploit his chance—very good, we will help him as much as we are able to. Let every one of us take his faith in his own hands, to live or to die. But we, as a unit, we must all of us together find a collective, unanimous answer to the general question.

"I certainly do not want to impose upon anyone, and so I shall not express my own opinion about this matter."

IZHAK ENGLEMAN: "We have to choose one of the two roads. Either one leads to death. One way we take a stand as fighters, and that is sure death. The second way we also face death, but it will come after several days or some time. We have to analyze these two ways. Perhaps we will reach our decision by knowing what has already been done. Because I do not know the details exactly, I would like to hear frank words from my colleagues who are acquainted with these matters and are more familiar with them. If there are those who think that they can remain alive, we have to take that into consideration."

HERSHEL ROSENTHAL: "It's still too soon to review everything that we have passed through in the last year and a half. But when we are to make a decisive and final decision, we must give some reckoning of what has been done up till now.

"In the past year, hundreds of thousands of Jews were slaughtered and murdered. The enemy, with great ability and by practical deed, succeeded in confusing us and led us like animals to the slaughter houses of Punor, Chelmno, Belsen, and Treblinka. The destruction of the Jewish communities in Poland will not only be the most tragic chapter in the history of the Jewish people, but obviously so, most obviously so. It is a story of Jewish fear and Jewish helplessness.

"Even our movement was not always adequate to meet the needs of the hour. Instead of immediate resistance, it was the custom to delay action, to put it off. Even in Warsaw, the resistance would have brought different results altogether if it had started not at the annihilation of the Ghetto, but in the beginning, when they first set up the Ghetto.

"Even in Bialystok it was just luck that we were the last to survive in that bloodiest of tragedies. What should we do? What are we able to do? In my estimation, speaking objectively, the situation is like this: the majority of the people of the Ghetto and even our own families are sentenced to death. Our sentence is absolutely final and definite. The forest we have never considered a place of shelter. The forest has always been to us a place to hide in until we could take revenge.

"But dozens of young people are today turning toward the forest. They are not looking at it as a place to fight. Most of them are living there like beggars, and their end will probably be a death in poverty. Unless we decide today on a better course, we too are going to share the same lot and be beggars.

"So now, only one thing is left to us, and that is to organize a collective strong resistance movement in the Ghetto no matter what the price, to see in the Ghetto our Musa Dagh, and to seek to write a gloriously honorable chapter in the history of Jewish Bialystok and our movement.

"I imagine that the natural reaction of any human being, if he should see such things done to his relatives as

98

we have known were done to our own brothers, to our own flesh and blood—a plain ordinary non-Jew would surely have despised himself for living, and would have cut out the heart of the murderer with a knife.

"It's natural that the only emotion that would surge through him would be this desire for revenge.

"To us the decision is clear. When the first Jew is taken from the Ghetto we must start a counter-action. If someone succeeds in getting hold of the ammunition that the murderers possess and in escaping to the forest, that's wonderful. A young man with arms in his possession will find a place in the forest. But my opinion is that we haven't enough time to prepare to go to the forest and meanwhile to prepare for this more necessary matter. I see this as a time and a place to fight and take revenge on the enemy.

"I have lost everything; all my relatives have been killed. In spite of everything, subconsciously there exists in me this great desire to live. But there is no alternative. I can see that only a few individuals will be able to save their lives. If there were a chance that 50 or 60 percent of the Jews might be let live, I would say that the movement should try to remain alive, under any and all conditions. But our fate is sealed and our luck has run out. All of us are sentenced to destruction."

SARA: "Colleagues: about honor there isn't anything to say. This we lost long ago. In most of the Jewish communities the Germans went through with their plans with no obstacles, without any resistance whatsoever. Sure, it is more important to remain alive than to kill five Germans. There is no doubt about it. There is also no doubt that in a counteraction all of us will be killed. In the forest, there is a possibility that 40 or 50 percent of our people will be saved. That will be to our honor, and that will be an important page in our history and a page of greater glory. There is still a need for us; and why do we speak of honor? We have no honor, it is gone. To remain alive, this is our duty, and fate."

CHANOCH: "We must not fool ourselves. Here complete destruction awaits us, to the last Jew. Before us are two ways, both leading to death. The forest won't save us, nor will an uprising or revolt in the Ghetto. All we have left to us is to die with honor. The chances are very slim that our uprising will succeed. We do not even know if we have enough ways and means to fight. All of us are at fault, that we find ourselves with so little means. But this is how it is. But this thing we must and we shall do.

"Bialystok will be annihilated completely. Just the same as it happened to other cities. At the time of the first action, they left the factories and the workingmen so they could use them. But now no one believes that there will be any exceptions.

"It's understood that in the forest there are great possibilities and opportunities to take revenge. But we should not go there, if only because there we would eat only as much bread as would be given by the grace of the farmer. What do we buy at such a price?—food and life. To go to the forest means to start the activities of being Partisans, and to carry it through we would need a lot of ammunition.

"The ammunition that we have here is no good for what must be done in the forest. If there is time, let us use it to obtain ammunition, and with it, go to the forest. But if the German action against the Ghetto comes before we have left, then we must act immediately, at the time of the first aggressive act against even one Jew."

CHAIM: "There aren't any more Jews, remnants only are left. There isn't any more movement—only a few left-over participants. It's not worthwhile to talk about honor. All we can ask is that our lives be saved. It's not important how they will judge us later on. To hide in the forest . . ." (there was constant interruption by the members participating in the meeting).

MORDECAI: "If seriously we have wanted to resist and if truly that was our aim, then we still have to watch over the lives of our people so long as there is one Jew alive in Bialystok. I'm asking a direct question: is it the opinion of my colleagues that we should go to the forest, that now we must do nothing but hide? Do they want to fight only if there is aggressive action by the murderers, and have they only one thought in their minds, that eventually they will anyway go to the forest?" (Voices from all sides, "No, not this!")

"Well, we hear two opinions. One of Sara and Chaim, and the other of Hershel and Chanoch. Now it is up to you to decide. One thing is clear: we will not go to the factories, there to pray to God that they catch the people in the bunkers in order that through and by that we shall be saved. We surely do not want to stand in the windows of the workshops and watch our brothers in other factories being carried to their deaths.

"We can set up a plebiscite: Hershel or Chaim?"

FANYAH: "'I represent the branch. I agree with Chanoch. It is up to us to decide—one great decision now and we will all attack at the same place; or separate activities on a small scale in the forest. In the end there could be greater possibilities in the forest. But as long as we are not able to go to the forest immediately, and the condition is very serious and the tension very great, should we throw all our strength into a counter-action, when the first Jew is sent to his death, and sound the cry of revolt, with all its results? If the let-up in action continues for another several weeks, we can do everything necessary to enable us to go out to the forest."

ELIEZER SUCHANITSKY (also from the branch): "Colleagues: my opinion is that we won't accomplish anything in trying to go in two directions at the same time. The forest is a very nice idea. The forest gives us a chance to remain alive. But with conditions as they are today, the German action against the Ghetto is a close reality. It's an illusion to think they will delay. Even if we had time on our side, say a period of three or four weeks, it would be impossible for us to obtain all the necessary materials to go out to the forest. Therefore in my opinion, there is only one thing to do: to answer German action with counter-action. I think that we must decide on this and give a frank answer which, with the means at hand, however little, we will abide by."

YOCHEVED: "Why are we talking so much about death? It is not natural. Every soldier at the front, or Partisan in the depths of the forest, has only one thought, even in the most dangerous hour: to live! We know exactly what our situation is. But even though we'd have a better chance of surviving if we fought in the forest, what meaning would that have compared to the idea of mounting a counter-attack here in the Ghetto? And fighting in the Ghetto doesn't mean that we would necessarily be destroyed; all our words to that effect lose sight of the natural primitive instinct that is inside all of us."

CHAIM: "I do not agree with Yocheved. Be logical, it's true that we are not allowed ethically to give to any person a permit to escape. There is no compromise possible. If we must fight then it is a fight to the death—it means we will be killed. In my opinion, the best way is to remain alive—to go to the forest. I suggest preparing a hiding place outside the Ghetto, and continuing our fight from there, with sabotage. Afterward we will carry out the counter-action."

MOSHELE: "First of all we have to start with counter-action, and if possible prepare to go to the forest. Every one of us must speak and tell his opinion, because the life and the death of our colleagues and members is being decided at this meeting. We must come to a decision even if the meeting goes on continuously until tomorrow."

CHAIM: "You are forcing all of us to speak, so the meeting shall decide 'No.' You say 'No' yourself, and you want others to say 'No.'" (Interruption.)

DORKA (also of the branch): "I think that our stand is the decision of people who have knowledge, who realize what happened to their people and to all their own relatives. We want to die with honor. In the forest there is more possibility for revenge. But we are not allowed to go to the forest as beggars, only as active Partisans. As of today we have no ways and means properly to prepare ourselves. And therefore it is our obligation to devote all our energies towards counter-action."

BERMAN: "It's hard to say anything. It is very difficult to choose for one's self a bed of ease. I feel as though a fight were going on in the depths of my heart, a fight between life and death. It's not important to me whether I or someone else survives. After all that we ourselves have gone through, and all that we saw with our own eyes happening to others, we can only conclude that all law is unenforceable and that we are living in a state of anarchy. Everyone must decide some things according to his own beliefs; but what we must decide here is the future of the movement.

"We are proud that our movement didn't cut its thread of life even under the most difficult conditions and the trials of the kibbutz in Poland. I and many others were brought here from Vilna. We were sure that many who were more important would be saved. Truly not only me and you have they brought over to Bialystok; they have also brought the movement itself.

"Now it is for us to decide what is to happen to the movement. Is the movement also on the threshold of destruction? And is the movement to be allowed to reach a point like this? Our movement belongs to the people of Israel, and we have only a share in its great history. In the full meaning of the word, we have to take part in the sorrows and pains and struggles of our whole nation.

"But if it is to be decided here whether we have a right to remain alive, I say yes, we have an absolute right to life. Our movement will perhaps be the only one that will leave a record of these hours and days and years of sorrow. The activities of this movement have meaning: that as a nation we should continue to exist.

"To exist not only for the sake of living, but to be able to continue our activities. We are a link in a chain that hasn't been broken for one minute even in the darkest

103

days. There is a minimum chance that it may still not be broken; that, if our strength is devoted in the right way, we shall succeed."

SHMULICK ZOLTY: "It is the first time I ever participated in a meeting dealing with death. We are preparing for counter-action; not to live historical deeds, but to die with honor, as is our duty as young Jews in these times. And if the hour is so appointed, some of us will accomplish deeds of historical importance, and that will be a history far different than that of the Jews in Spain, where they jumped into the fire with the cry 'Shma Israel' on their lips.

"Now about what we should do. We have been taught by experience, and we know that you cannot trust the Germans. They promise shelter in the camps, and that only those who are not working are to be sent to the camps, etc. Through slyness and the confusion they created in our brains, and by appealing to our instincts, they succeeded in carrying thousands of Jews to slaughter. In spite of all, we have a chance to maintain the peace and come through the approaching conflict. Everyone is putting his trust in time. Let us do the same. In the short interval that remains, let us obtain more ammunition and hoard it up, for our supply as of today is very little and poor.

"Also as to going to the forest, we would have to do a great many things in preparation. I don't want you to misunderstand me, and think my suggestion is that you hide during the coming action, for that would show timidity and apprehension.

"No, no! the instinct of a human being to live is tremendously strong, and it is impossible in the present circumstances not to be an egoist. I don't care if on our account others don't get to go to the forests. We have more right to live than others.

"We have set a goal for ourselves and we must remain alive to achieve it. We were brought here from Vilna because there we were due for complete annihilation, and it is a must that we remain as living witnesses. Therefore we must make every effort to strengthen ourselves, hoping only that evil will not hurry toward us and arrive first. So we must wait and hope to gain time.

"But if action comes quickly, then all of us as one man must counter-attack—and I too shall die, even as the Philistines."

SARA: "I want my colleagues to know that I know in advance what they will decide. I am only surprised at the calmness with which we speak. When I see a German my very bones seem to fall apart. I do not know whether all of you, especially the girls, will have enough strength to hold out. I have said what I feel only because I do not trust my own strength."

EZEKIEL: "I don't agree with Sara. Staring death in the face, one can be overwhelmed and rendered helpless. But one is able to reveal the great strength one can muster when there isn't anything more to lose. I agree with Shmulick, that we must start counter-action only if complete annihilation is the only alternative."

ETHEL SOBOL: "Let us get to the point. If action starts in a few days, then we have no choice but to initiate counter-action. But if we have at our disposal a longer while, then we must get busy in preparing to go to the forest. I wish I had strength to carry out what is placed upon us to do. Perhaps when everything starts to happen I will strengthen myself. But anyway I have decided to do everything that it is necessary for me to do. Hershel's words are true: we are not staying to face nothing but desperation. This thing is not a mere choosing on our part; our fate is sealed. Now we can only choose how we die. I feel quite calm."

MORDECAI: "The stand of our colleagues is clear. We will do everything we can to bring the largest possible number of people to the forest to engage in Partisan activity. But all those who are in the Ghetto when they come to catch the first Jew must react immediately. There is no place for anyone who places a price on his life and is ready to barter with it. It is true we have to approach the problem objectively. Most important of all, the proud record and the stature the movement has attained must not be diminished even at the last moment.

GRODNA AND BIALYSTOK

We decided to make contact with some Partisans in the forest, to get some ammunition. The assignment was given to Hershel Rosenthal. I traveled to Grodna to transfer someone there to do his work in the kibbutz and in the branch. I found the kibbutz and the branch in an exemplary state of discipline. Most of the members were new, but all of them were faithful and good.

I was not allowed to live many days in this branch, to enjoy its activities. Action had already started here also. Again, the Ghetto gates were locked like those of a cage; no one was allowed to go out to work. One could not find out what was going to happen or when. Through the reinforced fences at the ends of the street we could see families being taken away in vans. They were frantic and cried out, "Where are they taking us?" A fearful show.

We must try to save them, they must not be taken to Treblinka. With our own hands, we made a forged German seal, and with the help of members of our party who worked in a German printing house, we made false documents for them.

It was very hard to get any news about what was going on in Bialystok. But unexpectedly news came from Mordecai: he had been able to leave Warsaw and had reached Bialystok, but he could not come in to the Chetto. He went to Grodna but Grodna was also surrounded. On the way he had broken his foot, and now he was lying ill at the home of a peasant woman, without any belongings and without money. We immediately tried to bring him in. Without a shirt to cover him, sick and ragged, he came to the Judenrat, but was afraid of being followed. Later, we learned that he had fallen into a trap. He had lost his documents and was picked up by the Gestapo. While he was trying to escape, they shot at him; but he succeeded in getting away.

There was a consultation. There was no other way but

to go to the forest and contact the Partisans. We dreamed about independent Partisan units of our own. Our members were ready for anything. Through members of the party in the Judenrat, we received money for this purpose.

The German systematic destruction went on continuously; the second Ghetto was already annihilated. All our men, however, were saved, some with their families and some by themselves . . .

The quiet in the first Ghetto did not last long. Its inhabitants were still mourning their dear ones when relatives were taken away to be killed; and they were gone only a matter of hours when the news came of fresh German activity. Everybody now knew that everyone taken out of the Ghetto was being shipped to Treblinka. Many rebelled. "We shall not go! Let them rather shoot us here on the spot!"

But their words fell on deaf ears. All of them went. They hoped that some miracle would occur on the train. They waited to be saved by a miracle—and they went to their death.

In co-operation with the people from the Hashomer Hatzair, we sent the first group to the forest. It was hard to bring ammunition into the Ghetto and we said that they should obtain some on the way. We equipped them with money and everything that we could. We had to find help for ourselves, too. They left for the forest but they did not reach their destination: four fell wounded, one returned. Horrifying were the stories Leizer Reisner told about the road. He had seen hundreds of dead Jews lying uncovered in the forest of Martzikantz; others tossed about in their death throes, asking only death for themselves. The hope that we had had in escape to the forest lessened. Without ammunition it was impossible to get anywhere; and winter was coming, and there was nothing to hope for, no possibility of saving ourselves.

Mordecai finished what he had to do in Grodna. He got money, and prepared various documents and permits to pass. Despite his broken foot he set out for Bialystok. It was very difficult to get out of the Ghetto with its locked and guarded gates—but he broke through. He traveled by train, in his hand a forged permit to travel that he himself had prepared.

The defeat in the forest shattered our spirit. There was nothing left for us but to die an honorable death. We prepared our counter-action. Not everyone agreed with us, we who could only look forward to total annihilation within a few days; there were those among us who hoped that after all there would be several thousand left alive. They tried to find ways to be among those. The desire to live when death is fast pursuing one gives one a sudden last minute strength. We decided that the girls should try to break through in an effort to reach Bialystok; the men would remain to face the enemy. Along with many other girls, I too left.

In Bialystok everything was comparatively quiet. The kibbutz received us as a mother welcomes her children. We met many other refugees, made many new friends, and enlisted members. Some of them had been saved from the concentration camps. Everyone found shelter in the kibbutz. Day and night we lived in the shadow of the coming action drawing closer and closer to Bialystok.

All of us worked in the factory, preparing to wrestle with and fight the enemy from there. But we didn't have enough time to muster our strength. The Germans came at once. In the Ghetto itself an epidemic of typhus had broken out. Mersik was now taking care of the gathering of historical documents, and he fell ill: His fever kept rising but it didn't stop him from working. He managed to gather all the data he was interested in and send it to safety. His fever had climbed to 104° when he came to the final meeting that had been called in the kibbutz; he had to clear up some matters.

A few days after he fell ill his illness had been diagnosed as typhus. Mersik gave Mordecai precise instructions about everything; he didn't miss one detail. He must have felt that he would not return from the hospital. Two weeks after he was stricken, he died. The kibbutz was shocked, no one could weep. Mersik, the father of the kibbutz and our branch, the faithful and devoted Chalutz. "A pioneer among his people," said the death announcements. On the day of his funeral the entire Ghetto gathered in the court of the hospital. Everyone grieved, and praised him. Truly, he lived too intensely, he suffered too much pain in behalf of Jewry, and he hadn't enough strength to fight his illness. Even in the most terrifying minutes he believed that he would be able to get out of the Ghetto and reach the Land of Israel. But his soul left him, and we lacked even earth from the Land of Israel to put under his head.

We didn't have time, as the seven days of mourning finished, to set a marker over his grave; for the Germans' attack on the Jews of Bialystok had started. For eight days they took people to Treblinka to the slaughter. It wasn't easy to take the Jews out of Bialystok. Thousands dug in underground, and there were even many cases of armed resistance; and, too, many committed suicide.

We remained alive. Not one of those in the movement fell into the German trap. At the end of the action, the Ghetto looked like a big blob of blood. Thousands had been shot, many had committed suicide, and blood ran in the streets like water.

The Ghetto was a mess of blood: soaked pillows, shattered buildings, personal possessions lying sodden in the mud, bodies crumpled on every doorstep.

We heard nothing from Warsaw. They had been organized by our members, but all of them must have been killed. Tema Schneiderman had gone there, and from her there was no news either. There was a terrible feeling that we were the last Jews left. It seemed that in Bendin also there was no one left. We will truly be the last, and there will be no one after us. There will not even be anyone to bring us to our graves according to Jewish ritual.

It was not that we grieved in our hearts that we were to die. Why should we fare better than all those thousands who had been killed and murdered day after day? Only were our hearts bleeding that there would be left no sign, no remnant, no symbol of the resistance movement. We had not stopped working for a minute, we had done our job thoroughly, selflessly, under all conditions, openly and underground. And we would leave no trace.

As I am writing, Mordecai, one of our comrades, is preparing with another colleague for the revolt. They are making hand grenades. Mordecai graduated as a chemical engineer, so he is testing, and only one out of every six tested is good. They are preparing weapons to kill the German murderers. We will be killed, yes, but together with us many of them will die too. There is no other way; so it must be. I shall die with the Philistines.

Yesterday we tested new grenades. They didn't explode. One was too weak, another was screwed up too tight. They are looking for defects of construction. They have become real specialists at it. The room looks like a machine shop, and Mordecai like the head engineer.

The window of our room faces the Ghetto. Below us in the street is a German guard. They don't know where to search for us. One floor above them we sit, preparing grenades to use on them, and we are deciding which way we should throw them. Our work raises our morale. But what is more important is that our grenades should not disappoint us and that they should explode in their dirty German faces.

ZIPHORA BIRMAN

Kibbutz Tel-Chai, April, 1943

THE DAY OF THE UPRISING

It happened on August 15th, 1943. It was a beautiful summer evening. We had gathered for a meeting of the high staff of the resistance, in the lonely room of Mordecai Tennenbaum on Polna Street. The meeting dragged on as usual and it finished long after midnight. We had no permits to move around the streets at night, so we were forced to sneak through the courts, hugging the walls of the sleeping buildings. It had been the first full meeting of the high staff. At the end we had divided the roles among our members. Practical experience and realistic planning had taken up the entire evening. When we reached our room on Bialystokzanska Street it was already very late. We hadn't had time to fall asleep when Gedeliahu, the policeman, walked into the room. It was probably about two o'clock in the morning.

"Hurry up, dress yourself!" he said. "Through the gate on Yourovetska a unit of German S.S. troops has come in and posted guards at every workshop."

"What does it mean?"

"Don't ask. You must dress and alarm all the underground. I will go and notify Mordecai."

On the surface everything in the Ghetto had been quiet for the last few days. Life had been going along as usual. More than that, lately new orders had come to the workshop from far away, even from Koenigsberg and Berlin. How happy we had been lately as the news came to the Ghetto about the victories of the Soviet armies and the downfall of Mussolini. And now suddenly, a raid. All our plans were smashed: for instance, the plan to surprise the Germans before they had time to deploy themselves around the Ghetto, to attack them at once as they came through the gate—that couldn't be carried out any more.

Four o'clock in the morning. The rays of the sun had not yet reached the Ghetto streets when announcements were pasted up on the walls and buildings. They stated that all the inhabitants of the Ghetto, without exception, were to report at nine o'clock in the morning on Yourovetska Street, and that they were to bring with them only hand luggage. From there they would be taken, together with their tools and the equipment from the workshops, to Lublin, said the notice. It was signed by the commander of the Storm Troopers (the S.S.); and for the police, by Dibus.

Now we knew: the hour of annihilation was upon us. It was a very cold morning, but the sun rose into a clear pale sky. The streets filled with Jews who gathered in crowds around the announcements, reading them over and over again; then dispersed, shocked. This was no place to ask questions, there was no time for words. Anyway, the announcement spoke for itself. The Jews read it and turned quietly, each one returning to his own house. They didn't make any outcry, they were not hysterical. They walked blindly in the morning light as though they were groping in complete darkness. Their senses were not awakened yet, and the web of sleep and calm had not yet been dispelled. Only silent sadness enveloped them as the hours crept slowly by.

We gathered at the previously chosen spot at 1 Piotre-kovska Street. Mordecai was also there. He suggested dividing the members of the general staff so that some would be on either side of Yourovetska Street: for the Germans had chosen that street as the central point. Possibly the streets would be cut off, and so it seemed better to separate the members of the high staff, Mordecai argued. His suggestion seemed logical and we agreed.

Also we decided to divide the ammunition that was in storage. The ammunition on the other side of Yourovetska Street was given to the fighting groups who were positioned there. But ammunition in our quarter was to be divided among the units and positions on our side of Yourovetska.

Mordecai took up a position at 13 Tzyepla Street. We remained on Piotrekovska Street. We set up contacts with various hiding places. So we had fighting positions and a center for the high staff in touch with and commanding the whole quarter.

The hours were getting fewer. At nine o'clock the fight would start. People were only waiting for ammunition.

Our chosen positions were on alert; people ran out for supplies, then ran back to their posts. We had too little ammunition in our possession for the space we had to cover. People were accepting revolvers, but they requested heavier ammunition for the attack; and Kouba was furious, his hands working with the metal and Meyer helping him. Everything was rationed out to the positions; but still Kouba was busy, his hands moving up and down the length of a gun barrel. It seemed as though he were petting it, as though he wanted to breathe life into it.

There came Haska B'yelitzka. What was she doing here? How was it she was in the Ghetto just now? Yesterday she had come here for a visit, to relax among friends. Gedeliahu ordered her to leave the Ghetto immediately. There must be some exit from the Ghetto still open; until sun up she could get out. But Haska didn't want to go. I went over to her, for Haska was very dear to me; but dearer to me was her refusal to leave.

"Haska," I said, "suppose some of us do get out peacefully and so escape this slaughter. There won't be anyone to receive us, to extend to us a hand outside of the Ghetto. We have friends in the forest; someone has to establish a contact between them and us. We will be able to hold out for some time. Haska, you must get out! There is no other way!"

They took her out only after they were ordered to do it. We parted quickly. Haska finally walked away. Who knew whether we would see her again? She walked toward Bialystokzanska Street to the court of Ola Grigorchik, a Polish woman. As she walked she turned backwards. All the while as she kept on going she turned her face towards us.

"Haska, hurry up. It's almost morning!" She clambered up onto Gedeliahu's back and onto the roof of the toilet in the court of Ola's house. We stood for several seconds and listened. In the court, which was just outside the dividing line of the Ghetto, there was silence. No shots pierced the

114

air, no movement was heard. Haska had passed through, we dared to hope, peacefully.

Light started to come in at the windows. Gedeliahu turned his face toward me. His eyes, oh God! How much kindness came from them, how much warmth and goodness. Gedeliahu called me to one side.

"Chaika, I spoke with Zorah a few minutes ago and with the rest of the general staff and our executive committee; and we came to the conclusion that you must leave the Ghetto immediately. Maybe it is possible to get through the gate even yet. Haska had time to go out, and we made her go. It isn't sense for you to remain here."

"I don't understand you. You embarrass me very much. Do you want to send me away at such a time? Can't I fight with the rest?"

"Chaika, I didn't mean to embarrass you, or to offend you. You must understand that someone has to come out of this debacle alive. *Nu*, how shall I explain this to you? The world is not coming to an end, there will still be Jews and a movement and—in short, we think that you are the one who is most fit to go out of the Ghetto safely and have the privilege of seeing the victory."

It seemed to me that the ground had sunk under me. My brain felt thick and my muscles convulsed. I wanted to fall upon Gedeliahu and kiss him, kiss him for his greatness of soul, because of his delicacy covered as it was by his crudeness. How could it be that Gedeliahu could suddenly rise above himself and sacrifice himself for the world which should come into being after us!

I shook hands with him and turned away. I just couldn't look him straight in the eye.

I murmured over my shoulder, "I will not go!" Then we said nothing more about the matter. I met him several times, as he rushed from one place to another, bringing messages, estimating the situation, repeating instructions; and sometimes I heard his laughter, as he goaded them on, and tears welled in my eyes, particularly when I saw him at the fence shooting through it at the enemy.

Our positions were not thoroughly covered. We had no intention of hiding. We had in mind throwing ourselves upon the backs of the soldiers and the S.S. troops when they came to take their victims by force. The Germans would spread out, when, after the nine o'clock assembly, the place on Yourovetska hadn't filled up. Even when the first action took place no one had wanted to give himself up of his own free will. Every house would be turned into a fortress. The positions had been set up in high, strong buildings. They wouldn't be conquered so easily.

The position on Czenstochovska Street was on the third floor, and that on Piotrekovska was on the top floor; and so it was in several other places. If the Germans tried to approach a house, a rain of shot and grenades would greet them. The plan was very simple and plain, and everywhere in the Ghetto and at the gates the fighters were at their stations.

It was exactly seven o'clock. The entire Ghetto already knew what to expect. Germans had not yet appeared in the Ghetto, except the guards at the workshops and around the building of the Judenrat. We had another two hours.

From the place where our high staff was stationed, on Piotrekovska Street, messengers were sent into the streets of the Ghetto, to check on the morale and determination of the Jews. Two of our members were sent to Polna Street, to the fire station, to order the firemen to leave and return to their homes, and to warn them not to dare put out the fire we were about to set in the workshops. We had to get some gun parts out of the shops before the Germans started moving the shops. And most important, we had to get benzine for our own purposes.

Half an hour later all our messengers had reported back to Piotrekovska, and terrible news they brought with them. Masses of people were streaming to Yourovetska Street, crowds of people, taking their belongings with them! It was impossible to believe! How could it be? They were running away from safety! From the firemen also came a very shameful report. They didn't want even to listen to the pleas that they leave the fire station and let it be taken over by our colleagues. They said we were nothing but mad young men. They would not wreck their equip-

116

ment and they would not give us the benzine they had stored there. The firemen had disappointed us; they were scared of the Germans.

Eight o'clock. Our messengers were speeding to every corner of the Ghetto, explaining, trying to persuade.

"Jews, don't go of your own will. This is not an evacuation to Lublin. Every time they take anyone from the Ghetto it means death. Don't go! Hide yourself! Fight with everything that comes to hand!"

Our colleagues turned from one group of Jews to another, exhorting, berating. But the wave was streaming into the streets, which were filled constantly with Jews carrying blankets and pillows, wearing winter coats. Children and young boys, crying, getting lost, calling their parents' names, and again finding their parents. Here a wagon load of goods passed by, its wheels actually bending under the load put on them; and atop the belongings a small child moved to and fro.

A family marched along in the sun. It was easier to die among many than to fight and suffer alone. As it looked, it was easier to die soon than to live a long, tortured life. Truly, living in a hole, in a cave, under a wall, in colonization sewers, in pits and cellars—this was perhaps a curse to be weighed against a quick death that redeemed. Life without hope or way out, without a possibility of fighting: of what use was it?

Perhaps that was why the crowds marched forward to death. How else could you explain the thousands running to Yourovetska Street? Like lunatics the crowds ran. In vain our members stood at the entrances to the streets, in vain we blocked the three beaches that cut off the stinking B'yalka, in vain we tried to send the Jews back to their homes. They didn't want to listen to us, they closed their ears to our entreaties.

But our general staff did not give up; they met again on Piotrekovska Street. Now it was clear. Our fighters and our positions were only isolated islands in a desolated, lonely Ghetto. We didn't have the masses behind us. There were no Germans to be seen. They would take the transports out today and we would remain—small forgotten groups of fighters, people who were committing suicide, benefiting no one thereby. It seemed there was no reason for our fight; it had been taken away from us. The Germans, who had had experience in Warsaw, knew how to confuse people, and had destroyed our plan. They were succeeding in emptying that part of the Ghetto where it was possible to arrange a street battle, where it would be possible to turn every house into a fortress. They were massing the Jews on Yourovetska Street and east of it, in a suburb of parks and empty squares, where there were only wooden huts that could be used neither for ambush nor for shelter.

The situation was very grave; the high staff had to decide immediately—but what to decide? Should we continue with the old plan, though the main reason for our fight had ended—that is, the defense of the masses, now cut off from the fighters? Should we remain just as a band of honorable suicides? Or should we change the plan? Then we would have to go with the people to encourage them, and we would have to revolt in the concentration camp.

This change would mean giving up the protective walls of the city, and reducing the possibilities of a street battle. We were not strong enough to risk an open battle, hand to hand. Abandoning our first plan would take the reins out of our hands—we would not be able to direct the strategy, and we could not take the offensive. This was a serious decision, and time was running out. The clock, the clock —it was our first enemy. The large hand had already reached a quarter after eight; 20 after; 21. It was difficult to weigh the matter, and any decision was a challenge.

Thirty-five minutes before nine o'clock. Were we right? Was our new plan more fitting under the circumstances? But was there any reason for anything whatsoever more important than defending the masses of our people and rescuing them, organizing them and leading them in the battle for liberation? Even if they were liberated from a life of slavery, merely to die honorably.

In those precious 35 minutes all the fighting units were moved to the other side of Yourovetska Street, to the side where the people had been massed, to part of the Ghetto

118

full of parks, grass and open squares. Actually right under everyone's gaze, we had to move the ammunition, for we didn't want to reveal it until the battle started. Group after group of our fighters walked boldly through the streets, concealing themselves by mixing with the streams of people who were also loaded down with packages, quilts, pillows and blankets; but in the case of our brave fighters, inside these bulky dry goods was hidden ammunition, real ammunition, for long distance and short distance, grenades and equipment.

Our units were packing up their equipment and clearing out of their stations, one by one. I had one duty left to perform and I wanted to get to it as fast as possible. It took me across the bridge on Bialystokzanska Street and through the garbage dump to Yourovetska Street. As I walked it seemed as though I was the last person who would be traveling this route. My hands were as empty as the streets; I had no bundles, I hadn't even stockings to cover my legs, I was wearing some rotting shoes and I hadn't had them off since yesterday.

Yesterday! Yes, it was only yesterday that we had had a meeting of the general staff. Just yesterday the Ghetto had been full of activity and lively noise. Today it seemed I was at the end of the bloody march. The main streets of the Ghetto remained, but they were behind me, denuded, abandoned and drenched in sunlight.

All our fighters had already crossed the bridge and left. Only a few small groups, of one or two people each, were left behind. One was ready to move against the Judenrat, for that seemed to be annihilation headquarters; and it was thought that Freidel was the head. Another group had been sent to the workshop on Rozanska Street, where our Jewish labor had made boots for Nazi soldiers. It seemed that tens of thousands of boots had been left in the warehouse there. A third group had gone to the textile factories on Polna Street, and to the fire station on the same street.

The rest of the factories were at the other end of the Ghetto—to which now, the masses of summoned Jews were streaming. When the fire broke out on Fabritzna and Tzyepla Streets, our units were to carry out the planned

119

acts of sabotage. Mainly, they were equipped only with grenades and revolvers. The plan was for them to approach the buildings from the rear and toss a grenade so as to kill the guard and to damage the cars parked in the yard and any machines that might be close to the wall. The lay-out of the factories had long been known to us. So with the guard out of the way, we knew it would be easy to set fire to the inflammable materials lying around in the factories and workshops and warehouses. The groups chosen to do this were made up mostly of young girls. They were from all parties and branches of the opposition. I heard that Milka Datner and Fanka from D'ror were among them. All of them were very young. All of them fell in battle. Sonka, Milka, Fanka, and Yentel! All of them helped to set this great and holy fire.

You carried our flag high, very high above your young heads, dear, dead comrades-in-arms!

As co-ordinator and assistant to the high command, Mordecai had set up his living quarters at 13 Tzyepla Street.

Rubchok (Reuben Rosenberg) had been given the special mission of directing the activity and action against the building that housed the Judenrat. This building we wanted to blow up at a moment when all the members of the German general staff had assembled there.

So Rubchok cut through the streets of the deserted Ghetto. Yourovetska Street was already full of the assembling Jews, pressed close together, standing side by side. Whole families grouped together; the place was too narrow, so they spread out down Fabritzna and Tzyepla and overflowed into the side streets.

Far off down Yourovetska Street appeared a closed column of S.S. troops, crossing the roads that transversed the urban part of the Ghetto; for they had already been closed off. Rubchok had just time to get through. He disappeared around a corner and we couldn't see him any more; and that was the last time we ever saw him. What was his end? We tried to imagine by recalling the echoes of the explosions we heard and the billows of smoke that showed where fire had broken out in that part of the Ghetto.

All of us gathered at Mordecai's place at 13 Tzyepla Street. The occupants of Number 13 were still there. They trusted us, but at the same time they were afraid of what we might do. To get to Mordecai's room one had to go through the kitchen. The tenants saw the young people coming and going, with ammunition making their clothes bumpy; and they saw the guard near Mordecai's room. They decided that it was going to be worth while to stick with us, so they didn't leave to join the Jews in the street.

I pushed myself through the crowd, shouldering my way through closely-packed groups, on my way to Tzyepla Street. I hurried because the last minute was fast approaching.

Suddenly, in the crowd I saw my mother. For a moment I was tempted to pay no attention and pass by without stopping. I had been afraid of myself if I should see her in a transport. But I couldn't control myself, I didn't have enough strength to walk away from her wrinkled face that had aged before its time, to disregard her gray hair. I was ashamed of myself as I saw her in her loneliness. I was shocked to be so weak, I felt like a deserter from the battlefield. But seeing her so, and alone, pulled me apart inside; and I went to her.

"Chaikale, where are you going?"

I did not answer. I kissed her dry lips, her gray hair— and I ran, ran away. I never again saw her.

When I reached Tzyepla Street, the crowds thinned out in the triangle made by Tzyepla, Novogrodska, and Smolna Streets. Our colleagues were walking around with members of the Fighting Organization. Guns and clubs stuck out under their jackets. Group by group they came in, stood and listened, and were told the plan.

We were to storm the fence and make a break-through for the masses who were concentrated behind it. In the Ghetto itself no Germans were to be seen, except those who stood like wooden soldiers evenly spaced all the length of Yourovetska Street.

We were watching the other side of the Ghetto through binoculars, checking so we would know the exact size and strength of their forces; but we couldn't estimate it very well, so we decided to open with as strong an attack as possible, and not to take into consideration the strength of the enemy. There was no alternative; that was the last possibility. We knew that all of us would be killed. We knew that those who did break a way through the fence, the attackers, would be wide open to the hellish fire of the enemy, and that at best a few might get through the rain of fire.

But the masses were behind us. We had to open the blockade and let them run; with good fortune thousands of them might escape. Assembled there at that moment were more than 20.000 Jews; so hundreds of them might fall, but maybe hundreds of them would also get out of there. Even if hundreds fell, there were thousands left to try to get away.

All the members of the high command were unanimous in approving this plan. The ammunition was divided. One hundred pieces of ammunition for field use were given out, besides revolvers and grenades. Over two hundred people were left unarmed, or were armed only with equipment fit for close-range attack, for self-defense. One machinegun was put in the hands of Nachum Avelewitz. As he left the room his face was shining, he was so proud. Many of the girls were left entirely without ammunition. Most of the girls had been messengers or had been used for contact purposes, and some were nurses. The girls started to rebel; they wanted to be part of the armed attack. But who wanted to give up, men or women? And someone had to. The high command didn't want to yield. The members of the high command were themselves to break through first.

Finally, the only ones left in the room were Mordecai and Daniel Moskowitz. They named runners and communication people, and decided how the units should be divided so that the break-through would occur along the whole length of the fence. The divisions were made according to the quarter where each unit had worked in the past. I was placed in the unit of Smolna.

We found ourselves a house suitable for a lookout, on Smolna Street. It was a wooden building only one story high on the very edge of the large garden of the Judenrat.

122

Only its front faced the fences. Its inhabitants had departed. Their belongings were spread all around, and some were spilled onto the unmade beds and on the large family table. Pillows, mattresses, blankets, were everywhere, and on the table were the leavings of food from yesterday's meal. The tenants had left, and surely they too were doomed to be transported.

We had to wait for a signal. Meanwhile we tried to observe what was happening on the other side of the fence. Somebody went up on the roof. From the ramparts he could see the railroad. The military were well concealed, not one could be seen. But nobody knew what was going on farther away. Suddenly a pillar of fire mounted to the sky not far from us. this was the signal. They had set fire to the pile of straw near government houses to notify all the units, all those at special positions, and all the groups engaged in sabotage scattered in all the corners of the Ghetto. Immediately tremendous blasts could be heard on the other side of the Ghetto, and right afterwards tongues of fire licked the sky far away. Our girls had accomplished their assignments well.

But where was Rubchok? And what of the Judenrat? From Fabritzna Street we saw flames, and we could hear loud explosions. The felt factory was going up in flames; it wouldn't be left, a Jewish inheritance for the Germans to enjoy. Fires were breaking out inside and burning up the felt.

Another explosion. The barn was burning. And from the unit on Novogrodska Street could be heard a loud "Hurray!" An echo came back, "Hurray!"

"Hurray!" we answered the echo. We broke out. There right in front of us was the fence. Steadily we shot our way forward. For a moment nobody shot at us, there was no answering fire. Where was the enemy? Where was he hidden? We reached the fence itself and, keeping up a constant fire, we started to climb it.

"Oh God!" the outcry came from very near. The enemy was concealed right near the fence. Hearing the shots so close, they had evidently been startled. Some had been shot. Or maybe the strong ones had gotten scared—the trained soldiers were afraid of defenseless Jewish youngsters who had the spirit to resist! Hurray!

The whole world started to quake, and it shook as though drunk with the power of ammunition that was thundering through all its sinews, and particularly through the entire length of the fence.

Shots started to hit us. A rain of shots, and our first colleagues fell wounded. Not far away a fellow was rolling in his own blood. The house burst into flames. The nearby buildings were also burning, like boxes of matches that had lighted themselves up. The house was no longer a shelter.

We attacked again but were pushed back. Now we had to retreat. We left the burning house and reached the gardens on Novogrodska Street. Other units also started to retreat. The fires were eating up the buildings. We stood in the open fields, in plain view of the enemy. The battle raged face-to-face. We started to shoot from the catwalks on the top of the fence; they retreated behind the fence. We couldn't see them. We started to attack more to the west; they answered with heavy ammunition. A cannon spat bundles of fire. Those behind the fence were shooting with rifles. The shells rolled over our heads. We stormed their positions but had to retreat. That is what we did continuously: storm and retreat.

I kept on shooting. I fell, I got up and ran to the fence. I retreated when the wave of bullets forced us back. I stumbled on the broken fence and it stung my flesh, my feet bled. I became covered with mud.

I cried, "Hurrah!" and I flattened myself on the ground with the rest. The German fire became stronger. I heard the cries of the wounded, and near by I saw a colleague fall. His scream was cut short. I could see Zorah passing, his jacket waving in the wind. And then appeared Gedeliahu, who with quick movements, daring, and dash led the storming unit.

Before us the field was full of dead bodies. The battle was becoming hotter, and the day also was wearing on; the sun was higher and it burnt our skins. The rifle fire was more frequent and grew stronger. A heavy cannon thundered in the air, and silenced the voice of revenge and defense. The garden on Novogrodska and Smolna Streets was being planted with dead people. They were stretched out along the whole length of the fence, with rakishly extended hands and feet. The rays of the sun lit up their faces, their hair, and their bugged-out eyes.

The sun climbed very high and the shooting on the Ghetto side became less frequent and weaker. Our fighters became fewer, and the ammunition began to run out, particularly that for the heavier pieces.

And then, the gate on Fabritzna Street, which was always closed, was suddenly broken open. Through it a heavy tank crept, nosed its way as far as Tzyepla Street, and then stopped. It looked as though somebody had hit it with a benzine bottle. Tanks facing our few hundred fighters, pioneers of an oppressed people and a persecuted nation! Ha—ha—ha! It was the laughter of death, that walked around in alleys and gardens; this was the battlefield of the weak.

People from the crowd joined us—plain ordinary people, not organized or armed.

A woman whom I had seen almost every day started yelling to the people, "Come on! What are you waiting for? At them!" She rushed past me with several policemen. I recognized all of them: faithful people from Gedeliahu's squad. They were always obedient to him; he had helped them and they him.

Here were the factory workers. Their faces were wreathed with wrinkles, their clothes worn out. Not many joined us, only a few dozen; but their joining was a special kind of encouragement.

We would try again to break through the armed chain of German soldiers, to carve an escape for the masses lying on their packages on Yourovetska Street—so near, yet so far away.

Above our heads a plane buzzed. It flew very low, circled several times, then disappeared. Had it come only to fill us with fear? No, there it was, returning—diving and shooting. With a heavy machinegun it strafed the fields and alleys, but not the crowded victims. Even the Germans on the ramparts didn't shoot on the people crowded nearby. Was it for strategic reasons? Yes!

Two rows of S.S. troops started to approach, one from Tzyepla Street and one from the corner of Tzyepla and Yourovetska. Two rows, one after another, carefully smuggling themselves in, their automatics hanging at their belts. We shot at them, but the extent of the battle became always narrower. Many had fallen but the enemy lines were long. They walked, shooting all the while, coming closer and shooting again. Another little while and we would be cut off and encircled. They were coming now, just in front of us, from Yourovetska and Smolna Streets, cutting an aisle for the masses to pass through; they encircled us with a wall of gun fire.

One row of S.S. troops already was between us and the crowd. They ordered the crowd to lie down. We could hear the orders being shouted over near Yourovetska Street: "Lie down. Don't raise your heads! We are shooting at the rebels. Be careful!" They were trying to cut us off from the crowd, and were sending deadly bullets toward the wild rebels.

"Hey, brave one, attack again!" We had been encircled and cut off. Ammunition was running out. There were many casualties. The masses would not follow us. We couldn't carry them to the forest, not even to the last fight. We had killed Germans, we had fought, we had made a bridge of our bodies; but the masses would not take advantage of it, they wouldn't break through. The Germans were prepared to face our revolt, they had brought heavy artillery. The crowd didn't dare to break through behind us, they wouldn't move forward, their chests bared to the gun fire, wave upon wave, as we did. The battle lines were closer and we were almost surrounded. But no! Now came the order to try to break through the rows of soldiers closing in on us, and to join the units on Grodna Street. A single machinegun bore the burden of covering those who retreated.

I saw the faces of the S.S. troops. I could recognize them just by the color of their hair and their skin, and the freckles on their ugly brutal faces. I jumped up and ran like mad. I reached a house. Behind me I heard shots. I pressed myself to the wall and I felt a wave of heat, and right afterward there was whistling above my head. The bullets hit the wall only a few millimeters from me. The house was made of brick and stone, and it faced Yourovetska Street.

The revolver in my hand wasn't of any use to me. My grenades and bullets had run out. My coat was worn out and on my feet were only summer shoes. From head to foot I was covered with blood and mud; my throat burned and my heart was pounding. Behind me were the battlefield, the storming Germans, and my colleagues who were trying to break through the encircling S.S. Before me—was the frightened, shocked crowd, spread out upon its packages on Yourovetska Street. Now Tzyepla Street was also closed and empty. The second row of S.S. troops had closed this street off, and there wasn't any possibility of going up Grodna Street any more. From far away, single shots could be heard on Smolna and Tzyepla. It was the shooting of our members who hadn't succeeded in escaping from the iron S.S. circle, and who were shooting at the enemy so long as they had a single bullet.

I tried to smuggle myself through Tzyepla and reach Grodna Street, but I did not succeed. My group was lost, my colleagues were lost. Before me was the transport. Probably it was now between three and four in the afternoon. I stood among the crowd of poor massed Jews and I looked around, searching for my colleagues; perhaps someone, another one of us had reached here, another one who could not escape.

The people were standing and sitting cramped up close to each other. Except for my closest neighbor, I could not recognize anyone. Near me stood a young girl; she too was searching. Mild echoes of single shots reached our ears; but it was clear that the battle was over. Where were they, all the fighters that I had seen alive even in the last minutes of battle? Where were you, my dear ones? Without you my life wasn't worth living.

But I was there, among those to be transported. A thought grew suddenly in my mind. Should I go out with the transport? "All your days you were active in the underground; you fought against the transports, saying like sheep they went to the slaughter. Day after day, night after night, you talked to yourself and to others; let us not let them be taken!"

My eyes searched the crowds. Except for a black cloud of people that moved slowly with itself, I could see nothing. These living beings of flesh and blood were walking to their end. Yourovetska Street.

The clear sunlight hit the black mass of people stretched out on the ground, in the street, Yourovetska Street.

CHAIKA GROSSMAN

2 : IN THE FORESTS

INTRODUCTION

THE FIGHTERS IN THE FORESTS

Jewish resistance to the extermination program launched by the Nazis assumed different forms at different times and places.

In the Ghettos, the fight of the Jews crystallized in an underground movement that linked each isolated community to the outside world through a system of couriers, and which organized the people into effective combat units. The basic aims of the underground were: to see that the Ghetto dwellers were not abandoned behind the walls and to unify them in active opposition to their German oppressors.

Another phase of the Jewish resistance was the Partisan movement, based in the forests and swamplands of eastern Poland, along the lakes in the districts of Vohlin, Polessia and the northern sections of Vilna, the Ukraine, and Byelorussia. The rugged terrain of these regions lent itself to the tactics of guerrilla warfare. In these areas, Jewish and non-Jewish Partisans banded together to fight against the Nazis.

The Jewish Partisans were mainly Ghetto escapees. A few Jews who refused to be confined in Ghettos fled to the forests immediately upon the Nazi occupation of Poland. The majority of the Jewish Partisans, however, came from the Ghettos near the borders of the forests and swamps. As the occupation forces practiced ever-increasing brutality against the Ghetto dwellers, a steady stream of Jewish fighters, escaping alone or in groups, entered the forests to form guerrilla units. Their activities followed a prescribed pattern and plan: to transform their escape from a passive, personal defensive measure into an organized combat operation. As guerrilla fighters, the Partisans terrorized the enemy, struck at his rear and flanks, sabotaged his sources of supply, and in general drained his strength.

Gradually the small scattered groups banded together

into larger, more effective units; finally they became a well-defined Jewish combat force. But the time came when the overwhelming numerical odds and equipment hurled against them by the German enemy, and the hardships imposed by the hostile terrain, were too much for the Jewish force to handle alone. The Jewish Partisans were forced to seek allies, and this meant linking up with the general Soviet Partisan organization, the only other Partisan operation in this area.

The Soviet Partisans fought under the command of the Red Army. Their organization was comprised of Soviet units trapped in German-occupied territory when Poland fell. Cut off from their homeland, they fought the enemy behind his own lines. The Soviets welcomed allies in their battles, but they forced their fellow-Partisans to fight under the Soviet banner. It was the Russian scheme to absorb and assimilate into their forces all independent units; to obliterate whatever national aspect set one group apart from another; to identify all units as part of a regional force whose designation was determined by the particular geographical area it was in; and thus to account for these units as forces of that Soviet Republic within whose administrative jurisdiction the units operated.

Even the largest of the Jewish units could not hold out for long as distinct national groups. They were assimilated into, and absorbed by, the Soviet majority. However, it should be noted that some of the Partisan units operated to the very end of the war with Jews making up the large majority of their membership. But the many smaller groups were completely swallowed up in the general Partisan forces. They lost their identity as fighting Jewish units; they fought and died or survived as Soviet troops.

As the national character of the fighting units became increasingly vague, the whole story of Jewish participation in the battles was deliberately hidden, and eventually buried, in the loudly-extolled glory of the Soviet accomplishment.

But when the fighting was over, the record came to light —in tiny segments at first, but finally the full story of the Jewish Partisans was revealed. These pages chronicle some of the events of the period. It is a sad commentary that in addition to stories of heroism and courage, these pages must reveal the cruel disappointment of the Jewish Partisans when their comrades-in-arms, the non-Jewish Partisans, took time out from shooting bullets at the common Nazi enemy to direct arrows of age-old hates and anti-Semitic bigotry at their Jewish allies. Non-Jewish fighters took every opportunity to belittle, malign and ridicule their fellow-Partisans, for the sole reason that they were Jews. They tried to diminish the stature of the fighting Jewish Partisan, whose bravery and devotion to battle at the very last equalled, and often exceeded, that of any other Partisan group.

You will also read in this section of the super-human effort made by the Jewish fighters to help individual Jews in Ghettos within the areas of Partisan operations. They shared food, saved lives, and took care of the old, the sick and the very young. This they did as individuals and as units. Often this help was tendered over the protests and prohibitions of Soviet commanders, who saw no point in helping anyone who could not fight, and who urged that the helpless be left to their destiny, to shift for themselves as best they could. Food and other necessities were scarce, and the Soviet officers considered it wasteful to share supplies with the disabled.

But the Jewish Partisans were not fighting for themselves alone; they were fighting for the life of Judaism. Helping fellow-Jews was just another phase of the resistance to the Nazis, another victory against extermination.

ORGANIZERS AND COMMANDERS

A large number of those who organized and laid the foundations of the Partisan movement were Jews. At first, the groups were small, armed only with old rifles, able to act only at night. Gradually they formed small garrisons. Their battle cry "Hurrah" soon brought the chill fear of death to enemy hearts—long before there was a mass Partisan movement. Only later was that well trained and armed by the Soviet Army itself.

The massacres in White Russia and the Ukraine took place early in 1942. A few stray survivors of the Russian Army were left wandering, aimless and leaderless, in the forests. It is difficult now to reconstruct how the closely-knit, tough, effective fighting units of the Partisan movement came into existence, and the origin of many units is lost entirely; but some information has come down to us.

For example, when the Jews of Derechin (a district of Slonim), survivors of the May 22, 1942 slaughter, reached the forests of Ruda-Dobroscyzna, they met small groups of poorly-equipped Russians under the leadership of Bulat and Bulak. They had had no pitched battles with the enemy. Hundreds of Jews, refugees from the Ghetto of Zhetl, joined them in the Forest of Lipyetzan. They brought fresh blood and new courage into the guerrilla band, and they pushed for more action and fighting.

A few dozen Jews had escaped from Radun even as they were digging graves on the day following the massacre there. They met some Russians wandering in the forest of Natze and together they formed the nucleus of the Partisan unit known as Leninsky-Konsomol, which later grew to be one of the strongest fighting combinations.

Tuvia Belsky's group was scattered for months in the large forests of the Novagrudak district. Its members joined the Russian group of Victor Pancenko and so were able to engage the foe in actual battle.

Jews from the vicinity of Manevitz (Vohlin) attached themselves to the Soviet fighter Kanishtzuk Mikolay, who was known as "Kruk" in the Partisan movement. Mikolay was then being hidden by farmers, and his units met in the forests and organized themselves into battalions. They founded the famous Division Kruk; at the outset, this division was made up wholly of Jews.

Jews from the Ghetto of Poborsk (Vohlin), led by Misha Adelstein, were joined by Russian Partisans in the forest of Lubarka and together they organized the Kartuchin Battalion commanded by Bunsky.

Late in April, 1942, the Anti-fascist Committee of Slonim sent its first group, all Jews, into the Forest of Rafalovka, about 30 kilometers from Slonim. They founded Company Number 51 of the Sczores division.

Slonim, a Russian Jew who was a major in the Red Army, had been sent to the Ghetto of Novagrudak. In March, 1942, he got together a group of 15 men, who went to the Naliboki Forest. These men were joined on May 21st, 1942, by four young people from the Ghetto of Ivie.

One of the Partisans in the Forest of Lipyetzan was the teacher Sholem Bass from Zhetel. He had taken to the forest in 1941. When the German-Russian hostilities broke out he served as a lieutenant in the Red Army, and when the Russians retreated to the east, he and his company had been cut off by the Germans. They had remained in the forests. He was known by the Polish name Radetzki. Later on he posed as a Gruzinian and organized the Voroshilov Battalion.

Dr. Yechiel Atlas won fame as a commander. He organized many Jewish Partisan units. Born in 1910 in Tzarnitzky-Gura near Lodz, he was graduated in 1939 from the medical school at Bologna, Italy and later did postgraduate study in Poland. When the Germans invaded Poland he escaped to the western part of White Russia and settled in Kozlovshzisna, a town near Slonim, and practiced there. When the massacre took place there in May, 1942, his whole family, and in fact the entire Jewish community, was murdered. He lost his father, his mother, and a 17-year-old sister. The Germans let him live only because he was a medical doctor. He was sent to a village called Volia the Big (in the district of Kozlovshzisna, not far from the forests of Ruda-Dobroscyzna). From there he was able to make contact with the first small groups of Russian Partisans. He tended their wounded and helped them to get ammunition from the farmers, who accepted him because he was a doctor. Some young people who had survived the massacre at Derechin came to his village, Volia the Big, and together with him they left for the forests.

After careful consideration, Dr. Atlas delayed accepting command of the Jewish division, and served as commanding officer of the first company only. The commander of the second company was Eliyahu Lipshovitz from Derechin. The third company was led by a Russian, one Shobin, and from time to time Eliahu Kobensky from Volkovisk took over as commander.

Doctor Atlas won the love and appreciation not only of the militant Jews but also of the high Soviet commandants; for he was a giant of inspiration in all the fighting in which he participated, and was always an example of fearless courage. His heroism and that of the men in his company became famous, and their exploits were retold wherever Partisans gathered together. The head of the Jewish battalion of the Bulat division was the Russian Kola Konafleyov, but neither he nor Shobin—not even Bulat, who was a member of the general staff—ever made a decision on battle action without the advice of the Jewish doctor.

Dr. Atlas was short in stature. He seemed to lack the special make-up of a military man. Yet in some way, almost as if by magic, he was able to get rifles and ammunition for his own command, for the men of Kaplinsky's Partisan group in the Forest of Lipyetzan, and for Bulat's men. He succeeded in getting the farmers to contribute their own firearms; he found space in which troops could be trained in safety; and he taught those troops to fight without fear and never to retreat—always with the sole objective of avenging the innocent blood wantonly spilled by the German tyrants. He exposed the lie that "Jews are cowards and lack the ability to fight," and he aroused his people: their readiness to sacrifice their lives showed that they knew they were engaged in a holy task.

All the fighting actions in the vicinity of Dr. Atlas' camp were carried out at his initiative and according to his plans. He himself participated in the successful attack on the German garrison at Derechin (August 10th, 1942), the engagement at Kozlovschizna (September 5th, 1942), at Ruda Yovarska (October 8th, 1942), in the bombing and destruction of the bridge on the Niemen River, an event of truly strategic importance (August 15th, 1942), in seizing a German plane when it made a forced landing (September 28th, 1942), in the battle against a German expeditionary force (September 15th, 1942), and in the great December, 1942, siege of the forests.

He was very brave and a remarkable organizer, a commander with a natural talent. A Jew in every fibre, his soul cried out to revenge his fallen kinsmen. The Soviet government recognized his great achievements in the Partisan movement, and bestowed upon him, after his death in the great siege, the distinguished decoration, Hero of the Soviet Union.

The Jews of Derechin effectively organized the Soviet Partisan movement there; those in Bulat's division took an important part in battle, and perpetrated acts of effective sabotage against the enemy.

The lawyer Alter Dworetzki, a native of Zhetl and a graduate in Law of the University of Vilna, was very active in the Poale Zion and Freiheit (Labour Zionist) organizations during the German invasion. He set up a secret leadership of the Partisans and zealously prepared the Jews of Zhetl to resist the invader, and to move into the forests. He reached the Forest of Lipyetzan in April, 1942, and immediately set about organizing a widespread Partisan movement, with the objective of saving the youth and mobilizing them. But he did not have the satisfaction of seeing how successful the Partisan movement grew to be. He met an early death (May 11th, 1942) at the hands of Russian Partisans.

When the Jews of Zhetl reached the Forest of Lipyetzan, soon after the second massacre in the town (August 6th, 1942), a group of 180 Jews with fighting ability was organized. It was headed by the Russian commander Kolya Vachonim, who recognized the necessity of taking advantage of the power and strength of the Jewish community.

When, finally, there was the need of a high commander for the groups, Hirsch Kaplinsky, an energetic, wise and cultured man of initiative, was unanimously elected. Hirsch Kaplinsky was also a native of Zhetl, and had been the leader there of the Hashomer Hatzair (left-wing Zionist Labor movement). His plans to migrate to Israel had had to be abandoned when World War II broke out. He lost all his family, but he himself escaped into the forest. He proved his organizational skill and bravery, and became the commander of a group of Jews. Little by little he equipped them with arms, and joined forces with the Russian Partisans at the Lipyetzan Forest. They participated in many battles with the Germans. Besides planning attacks, he always personally led his men in actual combat.

The Jewish battalion took part in suppressing the Lithuanian garrison at Mirovscyzne Estate (about five kilometers from Zhetl), and the German garrison at Zakliscyzne Estate (eight kilometers from Zhetl), and engaged the Germans and Lithuanians in the battle of Patzatovscyzna, a village in the same vicinity. It also rushed to aid the villagers of Dubrovka when the Germans tried to annihilate them. It participated in the destruction of the strong German garrison at Ruda Yovarska, and later the garrison at Motzevitz. And everywhere it sought out the farmers who had murdered Jews and carried out acts of revenge. The General Staff of the Russian Partisans thus was gradually forced to pay more and more attention to the Jewish Partisans.

Kaplinsky was wounded in the great German siege of

the Lipyetzan Forest, as already mentioned. Though bleeding from his wounds, he tried to retrieve a sub-machinegun as he stumbled back to his unit. His death was especially tragic: some anti-Semitic Partisans killed him in cold blood as he called for them to help him (December, 1942). After Kaplinsky's death, the Jewish Partisans joined up with the Russian Borba unit (known as Urliansky) as a third Jewish company.

Tuvia Belsky, together with his brothers Zusia and Ashoel, became famous in the Jewish Partisan movement in the Naliboki Forest. The brothers Belsky were born in the village of Stankavich in the district of Novagrudak. Their parents were farmers and owned a mill. They were brought up and educated in the truly Jewish tradition and they were well-known in the nearby small cities. They lived a Jewish family life, a very nice one.

When the Germans invaded Poland, Tuvia, who was a leader in his community, moved with his family to the house of his parents in his native village. The brothers, who had grown up in the country, were at home in field and forest, and they knew every foot of the surrounding countryside. Tuvia won the trust of the General Staff of the Partisans when, in the Naliboki Forest, he successfully defended his group. Often he succeeded in so wording the sentences of Jews who had failed to observe martial law that they got off. He was even able to dismiss some death penalties.

Tuvia took upon himself the great responsibility of gathering all the Jews together and saving them, even those Jews who were not physically able to fight. This posed great difficulty, particularly in regard to supplying them with clothes and provisions. During sieges, while the Russian Partisans opposed him and showed their hatred of Jews, he would refuse to let them retreat; for he would not let an opportunity go by to save Jewish lives, even if it were but one old Jewish woman. At the time Jewish blood was being spilled like water, and any life, especially that of a Jew, wasn't a great loss and was quickly forgotten.

When Jews started to arrive from the Lidda Ghetto,

those close to Belsky, for example Jews from Novagrudak, opposed the newcomers' joining their group, saying that they would bring them all bad luck. Belsky answered, "I hope that thousands of Jews come! We will get food to feed them all." His group spread fear through all the Novagrudak district by its acts of revenge against the police and against those farmers who had delivered Jews to the Germans or who had taken it upon themselves to murder them.

He succeeded in saving more than 1,200 men, women and children, old and young, and was able to keep their bodies and souls together until the liberation. The younger brother of Tuvia, Ashoel, was also beloved by all. He was good-hearted, a smile was always on his lips, and words of encouragement never failed him. He distinguished himself as a commander of a combat group, and also served as substitute commander of the whole division. The Russians recognized and valued his great abilities and brilliant mind. Ashoel became famous for espionage. For quite a while he commanded a group of cavalry which was on an inspection mission in the Terov area.

Zusia, the brother of Tuvia and Ashoel, was the only Jew on the General Staff of the Jewish division known as Genekezer. He was placed in command when they were engaged in espionage, and he was authorized to act as the representative of the division's head Russian commander.

A man with great qualities as an organizer of Jewish Partisans was the Jew Zorin. He came from Minsk and was a Soviet Partisan in the Russian civil war from 1917 to 1920. In the Ghetto at Minsk, after the Nazis had invaded the city, Zorin was arrested and became acquainted with Colonel Samyonov, a Russian. Toward the end of 1941, both of them succeeded in escaping to Starolsolski Forest, about 30 kilometers from Minsk. A Partisan group was organized, headed by Parhomanko. The majority of its members, about 150 men, were Jews; but the General Staff was non-Jewish. Zorin was appointed commander of the group and more Jews joined up, though anti-Semitism had started to grow among the Partisans who were non-Jewish.

Late in 1942, and in January, 1943, many Jews from the Ghettos of eastern Byelorussia, especially from Minsk, escaped and streamed to the forest to join the Partisans. Most of them had no ammunition, and besides, were not fit to fight. After many arguments between Jews and non-Jews, and after a clash with the commander, Parhomenko, the latter took Zorin's gun away from him and arrested him. Samyonev, Zorin's unit commander, advised Zorin to gather all the refugees from the Ghettos, whatever their age or sex, and form a special group. This became famous as Group Number 106.

The Starolsolski Forest, because it was so close to Minsk, was frequently visited by the police; so Zorin moved his followers to the forest of Naliboki. There, under the protection of well-equipped Russian Partisans, they were more secure. The equipment of Group Number 106 was always inadequate, and the group's members remained dependent for food and ammunition upon the efforts of the few among them who were able to fight and forage. At the beginning, this fighting group was small, perhaps 60 people; but when the day of liberation came, 700 Jewish Partisans came from the forest under Zorin's command. In June, 1944, when the Germans started to retreat, Zorin's group ambushed German soldiers who were trying to escape through the forests.

In the heat of one battle, when he was attempting to overpower a group of 300 German soldiers while suffering from a wound in his foot, Zorin was forced to have the foot amputated.

In the district of Kapula Gilsick became renowned among the Partisans. The leader was Zukov; it was a unit of Major General Kapustin's command, and the commander was Brigadier Zapiev.

After the mass slaughter in Kapula, Nesvizh, Kletsk, Lyakhovich and Stolpce, many Jews reached the forests, among them quite a number who were not fit to fight. Major General Kapustin ordered Gilsick to assemble them in a special group. The group's most difficult problem was lack of ammunition. Paushenko (Kapustin's real name) did not pass out ammunition to the Jews, but ordered them to get it themselves by whatever means they could. This group, numbering 60 men at the outset, had but two rifles and four bullets. But very soon their number increased to 200 men—130 Jews and 70 Christians. Gilsick made every effort to get ammunition, and in January 1943 he had at his disposal 11 cannons, 23 automatic rifles, and 130 ordinary rifles. The Zukov group suffered greatly in the German siege and was in great distress. Nevertheless, Gilsick, a native of Kapula, led his group valiantly through all the dangers that beset them, and lost only a few men.

Jewish refugees from the Ghettos of Pahost-Zagorodsk (in the vicinity of Pinsk) and from the labor camp of Honcavich, formed, in July, 1942, a Partisan unit under L. M. Kahanowitz. They were cut off in the swamps of Pinsk and its forests. Kahanowitz himself went on several sabotage expeditions, and further, he was able to obtain ammunition from the farmers.

The leader and commander of the group was David Bobrov, a native of Pinsk, and a student at the Parbutz Jewish school and a Polish gymnasium. He had served in the Polish army in an artillery outfit. He was arrested by the Soviet authorities because of his "inferior" race. In the rush of retreat, the Soviets didn't have a chance to release him from prison, and he was freed by the Germans. But he knew the truth about the German murderers, and immediately called the Jews together to escape to the forest.

The Jews who ran away from Disnah, Mayor, Glouboki and Charkochizna were pitifully helpless in the forests and swamps in which they took refuge. Their group was attached to that of L. M. Kahanowitz, under the direction of Lieutenant-Colonel Komchenko. He was also the commander of the Spatack unit, and soon learned of the desperate condition of the Jews. Shlomo Mussin did a great deal to help organize this group. He had been a teacher in the Jewish school in Droyah before the war. When, in July, 1942, the Germans started to slaughter the Jews, he escaped to the forest with a group of 70 or 80 others. He was very heroic in battle. In its short existence, this group carried out very successful operations against the Germans and the police force, thus acquiring ammunition.

The leader of the 51st Jewish group was Yordarovich, a Russian Jew from Homel. They joined up with a group from Choraz (Wolcha Nora, near Slonim). In the war between Russia and Finland, in 1940, Yordarovich received a citation and the medal of Lenin, because he was one of the first few to cross the Mannerheim-Naume line. In June, 1942, he escaped from a camp of captives in Bialystok and reached the forest of Wolcha Nora, revealing great resourcefulness. Under his leadership the Choraz group carried out various battle plans, and initiated the strategy which saved the Ghetto of Kovel; and it was under his direction that the Byelorussian school at the estate of Havenovitz was destroyed. Yordarovich was a very warmhearted Jew who sometimes, around the campfire, told his men stories about the Land of Israel and its life. He wanted to go to Israel, by way of Bessarabia; but he lost his life October 14th, 1943, in a great battle that took place in the vicinity of the Sczara River.

Goaded on by farmers who told stories about the Russian Partisans, three young people from Zofyofka—Badish, Trockenbrod and Rolin—went to the forests to join up. For a while they acted on their own, without contacting the Russian Partisans. Their band grew in numbers until there were between 60 and 70 men. They appropriated their ammunition from the forest wardens and were able to take revenge on farmers who had killed Jews, and on robbers and murderers. They even had pitched battles with some of the small garrisons.

Later they joined up with a group headed by Kobfack. At the time of his famous march into the Carpathian Mountains, Kobfack took into his ranks many Jews who had hidden themselves in the forest or been concealed by farmers. After liberating some Jews from the Sealad German labor camp in eastern Galicia, Kobfack established a Jewish national group of about 50, known as Group Number 7, and assigned to command them a Jewish General Staff, all its members experienced Partisans from other groups. Group Number 7 suffered severely when, in the vicinity of Delatin near the Dnieper River, they cut through to the Carpathian Mountains. After that, it was decided that the group should disband; its members were assigned to various other groups. They are well remembered as a fine group of Jewish fighters.

Right after the horrible slaughters in the district of Lidda, in May, 1942, Jews from the cities and villages of Lidda, Radun, Baranova, Ashechok, Brasilichok, Sovakinsak, Zabeloch, and others, streamed to the forest of Naja; and, with some Jews who had been working for nearby farmers, they started their own Partisan movement.

A group of Russian Partisans appeared at the same time, but its main objective was robbery. The Russians suggested that the Jews join them. With the arrival of new refugees, they got ammunition and carried out campaigns against the enemy on their own responsibility; and so, late in February, 1943, a new division of Partisans came into being. Soon after, they went to the district of Zitomir. There, in January, 1943, they formed a Jewish division under "Uncle Mischa," and it was so called until the liberation.

Later that same year, Ziman Hanneck parachuted into the Forest of Bodunicki Yorges. He had been sent to organize a Soviet Partisan movement in Lithuania. In a very short time, he succeeded in setting up an organization with branches in the southern part of Lithuania, in which many Jews, especially those from Vilna, participated. The commander of this Yorges unit was a Russian Jew, Bobah, a captain of the Vasilenko Red Army who had succeeded in escaping from the famous Ninth Fortress in Kovna. The Yorges unit was active in the forest of Rudnicki near Vilna. It was Samuel Kaplinsky who made them victorious in defensive action, Aba Kovner who made them effective in revenge; both of these men were from Vilna. This unit of the Jewish Partisans was noteworthy in their engagements at the forest of Rudnicki, though their existence was comparatively brief. The unit included the Yechiel Sheinbaum of Vilna, who gave it a truly Jewish nationalist spirit and outlook.

One of the organizers of the Voroshilov battalion was Ephraim Bakalchok. At the time one of his militiamen was Risyanek, another was the Ukranian Maxime Misorah of Vichefka. When the Germans invaded, both Bakalchok and Misorah had escaped and fled to the east. When they reached Kiev they decided that it didn't make sense to continue running, since the entire surrounding country had been conquered by the Germans; and therefore they decided to return to their homes. Ephraim hid himself among the Jews of the city of Dombravitz; Misorah, the Ukrainian, found shelter with farmer friends. But they kept in communication with each other.

In the summer of 1942, both decided to go into the forest and organize a group of Partisans. Very soon some Jews from Sernig joined them. They had escaped from there toward the end of September, 1942. By the following summer, the battalion had acquired a name, Voroshilov, and had increased in size to 200 men, including Jews. This battalion was the strongest and the best fighting unit of all the Vhordoroff division. The Jews distinguished themselves in heroism; many lost their lives in action.

The Odessan Jew Valek Avogoff was called up in the beginning of the war as a reserve officer. He was sent to the front and was captured in Kovel. He succeeded in bribing his German guards, and escaped, with four friends, to the forest. There they met 50 Russian soldiers who had broken out of prison. Avogoff became the head of the company. He got ammunition, and they attacked German garrisons. In a short space of time this group numbered 65 Russian escapees. The Germans threw a great cordon around the forest near Briesk to capture them; but Valek led his company out safely, and they went to the forest of Pinsk. Late in 1942 a great Partisan encampment was established under the command of Generals Veitma and Fedorov. Avogoff joined them.

He was appointed commander of the expeditionary Voroshilov battalion cavalry, and after a period of time he became a General Staff Officer of this battalion. Soon he became famous for his heroic deeds, and General Veitma appointed him commander of all the expeditionary groups at the front. He served in this rank until the day of liberation. Even now, veterans of the Partisans in this area tell of his deeds with great respect.

In the Soviet Partisan movement among the Poles in Vohlin, the exploits of Robert Sadanofsky were noteworthy. He was an assimilated Jew from Lodz. Until the war he had been principal of a public school in Valhone, a village seven kilometers from Disofsk. When the Germans started to herd the Jews of that vicinity into the Ghetto of Disofsk, he escaped to the forest. Shortly, his friend, the Polish teacher Roskofsky, joined him. The latter was inclined toward the Soviets. Both of them commenced organizing a Polish Partisan movement. At the start their group numbered only 15, and called itself the Kosciusko unit, after the Polish hero. At the front, the unit was attached to the Russian Partisans of Sabaroff.

Sadanofsky was sent to Moscow by a Soviet plane that took off from the Partisan airfield in Katench near Yulsk in White Russia. In Moscow he completed a course in a military academy, and, with the rank of Major, he returned by plane to the site of his former activities. Because of the mass slaughter by the Ukrainians of the Polish minority in Vohlin, Polish youths started to stream toward the Sadanofsky camp. In the autumn of 1943 the Polish Partisans had grown to seven groups made up of 2,500 men. Their slogan was, "Poland is not lost yet." All these units later came under the supervision of Sadanofsky— even the Polish units behind the lines in the vicinity of Parcev—and they all remained active until the liberation. Today, Sadanofsky is a general in the Polish army.

In the Goldfalk sector, there were many Jewish commanders and leaders. Some did not know what their race was, nor who their ancestors were. Visacovich was provisional head of the unit's General Staff. Cimbal commanded a division. Kartenko commanded the Third Group, and among this group's number was Victor, the extraordinary saboteur. All of these men were Jews. For various reasons, sometimes because of the anti-Semitic spirit that was rife among Russian Partisans, sometimes because the Jews (especially those who came from the eastern districts) didn't have any pride—they did not reveal their race. It is difficult to identify all the many Jews who helped in building the glorious record of this sector.

MOSHE KAHANOWITZ

EASY REVENGE

One morning the courier awakened me to say that the spy had returned to the forest and with her a large company of Jews. Everyone was waiting at headquarters to learn about the mission and what had happened. I jumped to my feet, shook my coat which was covered with mud, and went immediately to the other side of the hill on the edge of our encampment.

How had this spy returned so quickly? Only the day before yesterday she had gone to the city on a dangerous mission. How had she been able to return so soon and bring with her a group of Jews? She had had but one revolver. Still wondering, I ran across the bridge. This bridge was a wonderful thing; it connected our base, which was in an isolated spot on a hill in the midst of the eternal swamps, with the dry land of a great yesterday— the dry land of the enemy. It wasn't really a bridge, and it wasn't really a passageway; it was a ladder made from pieces of wood and vines which for thousands of meters was laid over the swamp and deeper water. And we knew that one fine day when we could all leave the order would come to destroy it.

We jumped to the bottom of the hill opposite the bridge. A column of men and women, bent and rain-soaked, moved slowly closer. When they reached the end of the bridge, they stopped, and a heavy sigh broke from them. I didn't know why they were sighing. One girl fainted and fell into my arms on the bridge.

All of a sudden I understood what this great sigh meant, this sigh that had come from the mouths of these refugees who had escaped from the gates of Hell with the fear of a sword at their backs. Now their footsteps dragged as they neared our base, which to them was a haven; and I remembered that I myself had been but several days before as confused as they. I remembered how many people's fates were connected with this bridge, and how many had not had the luck to come over it; and some had gone over it but had not returned.

We had a system among the Partisans: to attack the enemy and then to disappear. For instance, if we succeeded in mining railroad tracks, we rushed immediately back to our base out of sight, and rejoicing because of our work was poured out by our comrades. It was really hard for us Jewish Partisans to leave our work in this way at a time when we were most eager to see the results. Though our fingers were frozen, we itched for more revenge, and wanted to lie down near the tracks and see what we had accomplished. Our faces might be buried in grass and mud, but in our hands was a string—thin and long, stretching from the edge of the forest to the mine under the tracks. The wire was in the clear, and in the wintertime, in the dark of night, we would stay on till the end.

This was our answer to the German guards who toured the prisons looking at their charges as if they were animals in cages, who made them dig trenches for their own bodies before it was time for them to die. Going past the prison cells, they would flash reflectors to find out what was going on, and then make their charges dance to miss their bullets. So we were glad to be trusted with missions and carried them through only too well. Little did the Germans know how much hatred bubbled in our hearts in the dark and the cold, and how it did not subside as the hours dragged on.

But now it was quiet. The railroad tracks seemed washed bright in the moonlight. The trains usually moved by, one after the other. But it was midnight, and no train came. Every nerve was tense in expectation. Longing started to burn in the heart. And what came was to us not a train of steel, it was an object of desire. A greeting came clearly to us from the tracks that stretched far in silence. A prayer went aloft while we held a wire in our sorrowing hands—a prayer different from all the prayers that had ever been said, a prayer of love for all human beings. Then the armed train came closer. Ahead of it the enemy had with cunning sent some empty old cars to test the tracks. Fence boards were set up and a group of armed

149

guards came forward in a special car. But the eyes of those holding the wires were clouded by a vision of a dance of death—what was about to happen when they should pull the wire. The Jewish Partisan not only wanted to sabotage the enemy, but was willing to endanger himself till the bitter end, just to see the final blast. For that brief moment he could feel in every drop of his blood the satisfaction, the glory, the retribution: yes, a year's revenge!

ABBA KOVNER

WHAT HAPPENED AROUND LUBLIN

My first contact with the Partisans was about the time of the Jewish Holiday of Tabernacles in 1942, when they were organizing the first group. It was in the Forest of Osmolycza. It happened after the Germans had issued a new decree that all the Jews of the small cities near Lublin must come and personally report in Belsyce. Many of the Jews, and especially the youth, were defiant. Some tried to hide with farmers, but some made up their minds to go into the forest and make a stand and fight for their lives.

But where could ammunition be found? Surely farmers had a lot of ammunition that the Polish army had left behind when it fell apart. But it took much wheedling to get a revolver or a gun from a farmer. The Jews received a little ammunition from various Partisan groups that existed at the time. These were made up mostly of Soviet prisoners who had escaped from the prison camps.

The group of Partisans I joined was organized in the autumn of 1942. I remember that the two Nudel brothers from Lublin and the Nachman brothers were among them. One fellow from Lublin, whom I'll call Zadok (I forgot his family name), was the son of a rope manufacturer in Lublin. He was the first to have a revolver; he bought it from a farmer. Later he went to other farmers and threatened them with this revolver, and so acquired several rifles and pistols.

So, armed, we went to the forest. Just as we were leaving, several other young boys joined up, and soon we had more than 20 fighters. Zadok was our leader. We collaborated with a band who were known by the initials A.K., who tried to exalt themselves by saying they belonged to our group. Together we attacked the Germans in the forests of Zavawhola, Osmolycza, Pietravitza and Techef. They also organized a combined action and attacked the Zavawhola estate. The manager of the estate was a German, who was known as a murderer. We set the building on fire, and took the horses, the wagons and many pigs with us.

At the time of this attack, Zadok chanced upon another leader of a Partisan group, Yanek Springer or Singer (I don't remember his name exactly, but I know he was from Lublin). His group included 12 Soviet war prisoners who had escaped from German captivity, and about 60 Jews, mostly from Krasnik and Lublin and the other small cities in that vicinity.

Two weeks after the attack, Zadok and several of his comrades met again with the A.K. group to receive some ammunition which they had promised to him. But the A.K., it seemed, was only a band of pirates and robbers left over from the prewar days. They met with the Jewish Partisans, and, acting as hosts to a party, gave them poisoned whiskey, and then killed them.

Henyek Zimmerman and Resnik were leaders of Jewish Partisan groups which were active in those days. Resnik had been a prisoner of war and had served in the Polish army. He had escaped from prison and had joined the Partisan group that was very active in the forests of Dombrava and Osmolycza.

Henyek Zimmerman caught seven of the band that had killed Zadok and his comrades, and shot them. He took the equipment they had hidden in the forest, some of it acquired before the war. He gathered some young Jewish boys who were hiding in the forest, and the remainder of Zadok's followers. His name soon became known and he was quite famous in this vicinity. Henyek Zimmerman's group numbered at one time or another 12 to 20 people, most of them young men from Lublin. They were, comparatively speaking, very well armed.

Henyek Zimmerman wanted to enlarge his activities. He wanted to act directly against the Germans, who threatened to kill every Jewish family and every farmer who hid a Jew. He also fought those farmers who accepted money for delivering Jews to the Germans. He also fought the civilians who themselves killed Jews in order to steal their money and clothing. Henyek warned the inhabitants of all the villages in the vicinity that anyone who aided in apprehending a Jew would be killed, and his house would be burned to the ground; and he was not contented only with warnings.

One farmer from Deshef delivered a Jew to the Germans. His house was set on fire, and he was taken out and killed. His body was put on display alongside a road that crossed through the fields and a note was pinned to it, "He was shot for delivering a Jew."

The news of this spread like wildfire, and the fear of Henyek chilled all the villagers of the vicinity. They started supplying food to the Jews who were in the forest hiding from the Germans. One day Henyek ordered the farmers of Benbinski to place pots of boiled potatoes outside their houses every night, and said that he would check to find out whether this command was fulfilled. So for several weeks the farmers really did leave pots full of boiled potatoes near their huts so that the Jews might eat.

In the early part of 1943, Henyek's group planned an attack on the Polish police station at Pietrowitz. This had seven policemen. Henyek took their ammunition, he burned all their documents and archives (so that forged documents could not be checked), and he told the police they would be shot if they bothered the Jews again. After this attack his group made several other successful attacks on police stations in the vicinity.

In April of that year I was hiding on the land of a farmer named Sackshebik near Osmolycza. I was using a hut built in the middle of the field at the time when the land had been divided. The farmer didn't know that my father, my sister and I were hiding there. One day, around noontime, I heard shots. I secretly came out of the hut, which was near the forest, and so was an eye-witness to a battle between seven or eight German gendarmes and Zimmerman's Partisan group. Four Germans fell, the rest escaped. Henyek took from them a heavy machinegun and other equipment that he had been looking for for a long time.

A little later, probably in June of 1943, Henyek was arrested by the German police when he was visiting one of the farmers. Luckily they didn't know he was a Partisan, they thought he was just a plain Jew. They brought him to Pietrowitz, and from there he succeeded in escaping.

Henyek fell in battle, his weapon in his hand. This is how it happened: at the end of the summer of 1943, a strong unit of the German army surrounded the village of Benbinski. It was a punishment expedition against the village. They set 12 buildings afire, and confiscated the corn, the wheat, and the pigs. Zimmerman and his group of 16 were hiding that day in a hut in a field near the village. The Germans surrounded the hut. Zimmerman and his comrades came out to make a dash for the forest. A struggle raged and continued for a long time. The Germans were forced to call for reinforcements from Behova and Glisk. Zimmerman, Resnik and several other Partisans succeeded, although outnumbered by the enemy, in breaking through to the forest. But at the last moment, Henyek was wounded. He died a hero's death, continuing to shoot at the Germans till his last breath.

In general, the Partisan groups that I knew, in the years 1942-1943 in the forest of Osmolycza, were small and scattered, and their main object was not a war to conquer anyone, but merely to defend their lives. Henyek Zimmerman alone tried to widen this. He set up for himself the goal of defending the Jews in the nearby villages.

It was not until 1944, when the general Partisan movement had spread and grown, that the remnants of this group became absorbed into the great Soviet Partisan movement of the A.L.

At the beginning of 1944, Yenek Kleinman and Gesek contacted the Soviet Partisans. These latter sent them on a mission of very special espionage in an area they knew very well. Soon the Partisans under Captain Chil (Yechiel Greenspan), part of the regular organized Partisan army, came to our district. A second group also came at that time. It was called The White Furs, because of the white furs its members wore.

I also met the Bolvotkin Ukrainian nationalist bands: these were attacking, killing and robbing everyone— Poles, Jews and Russians. Their commander was Feudov

In Feudov's group there was also a Jew, one of my colleagues, Berish Arbuz. I knew his family very well. His father, he and his two brothers had hidden themselves in the farmhouse of the Yablonskys on an isolated estate between Zambowitz and Kransnitzi. We had all hidden there for several weeks. This farmer was really a very decent sort with a big heart. He had done a lot of favors for persecuted Jews. For fear strangers would visit him, he had made a special hiding place for us behind a closet. He always fed us the best food he had.

He boarded a lot of other Jews for many weeks, even Jews who didn't have any money to pay him. But Berish Arbuz hadn't wanted to continue hiding any longer; he was tired of sitting still. So he joined Feudov's band. I met him several times and I asked him, "Why are you wandering around with them? They are not Partisans."

But Berish didn't want to leave them. "Among them I'm a free man," he said.

Through Berish, the Yenek Kleinman and Gesek groups asked to join up with Feudov. But through great good luck, this matter was never settled. Berish Arbuz was killed by Feudov. Several days later Feudov's band attacked Gesek's group near the village of Zabavila. In this battle, among those who fell were Izhak Perelmuter and his brother Berek. The rest got away. The Soviet Partisans soon liquidated Feudov and his band.

MOTEL STERNOVLITZ

NO MORE RETREATS

In November, 1942, we went to the forest. There were six of us: my sister and her girl friend, Sima Bronsky, and my friends, the brothers Lox and Samuel Rubenstein, came along. We hid ourselves in the forest of Koslofka (the district of Lublin), about seven kilometers from Lubatov. We lived in hovels carved deep in the ground, and many times we slept under the open sky. Not once during the winter did we find ourselves snowed in completely when we woke up. But often we had to lie down in mud, surrounded by swamps. We were pursued by enemy groups of greater numbers than we, and who had better equipment. In the beginning it was very difficult and hard. We had only seven men and only four rifles among us, and just 20 bullets.

To engage the enemy in actual combat was an impossibility. We watched our bullets as if they were the rarest gems, for they were all that stood between us and death. In the beginning our activities were confined to the business of obtaining food. Even this was far from simple. Many times we were forced to shoot people to get even a piece of bread or a bit of meat. Besides, we didn't dare leave the forest except at night.

The Partisan movement was still in its infancy. We had no contact with other groups. But little by little things changed. It was a great step forward when almost 100 Jewish prisoners of war escaped from Lipova and Lublin in December, 1942. Most of them were single and soldiers, and they came to us to join the movement. Their leader was Kadanovitz, who was killed several weeks later. These escapees divided themselves into small groups and kept in contact with each other.

Ten of them immediately joined us. They were commanded by a very talented and experienced army man. He had been a Soviet lieutenant. We called him Tolyek. At the same time a second group, under the leadership of a fellow from Makushoff whose name was Kashenblott, was also active in our vicinity. This group didn't last long. In December, 1942, or the following month, they were boarding with a farmer who delivered them to the Germans. Only two of the original 12 survived.

Kashenblott and the other survivor joined our group. Under the command of Tolyek we commenced weekly operations. I had the privilege of participating in the first battle. It happened this way: five of us were ordered to go out to a certain place, 12 kilometers away, to capture a heavy machinegun. By the time we reached there dawn had come. Somebody observed us and notified the Polish police, who were stationed about five kilometers further away. Eight policemen came on the double and fired on us. We chased them off and they escaped, to the thunderous laughter of the farmers.

That same day we set out on our return trip and passed along the main Lublin-Warsaw road in the middle of the day. The farmers were cleaning the snow off the roads, and around them stood German guards. The Germans were so completely surprised that they didn't dare to challenge us. A little later we turned into one of the towns to get something to eat. There, the Germans attacked us. The bullets whistled around me. I aimed at the place from which the Germans were coming and fired. I felt very alert and awake in a wonderful way.

After three-quarters of an hour the shots ceased, the Germans disappeared and the road was clear. Only one of us, a prisoner of war from Lipova, was wounded; he had been shot in the foot. He died, because in those days we had no medical supplies.

The next day we came back to our base. Tolyek praised us. Our hearts were full of pride that we had withstood the first test of fire. But that same day we had to move from our base deeper into the forest. A German division had just returned from the front for a vacation and they were combing the vicinity, looking for Partisans and Jews. According to the news we received they admitted killing about 60 unarmed Jews.

Altogether in the Forest of Vohla (five kilometers from

Makushoff) 600 Jews, most of them from the small cities and villages in the vicinity of Lublin, hid themselves from October to November of 1942. And when the Germans decreed that all Jews should present themselves at Belsyce, they saved their lives by running away into the forests and small villages thereabouts. They were totally unarmed. The Partisans helped them as much as they could with food and even money, but there just wasn't enough ammunition to give them. Only a very few Jews who acted peacefully and did as they were told survived the war.

For instance, I learned about one group of 60 to 70 Jews, men and women, who spent the war in the forest of Povchek. The Partisans helped them with food, and when the Partisans had to leave they even left them a gun and some ammunition to defend themselves. A gun in those dark days couldn't be purchased for love or money.

The same day that the Germans routed about 60 unarmed Jews from the forest, they also attacked a bunker where six escaped war captives from Lipova had hidden themselves. All six of them put up a heroic defense. They quickly picked up the grenades that the Germans threw into the bunker and tossed them back among the Germans. They blocked the entrance to the bunker with their lone sub-machinegun and held out for eight long hours. When night came and darkness fell the Germans were forced to retreat. Only one of the defenders died, and he died later, of his wounds. The other five came out of the struggle alive.

During the winter of 1942-1943 we carried out several actions in collaboration with another group of about a dozen armed Jews, headed by Ephraim Bleichman. This group had been active in the vicinity of Lubatov-Kaminka. We met several times each month.

Several of our men came for one of these conclaves to the house of a farmer. We ate and drank some whiskey. Suddenly, at eight o'clock in the morning, a car appeared, and before we could look to see who had come two German soldiers got out of the car and asked the farmers for eggs and butter. Without waiting for his answer, they walked to the house. Instantly two of our men sprang up to guard the door, and when one of the Germans opened it, Ephraim Bleichman honored him immediately with a bullet from his revolver. The second German had a sub-machinegun. He took cover and started to defend himself. We pursued him. One of us, a short fellow, caught the broad-shouldered, tall German and tore the machinegun out of his hands. Then the rest of us reached them, and we finished the German off. That's how we had the luck to obtain our first sub-machinegun.

In February, 1943, we put up a new bunker, with a water supply in it, and shelves, etc. We were ten Partisans, and with us were 30 young Jewish men, most of them from Lublin; but they were without arms. There were also several girls with us.

At that time we set up a contact, through a farmer, with the leader of the P.P.R. underground of that area. He was known to us by the name Genek. Through him Tolyek contacted also A.L., who appointed him the commander of all the Partisan groups in a triangle bounded by Lublin-Makushoff-Lubatov. Also the Jews who were hiding in the forest were put under his command. Tolyek prepared to start sabotage operations against the enemy. But fate decided differently.

After several weeks of sitting still, four men took the initiative and went out and captured a machinegun. They took with them four of our ten rifles, and they promised to return them in three days. They did not come back, so some of us went to look for them. We left at three o'clock in the morning, and searched for two days before we found them. We ordered them to return immediately. Two days later all of us returned to the base. There was a terrible and strange silence, and we approached the bunker with pounding hearts. To our great sorrow, nothing remained of our base, and none of our comrades came to greet us.

A dreadful fear enveloped us. We didn't want to believe that all our comrades had been murdered, but it didn't take long to learn the terrible truth. Six hours after we had left a strong German unit had surrounded the bunker. Machineguns had been set up on all sides. Those who were armed had defended themselves to the bitter end. Then the Germans had piled straw before the entrance of the bunker and set it afire. The bunker filled with smoke, and all in the bunker had been choked by the smoke. Those who didn't die immediately were shot by the Germans. Every one had perished: six Partişans and 30 unarmed young people, among them my sister and our commander Tolyek. All this happened on the 19th of February, 1943.

That left only eight of us. We chose Yegar as our new commander. He was an escaped war prisoner from Lipova. We were determined to do more than just worry about existing. We started to look for new contacts. Two more Poles who had escaped from Germany joined us. Through the winter months we clashed many times with policemen and stray Germans. Once we had a skirmish with a group of the A.K., who had killed two Poles in Litvinov (the district of Poloff).

Finally, in the spring of 1943, we found Genek and renewed our contact with A.L. Genek had sent us to a certain place where we were to meet—according to his words—with the head of the Partisan movement of the Lublin district. His name was Meitek, but in the underground he was called Mauchaz. We went to the appointed place and we met with Meitek. He had brought with him underground newspapers and proclamations. He brought us greetings from a very large Partisan group under the command of Chil (Yechiel Greenspan).

Our group was given a different name, Ameila Plater. Meitek ordered us to remain at our base and from there to carry on sabotage. After a month had passed the renowned Jewish Partisan commander Bolock came to visit us. He was a colonel. Our base was in the forest of Povchek, on the banks of the Vieptz River. On the other side of the river, some of Captain Chil's Polish groups were camped. In co-operation with them we commenced a very intensive campaign of sabotage. We made repeated attacks on the Polish police and on German cars on the roads. We mined German trains, knocking them right off the tracks.

160

At first we took the railroad tracks apart with our hands, but later on we received dynamite and so we were able to set mines. There were ten people in our group. They were of various political opinions, but in our conversations we never argued about politics. We were like brothers, bound strongly together by our daily co-operation in actual combat.

Soon the group of Ephraim Bleichman united with us, and we increased in number to 17 men. The day after Bleichman's group joined us our combined groups attacked the village of Lukoff. This was held by the N.S.Z., an organization that worked with the A.K. and the Germans. We made more ambitious attacks and multiplied our activity. We smashed and blasted German trains more frequently. Sometimes we used 16-kilogram air bombs which were still to be found in those parts, although they had not been used by the army since 1939. In the summer of 1943 our activity was limited to places no farther away than about 60 kilometers. But we were going to greater and greater distances all the time, and in fact, were nearing Lublin itself.

In February, 1944, we were ordered to the forest of Parczed, where Captain Chil's group was based. The Polish groups went with us, and we found many Russian and Polish Partisans there.

As soon as we arrived we were given the duty of escorting Soviet parachutists to Ahpola, which was by the Vistula River. Our group was made up of eight Partisans: five Jews and three Poles, two men and one woman. We walked for about 15 kilometers and then stopped at a house near the forest of Volyah. In the morning, I stood guard. Suddenly I saw some Germans coming out of the forest. I awakened the comrades, but the Germans went quietly on their way. When they reached the village, they set fire to a building. We seized this opportunity to move into the forest. For three hours we lay hidden there, then sent a man to check the vicinity.

As soon as he had left, the Germans returned, appearing suddenly as if they had popped from the earth. Shooting started and a battle developed. We climbed to the top

161

of a hill, and from there we were able to defend ourselves bravely. Bullets flew around us. Our commander, Yegar, lifted his head for only a second, to take a bandage out of his pocket and he fell to the ground, dead. Only after it became dark did we succeed in retreating to safety.

Immediately upon our return to base, I was assigned to a group of four Jewish Partisans and two who were not Jews, to bring the political leaders, Brobna Hanneman (from the P.P.S.), Ousoufka Morotzky and Stiholsky, through the front lines. We brought them safely across the river Bolk to a Russian Partisan group and returned without mishap.

On the 15th day of May, Ola Zimesky came to visit our base. He gathered everybody together and made a speech. When we assembled there were more than 600 men, about 400 Russians and 200 Jews and Poles. Captain Chil had about 40 men. Ola Zimesky raised me to the rank of corporal.

Right afterwards we were ordered to leave the forest of Povchek and go to the forest of Yanoff. Only 30 men of Captain Haiel's group were to remain behind.

Several hundred men, well armed and with radio equipment, started for Yanoff. The first object of our journey was to reach the forest of Parczed, and from there to go to the forest of Koslofka. From there, we went to the forest of Volyah. Here the Germans stormed us. After first attacking us from planes, they surrounded us.

At six o'clock in the morning the battle was already developing, but it ended in a great victory for our people. About 40 Germans were killed. From the forest we could see the German planes landing to gather the wounded officers. We would have finished off all of them, but they were defended on one side by the river. After a battle that lasted 14 hours, the Germans were forced to retreat; and not one of our people was killed.

From the forest of Volyah we walked a whole night to reach the Vistula River. At four in the morning we came to the village of Rombleu near Nalentsu. But no sooner did we start to set up a place for our people to rest than six German planes started to bombard the village. We all rushed to the fields. The planes flew very low. The bullets set afire the house where the Partisan General Staff had its headquarters; the radio was smashed and the antenna was shattered. The only lucky thing about the attack was that a forest was not far away and all of us took shelter there.

The bombers must have seen us, for they flew over the forest and dropped bombs. In a few minutes all that was left of the trees was splintered wood. But they had only begun. Truckloads of German soldiers from the S.S. Vickin division started to arrive. They had light field artillery. They bombarded the forest for several hours. All around us was a hell of shells and bombs. Constantly the six planes circled above our heads, raining bombs on us one after another.

We lay still as if we were paralyzed, for the order was to save ammunition. After several hours our commander, Captain Zemsea, ordered us to use the flame throwers and set fire to the village, which was being used to conceal the German cannon emplacements. The Germans seemed not to be able to aim their cannon very well, because the shells were passing over our heads. Anxiously we waited for dawn. The Germans saw that we were not answering their fire, and they may have thought that most of us had been killed by the planes, the cannon shells and the artillery fire: for as evening came, the Germans came into the open to attack us. They started toward the forest. We had waited for this moment. All of us were tense, our nerves on edge, particularly after the hours that we had spent lying still during the bombardment. Now we had a chance to release our tensions. We opened fire. Like madmen we stormed the Germans. We hit them and beat them with everything that came to our hands—hatchets, sticks, knives. Scared to death, they raised their hands and surrendered. But their yielding did not help them. We killed about 150 Germans, and our losses totaled about 40 killed and wounded.

Our position was still dangerous. We couldn't get out of the forest. We were surrounded by the enemy, they outnumbered us many times over and they were very well armed. So Captain Zemsea commanded us to split into groups of ten. Each group was ordered to take one of the wounded and to break through the enemy lines. The plan was carried out really well. Many of the groups found their way to the forest of Yanoff, and some returned to the forest of Parczed, as our group did. But Captain Zemsea himself was not lucky enough to reach Parczed: in retreating, he was killed by a stray bullet.

When we returned to base, we started to re-organize our group. We were joined temporarily by the group of Captain Chil and a very large Partisan group under the command of the Soviet General Baronofsky. From that time on Partisans no longer worked in small, individual groups, but operated as a well organized, disciplined army. Its commanders were Soviet officers who joined us by parachuting from planes. Now there were thousands of Partisans.

To demonstrate how our prestige and morale had grown, I need tell but one incident: one day the Germans attacked us and tossed several grenades into the building that housed our General Staff. One of the Partisans said, "We must get out of here."

General Baronofsky answered him: "Those days are past and gone. The Russians no longer retreat."

MICHAEL LUDERSTEIN

there was no opening or weak point where we could launch an attack.

The battle was long and brutal. In the beginning we made use of our small cannon, a .45 millimeter. Unaish was among the first to break through into the village. He fought crazily; he fired point blank and he threw grenades so that they were exploding all around him.

Finally the battle was over. The safe nest of the enemy had been destroyed. But just then Unaish saw a German officer escaping from the village. He ran after him against an order to remain in his place. After a while we found his body near the body of the German officer. He must have been hit by a stray bullet, and his blood, his clean, pure, in fact, his holy blood, was mixed with the blood of the German. Our group really won fame in this encounter. Five of us had fallen.

Unaish was placed in a wagon drawn by a dark horse. A blanket of flowers made by the hands of his friends and comrades was spread over the wagon box. The commander of the group took formal farewell of the departed.

In deep silence we walked our five friends and comrades to their common grave. We looked for the last time on the face of Unaish, who had been so dear to us. We parted from him forever. A volley of shots was fired over the grave of Unaish as he went on his last journey. His memory will remain in the hearts of many of us. We knew how he felt toward us as Jewish Partisans and as soldiers, and the honor he gave us on that account. But the source of that honor was heroic action, like the deeds of Unaish, which earned respect and glory. These people died to give us an example, a criterion, so that we would be the kind of people Unaish was.

BORYA UDKOFSKY

JEWS OF THE FOREST

The Russian Partisans decided to get rid of us. The farmers complained of us, saying we were bandits; and the Russians believed them. Although I was very strict about who should be robbed and what should be taken, it was hard to draw a line, and we had to have food to exist.

The Partisans said that we could take all necessities, and anything that was surplus or a luxury to the peasants. But the definition wasn't the same as the definition of the farmer. He understood the situation differently, and he complained about the Zhids (Jews). Also, the farmer's thinking wasn't the same as that of the Partisans; the idea of the one giving the order is different from the one carrying it out. We held a meeting and I explained the situation. We decided to meet with the Partisans and argue it out.

Yehuda Belsky had an acquaintance with one of the farmers of Butskevitz, and he also knew some Russian Partisans. We sent Yehuda to arrange a meeting in one of the hortorim (isolated farms). We sent four armed men with him. All of us were very heavy at heart; for there might be a clash with the Russian Partisans, and there wouldn't be anything to do but fight. The spokesman for the other side was Victor Pancenko, the head of the Soviet Partisan group. He repeated everything that we ourselves had heard and said very plainly that they had decided to shoot it out with us.

I started to answer him. I said that I was the leader of the Soviet Partisan group acting in the name of Marshal Zhukov. "If you didn't know it before," I said, "you know it now: we are not bandits or robbers. And if you are a Soviet citizen you should know that the U.S.S.R. is ready to fight the German fascists, whom we are fighting; and your motherland does not discriminate between Jews and non-Jews, but only between loyal citizens who obey orders and bandits who destroy and rob."

170

"We have been told that you are burglarizing in the villages," he answered.

"Well, this we can find out and if it is true then we agree to fight with you," I replied.

He agreed. I said that we came from the vicinity, we knew all the highways and the byways, the forest and those who lived there; and we spoke the language and dialects of the district.

We made a plan to prove that the accusations against us were false, and one night soon afterward we went out to carry it through. Victor went with us. We walked to the village of Nagrimov, to the house of one of the farmers who had complained against us. We knocked on his window and one of us asked for some bread.

The farmer whined, "There is no bread, my friends, the Jews were here and took everything. They stole everything and left."

Victor got very angry and immediately drew his revolver. "I'll kill the son of a bitch." I didn't let him.

I said, "Kill him later, you can always do that. Ask what the Jews took?"

The farmer called to a girl who was in the house at the time when the Jews supposedly took whatever they took, and the girl said that the Jews had been there at one o'clock in the morning. "They took bread, fat, onions, salt, butter, and eggs, and even the table cloth."

"And what else?"

"That's all."

We went into the house and sat down. Victor yelled at the farmer, "From today on, if a Partisan fighter comes don't pay attention whether he's a Jew, a Pole or a Russian. Give him what he asks for. Give him food, also boots and even furs. Your life hangs by a thread. My friend stopped me from shooting you. Why did you make up such a huge lie about the Partisans?"

Then I said to the farmer, "I am Belsky." This announcement had the right effect: it made him quake with fear.

From then on Victor Pancenko and his people and our group were on friendly terms. We decided among us the zones of supply for each; the road from Novagrudak to Lidda belonged to us, and the Zhetl area belonged to them. We didn't go into Pancenko's villages, and he didn't come to ours. Victor visited us very frequently. A friendship grew up between Victor and the secretary of our group. Sometimes we visited at his place, too.

After the 1942 summer harvest we prepared to wreck the huge German granaries. The Germans had taken over the great estates and most of the *kolkhoz* farms, and they had plowed and planted the fields for themselves. The year had been a good one, the yield was large and the barns were full. Why should we leave food for them? The small farmer, all right. Let him have it; and also we would provide for ourselves. But the big estates were all in the hands of the enemy and their fate was decided: we would burn them down.

We divided the estates between the group of Pancenko and ourselves. A date was chosen for setting fire to all in the vicinity. We made careful preparations. Late one fall night all the estates that were worked by the Germans broke into flames at the same time. Ambushes had been set up so that we could easily shoot anyone who came to put out the fires. The skies above the forest and fields blazed red.

The farmers understood who had done this and why. The fame of the Partisans increased: We were challenging and harassing the Germans! We were joyous and fearful at the same time. Danger awaited us on all sides.

But starting a fire wasn't all; even now we do not know how it all happened. Terror enveloped the countryside: planes flew over the fires and dropped bombs! It seems that Russian pilots returning from bombing enemy lines must have realized the importance of the fires and dropped the rest of their bombs. Panic spread among the enemy: they knew the Partisans were a part of the Russian command, and they thought our actions were co-ordinated with the Russians'. In any event, the planes finished the work the Partisans started when they set the fires. We were in a way waging total war.

The farmers now regarded the Partisans with more respect. The Germans didn't have the nerve to challenge us immediately. They made careful preparation. Meanwhile bits of news and rumors came to us. We had now achieved a prominent place in the war strategy by these acts of sabotage.

For instance the brothers Belsky came to consult Pancenko about how to carry out a plan they had to kill all the mayors of the cities. The mayors were collaborating with the Germans and had to be done away with; and the same with the Soltisim (the village presidents).

Groups went out at night and searched out village presidents who were collaborating with the Germans. We killed about six of them. In each group there was always one of the brothers Belsky. Ashoel, the youngest brother, was a guide and was very helpful, often getting us out of great difficulty.

After we burned the grain we decided, for many reasons, to stop the Germans from gathering food from the villages. We had to keep the enemy from eating and destroying stores of food, in order to quiet the farmers, some of whom argued against us.

"You are taking, and the Neimetz (the Germans) are taking. How will we eat ourselves?"

We said, "Let's try something. We will set up ambushes and attack the German trucks which haul the food away. We will in this instance help Victor Pancenko's group."

Twenty-five of us, all well armed, with an equal number from Ashoel's group, formed a unit, with Ashoel as leader.

We chose to meet at a turn of the main Novagrudak-Novayelna road. There the trucks would have to show up. We prepared a proper reception for them: our group would attack, and Victor's people would act as reserves. If the Germans started a full scale battle, Victor's group, ambushed a few dozen meters from us on the other side of the road, would attack from the rear.

We returned to camp. Early tomorrow morning at a given signal, we would go out. We never hid anything from our parents, so we told them what we were about to do. Some of them begged that their children shouldn't be sent, and women came to ask if their husbands had to go.

I scolded them and finally had to threaten to shoot anyone who disobeyed or any who hadn't the right who mixed in these matters.

We had come together in the forest not only to survive and to get enough to eat. Were the mass slaughters so soon forgotten? We were going out ourselves and taking chances, why must we have pity on others and prevent their sharing in the revenge? Maybe we were to die in the attempt, but we had to avenge those who had been murdered.

We went to the spot from which the ambush was to take place, and walked into the forest to await our contact from the village of Radyoky. A military convoy came by, but it was too strong for us to attack. We were there to ambush the convoy of commandeered supplies. It would have fewer German guards and probably only local policemen.

Around noon good news reached us—a girl who was friendly to our cause brought it to us from the village. She said one car and a full truckload of chickens and eggs was coming from Radyoky, and in a short while they would be returning to Novagrudak. So we grabbed our guns to be ready to start. We lay in the underbrush about a half an hour. There was a whole line of us, each with his rifle, hidden in the grass and behind bushes, at a distance of ten meters from the road. I was about halfway down the middle of the chain, to enable me to command both wings. My brother, Ashoel, was to shoot at the front wheels of the vehicle; I was to aim for the driver.

In 1927 and 1928, I served in the Polish army and I was a very good marksman and received a special prize for marksmanship.

A car horn sounded. It would help to direct our aim nicely! It was a small and fast car. Four officers. We shot but we didn't hit. Our aim was too high or too slow. Victor's group also missed. Three seconds had not gone by when behold, a loaded truck appeared. This was the car that we were waiting for. Now we had learned how to aim and the target was so big and so slow, we couldn't miss.

Tak, tak! The truck stopped. We had hit the wheels and the driver himself. Then there was a hail of bullets. Eight

Germans and some Byelorussian militiamen jumped out of the truck, took up positions, and trained a machinegun on us.

"Hurrah," came a violent outcry from Pancenko's people, from around a curve in the road.

The enemy panicked and started to run. Afterwards we found out that most of them were wounded. We started to pursue them, but they disappeared into the woods. We rushed to capture the machinegun and the rifles, and the boots and the chickens; and we also found boxes of bullets.

We had trampled on the eggs and butter and they were squashed, but the bags of sugar we were able to save. We put bullets in the tanks of benzine and set them afire. They blew up with a glorious boom. All this took but a few seconds and we were left with two machineguns, four rifles, and thousands of bullets.

Excited, we quickly moved away into the forest. Our first victory over an armed unit!

German soldiers would come to gather up the dead and pursue the attackers. But our joy was greater than our fear. For the first time we had fought the German soldiers face to face! We had proved that it was possible to do so and that it was possible to kill them.

We had visions of meeting them again and killing more and more of them. But ordinary caution demanded that we get out of there and reach the other side of the forest.

We walked until dark, ate well and lay down to sleep. The talk about uniting and the joint victory had to be put off until tomorrow. But both groups had only words of encouragement, and decision, and the need to act. We divided up the ammunition: to us one machinegun, and two rifles to Victor and his people.

On one of Victor's regular visits he told me that a number of young Jews were living on a private farm near a hortor not far from Abellkewitz; they were doing nothing by day, but at night they were engaging in armed robbery. He said the local people were very angry at them. They were afraid to turn them in to the Germans for fear of reprisals from the Partisans, but they had inquired whether Pancenko was protecting them. It seemed that if not, they would get rid of them, one—two—three. Victor said if they wanted to live as Partisans they should combine with our group. Otherwise, Victor was willing to finish them off himself. On the one hand, maybe this was a large group of Jews and he would have difficulty; on the other, perhaps they were Partisans at heart, and we could greatly increase our fighting force. Anyhow, I told Victor that we had no responsibility for these Jews and as soon as he told them so, many volunteered to help us.

About 20 men with three machineguns and some rifles and revolvers started out one very cold, snowy night. It was dawn before we reached the hortor. It was a large estate. We put guards all round; it was so cold we had to change the guard every half-hour.

The owner of the hortor greeted us cordially and gave us food. When we told him about why we were there he put on a poker face as though he knew nothing about it. He swore there were no Jews there. I explained that we hadn't come to kill anyone. "Just the opposite, I myself am a Jew, the commander of a group of Jewish Partisans. I can take them away, but if they don't want that, I will leave them here." I told him also that I didn't want to bother him at all. Nothing would make him tell the truth, so finally I placed my revolver to his temple. "Come," I said to him. This softened him up.

He said, "Search, master, perhaps you will find something."

"Where?"

"In the barn," he answered.

We walked into the barn. I shouted in Yiddish, "Let the Jew hear and take heed." No one answered and there was no sound. We started searching. In one corner we found, hidden by some straw, a wooden trap door, which when opened disclosed a hole, the entrance to a tunnel. Benzion Golkowitz leaned over and shouted: "Jews, come out. There's nothing to fear." Still there was no answer. Benzion went into the hole by himself and to his surprise found a group of armed men. Each was in position, rifle in hand. "Comrades, Belsky is here, the commander of the

Jewish Partisans. He wants to speak to you. Why don't you come out and meet him?"

One of them spoke. "Kessler is my name. I am the leader." And then to the others, "All right, let's go." He came up out of the tunnel, rifle in hand, and shook hands with me.

"You're not afraid any more?" I asked.

"Ah, Belsky, I have heard about you. Come, let's talk."

So, I climbed into the hole. Shumansky's wife was there, and her two sons. The Shumanskys had owned a large mill in Dworetz. The father also came over and shook my hand. All of them were overwhelmed with joy. Abraham from Butzkov was there and recognized me. He asked, "Don't you remember the son of David of Stankavich?"

"And who are you?"

"The brother of Moishke."

"Avremel?"

"Yes."

Altogether there were about 20 men. Of course, I didn't know them all.

"You good-for-nothings, why didn't you answer me when I called you?"

After we had had a rest and sleep, we ate with them, and then we really talked. We said, "Here they kill you with bombs and grenades."

"They threw them right into the midst of us, in a cave."

"I have a big group," I said, "several hundred people. You can live with us. Take the women and the children, the horses and all your belongings, and come to our camp. In the forest you will be free as the birds. There is no fear, and there is no Ghetto. If the pirates and barbarians come from one side—we can run to the opposite side. We have power enough to fight them. They can't kill all of us. Here, you are lost. Victor Pancenko is our friend, but he was going to finish you." Kessler left.

I continued, "We have rifles, but we don't want to use them to fight Partisans. The farmers are complaining about you and plotting against you. We have non-Jews faithfully fighting beside us. You have been alone long enough. There are no areas of influence. This is not a principality. Join with us and let us start on our way to camp. There are enough shelters for all of us. It's only good sense."

"Let us consult among ourselves," was their answer.

"All right. I will give you half an hour. But your answer must be definite. I came here at great danger. I'm no child, I didn't take the chance for nothing. I came to find out where you stand."

They went out to talk it over. When they returned they proposed to send four people to our camp to see how we lived and what they might expect.

"Did you study the Bible? Joshua sent spies to Jericho and they fell into a trap. Afterwards they were forced to go to Rahab, and they had to hide up on the roof under the eaves. That way Jericho could not be conquered. You should join us. We have our own special code by which we live. There is strict discipline. You would be living with us as we live. If you don't want to, I am prepared to take your ammunition from you by force. To the road!— March!"

Shumansky interfered, "Why are you getting angry, Belsky? We will go, but let's see first what it's all about. I'm not a German. You haven't anything we can't look at."

"We have huts ready and waiting. You will live just as all Jews. What's the matter with you? Non-Jews come to us and they don't negotiate this way."

They saw that I wasn't pussyfooting, and that I was quite serious and would not soften. So they began to give in.

Another, Chanan Presman, said, "Comrade Commander, we are coming. But we have a score to even before we leave. We have to finish off one farmer, Abellkewitz."

"Why?"

"He's the captain of the local German guard unit. He has delivered 20 Jews—women and children—to the Germans. His house is a half a kilometer from the village. He has ammunition as well. This seems to me a very good thing to do, to pay off an evil man like this; and it's good that in this vicinity they should learn that Jewish women and children are not helpless and defenseless. This can be done in a united front as though done in co-operation with you."

"Do you know how to go there?"

"Yes."

And so it was that toward evening, after we had had something more to eat, we went. Izhak Berkowitz, a very tall, muscular man, was the guide. They called him Itzinke Bolshoy (the Tall One). Everything was very quiet; all we could hear was the crunch of the snow under our boots. It sounded very loud in the still air. Though we were still far from the farmstead, dogs barked; but our horses were good, and we closed in quickly.

The command had been given that the family must be annihilated; not one should survive. When we reached the house, I put guards near the windows. Ashoel, Pesach Friedberg, Benzion Bolkowitz, Michael Lebowitz and I entered the house. Pesach Friedberg was assigned to engage the woman of the house in conversation. Benzion knocked, and called out, "Open up!"

At first there was no answer, but he knocked much more loudly. A voice answered, "Why are you making so much noise? I'm coming."

A bald farmer opened the door. We asked whether there were any strangers in the house. He answered that there weren't. So he had sentenced everyone to death. The whole family was in one large room, in beds lined up along the walls. There was a large oven and near it were metal tools of all kinds; we had to be careful that one of them didn't get his hands on them.

Pesach sat on the bed nearest the farmer. "So, what's new?" he asked.

The answer was brief, in Byelorussian; "We shall go at once and beat up some Jews."

"Quite so, and so you will be one of us, a real hero. How many Jews have you murdered?"

"I don't kill them. It's not worth while to dirty your hands on them. I deliver them to the militia, and they make short shrift of them."

"How many Jews have you caught?"

"Four days ago we got a woman, two children and two men. Several weeks ago, we got 11 men. I don't remember exactly."

"And before that?"

"Several days earlier we had ridden after them and we took a pistol from them. Eventually, we delivered them to the local police. The women and the children and even the men I locked up first in the cellar for a whole night. It was cold down there and by the morning they were almost frozen. So I was able to tie them together like lambs and bring them over to the army post in Dworetz."

I walked over close to the farmer and said, "Mister, aren't you a human being, and have you no conscience? How does your conscience let you catch living people and deliver them to certain death at the hands of the German tyrants and murderers?"

"What are you asking, sir? Hitler made a law, and we have to carry it out."

"What has this to do with you? What business is it of yours?"

"Well, I am the captain of the guard. We have to keep this area free of Partisans!"

"But you are a human being!" Here Pesach gave him a slap, the first, in the face, "I am also a Zhid (a Jew)."

I said, "Enough playing around." But then I told Pesach to hold off while I tried again to question him. However, he saw that the end had come and he stopped talking, except to beg.

When we had destroyed the house and everyone there was dead, I said, "So shall be done to every man that Hitler wants to honor." I recalled a similar decree in the Bible in the Scroll of Esther.

I wrote out a notice in Russian: "This family was destroyed for collaborating with Germans and for apprehending Jews." And signed it: "The Group of Belsky."

A great catastrophe befell us a few months afterwards. In March, 1943, we sent ten comrades, under the leadership of Abraham Polonsky, to get food. In the group were also Abraham's brother, my brother-in-law Alter Tiktin, one of the Shumanskys, and some others. They carried out the assignment, obtained the supply of food which they were to get, and returned.

Five kilometers from Novagrudak, they stopped off at a hortor of Byelousk, one of Polonsky's acquaintances, to rest for a day. Not far away was a garrison of soldiers from the post, and they thought it better to rest by day. Byelousk received them cordially; he gave them food and refreshment, and he also found places for them to sleep. It was understood that there were to be watchmen; but in the middle of the night the hortor was surrounded. (We found out afterwards that Byelousk had sent one of his sons to the Novagrudak police to let them know that Partisans were staying at his place.) Our comrades woke up in terror, and it was already too late to fight.

All of them were shot except Abraham. He hid himself in a chicken coop, under the oven. When the police and the officers had left and the Byelousk family was celebrating the death of our comrades, he came out from his hiding place and called to Byelousk, "The Partisans will avenge this." One of Byelousk's sons threw a hatchet at Abraham, hitting him in the head. We learned all this later from the nursemaid who worked for Byelousk and was an eyewitness of the whole scene; Byelousk had thought his murder of the only Partisan witness of the crimes had ended the matter.

We waited only two days for the return of this group. Not hearing from them, we made a search of the villages. When we reached the vicinity of the hortor we heard all the details as they had been told to the murderer's neighbors and friends by the nursemaid witness.

We could not let this go. If we did not take revenge on these vile informers, how would we all end? If such things were allowed to happen, every farmer would turn us in.

The first investigators that we sent to search for the missing group met some Jews in the forest. These Jews were hiding in one of the hovels of an out-of-the-way farm. Among them were Hirsch Berkovsky from Selyoff and his sister Yenta. When Hirsch Berkovsky heard about this terrible crime he also learned that the nursemaid had been present. They questioned her closely. At first she denied everything, but after she had had special attention by way of several beatings, she told the story. The investigators came back and told us all that had happened.

Ashoel took the 25 men of the first company, the best armed among us and very well trained, in wagons, to dispose of the family of Byelousk. I gave my orders to Ashoel: not a thing shall be taken from Byelousk's house. Everything must go up in smoke. I reminded him of the command of Joshua and the deed of Ahikam. I said, "Just as our forefathers did." And he promised me he would not forget.

Later, Ashoel reported that they came to the house in the middle of the night and surrounded it. Then he knocked so hard that they had to open the door. With him then were Israel Yankelevich, Michael Lebowitz and Pesach Friedberg. They spoke openly and bluntly. They had come to avenge the blood of their ten comrades.

Byelousk understood immediately and he resisted; when the four pointed their rifles at him, he grabbed at the four rifles and started to fight and wrestle. Even after he had been stabbed several times, he still fought. Ashoel shot him point blank in the forehead and commanded his comrades to get about their duty. Their work was finished in a matter of minutes, and the house, the barn, the dairy, everything went up in flames.

One of the group, Michael Lebowitz, asked Ashoel's permission and took a coat. In one of its pockets we found a letter from Froup, the German commander at Novagrudak, thanking Byelousk for delivering the ten Partisans to him, and expressing the hope that all Byelousk's neighbors would follow his example and help to annihilate the Partisan bands. Dr. Isler translated the letter for us from the German into Russian, and we kept the translation but turned the original over to the Partisan high command.

Returning from the Byelousk reprisal, the men stopped at a farmhouse where our people from Novagrudak had once had a lot of difficulty. In 1941, they had bought a pail from the farmer who lived there and had gotten into a quarrel with him. He had called the police and forty of them had responded. He told them that the Jews had stolen several things from him. The police lined up 250 Jews for him to identify the thieves, and he pointed out four. These four had been taken out and killed. Our people now paid him in kind.

The great siege started on August 1st, 1943. Ashoel returned from our supply zone, bringing everyone with him. Besides the regular food supply, he brought 15 head of cattle. Life in the camp went on as usual. Only the fighting units were alerted, but then they had learned to be ready for action at all times. A hundred of them, together with 200 fighters from a neighboring brigade, set up an ambush near Naliboki, about 15 kilometers away. We were to block the roads with fallen trees and rubble.

The ambush party took over the roads and planted mines. We could see the military cars while they were quite far away. Before the first German car reached our first blockade a bullet crashed into it. A Russian Partisan was the one who shot it. Later it was discovered he was a traitor, but at the time he apologized, saying he had made a mistake in firing that shot. The car stopped, and of course the whole German company. The soldiers jumped out of the cars and started to spray bullets all round. The Partisans didn't want to battle the German militia in the open, and we retreated. The ambush did not succeed, the mines remained in the roadbed.

Comrades told me later about the particulars of this ambush. All of them might have been killed on account of one traitor. They justly complained about him.

Meanwhile we moved deeper into the forest. I met with Kavalov, and together with Zusia and Ashoel, several hundred of us went on a mission of ambush close to the previous camp. We were all Jews. We were busy with the ambush for several days.

TUVIA BELSKY

WE ATTACK A GERMAN GARRISON

The snow had already melted. Only under the trees, and under brush where the rays of the spring sun didn't reach, did the snow still lie frozen and gray. The Partisans changed from their winter clothes to those of summer, and to all appearances seemed refreshed. No one sat, as they had in winter, near the fire; we walked around the camp or lay on our backs on the hillside, enjoying the warm sun and talking in low voices.

The Ukrainians were talking about working the fields, about their families far away, behind the front, about their womenfolk who were probably facing difficulties in getting the planting done. In their voices one sensed a longing for home and family.

Around me were several Jewish Partisans. Boris Goldfarb was stretched out on his back, and his large twinkling eyes were raised to the blue sky. Motel from Bereczetnitze was exaggerating, as usual, in a hot argument with Sasha from Odessa: after the war, would the nations of the world give Palestine back to the Jews who survived? Sasha from Odessa was a young man; his body was strong and muscular, but his manner was phlegmatic. He said that the remnants of the Jews would be able to live securely wherever they were. But Motel did not agree and called out excitedly that a people without a country aren't a people at all. In every discussion he bemoaned the fact that he hadn't taken his group with him to Palestine, before the war. He said he couldn't forgive his parents for preventing him from fulfilling the craving of his soul. Now all of them were buried in the mass graves of the Ghettos of Sarne, or had fallen in the forests. But Motel was very encouraged by being with Partisans, so he could take revenge in every possible way. After avenging his brothers he hoped he might still be able to reach the land of Israel.

The wild ducks coming from warm countries, quacking and beating their wings, stopped the argument. The Partisans turned to watch them as they flew above the trees. Benny was carefully watching them in their flight. They would soon reach their destination and be building nests. "They have a home," he said to himself and sighed deeply from his heart. The rest kept quiet.

Menachem Fink sat on the ground not far away. He was rinsing a big aluminum pot. "Are you cleaning the dishes for Passover?" Boris asked, laughing. "And have you already baked the matzos?"

Meantime Zeydel Green came over to us. On his shoulder hung a sub-machinegun; he held a sandwich in one hand and was chewing with great enjoyment. He had only just returned from a Partisan mission in which he had been a contact man.

"Uncle Mischa," Zeydel turned to me. "I will tell you very interesting news."

He said that two Poles from Cracow had joined the groups of the Sitovtsim. They had been drafted by the Germans to work in a tractor factory in Harkov. On the way there they ran away to the forest. They said they had been in Warsaw ten days ago, and that stubborn and hard fighting was raging in the Warsaw Ghetto. The youth was organized and fighting heroically. The Germans were using all kinds of ammunition in fighting them. The Ghetto had been set afire on all sides. The underground organizations of the Poles were helping the Ghetto fighters. Many Germans and a lot of Ukrainians and Lithuanians had fallen at the hands of the Jews, who knew that there was no hope for them, but in spite of it, were continuing to fight.

The Partisans listened to the story of Zeydel Green with bated breath. The spirit of the Maccabees had risen again, Boris Goldfarb pointed out—not for victory were they fighting, but for the honor of their people. "It's too bad that Warsaw is so far away We could have rushed help to them. We have plenty of ammunition, we could have helped them." Benny added.

At that time we had a very large supply of ammunition, that we had saved and hidden in the ground.

185

"To our great regret we can't help them immediately," I let them know, "because we have to go on a desperate operation; but we shall inflict such punishment on German flesh and bodies that they will know it is an expression of solidarity with our fighters in the Ghetto of Warsaw, and of revenge for the blood that has been let in their revolt and fight. They will know that this is a fight of many, not just a few."

So with this high purpose we left to attack the German garrison of Alexandrovka. This garrison was manned by two hundred well armed German soldiers. They were camped in the center of the village. The houses they lived in were surrounded by a very thick wall—two walls of heavy beams with a filler of earth between them. At the four corners of the village stood small wooden towers; day and night, watchmen armed with heavy machineguns stood guard, ready to spray bullets all around them.

The temporary fortress had a gate, with a guard and fierce watchdogs. It was impossible to reach the soldiers of the garrison except with hand grenades. Nevertheless, we decided to attack it on April 30th, 1943.

At five o'clock in the afternoon, a group of 70 Partisans, armed with machineguns, two tanks and plenty of bombs and grenades, went to the attack. We had prepared ourselves well. We had made trenches in which to hide, and we had made them without arousing suspicion because the village was completely surrounded by a row of green pine trees.

A farmer's wagon, drawn by a skinny horse and loaded with sacks, came down the road on its way to Alexandrovka. Atop the sacks a Partisan lay. It was Moshe Milard; he made out that he was sleeping. Popoff, as he was called because of his long beard that made him look like a Ukrainian patriarch, had been carefully chosen for this important job. The horse walked slowly; finally it neared the German garrison. Popoff appeared to be Ukrainian in every way: he knew the language perfectly and he was an authority on Ukrainian customs. As the wagon neared the village, Popoff hid his head under the sacks. He wrapped the reins around his hand and stretched himself out as though he were drunk and had fallen asleep. The wagon came within a few meters of the garrison gate. Popoff yawned and stretched as though he were waking up, and searched for his hat.

The German watchman ordered the farmer to move along. Popoff pointed to his uncovered head, and screamed in Ukrainian, "I've lost my hat." And he got down from his seat. He started to put the sacks in order. From the top sack he took out a green string at one end of which was a metal hook. On the other end was a detonator which connected with a mine hidden among the sacks in the back of the wagon. Atop the mine lay a sack full of explosives.

Popoff pretended to check a front wheel. It took but a second to attach the metal hook to the tire of the front wheel. Unconcernedly and quietly he laid the reins down on the back of the horse; turning, walked up the road along which he had come. He bent over searching for his hat every inch of the way. When he had moved about 100 meters away he could still hear the German yelling, but Popoff kept going without turning back. The blast, he knew, would go off as soon as the wheel to which the hook was attached moved. The thread would stretch taut and pull the wire that was imbedded in the magazine of the mine.

A few minutes after Popoff returned to us, we heard a tremendous blast. Our lookout, watching from the top of a very tall pine, reported that from the direction of the garrison enclosure heavy clouds of smoke were rising and great tongues of flames were shooting into the air. Afterwards, we could hear, re-echoing one after another, the storehouses of the German garrison blowing up. Later, there was a hail of rifle fire, and it continued for quite a while.

I divided the Partisans into two groups. One group was led by Benny; I commanded the second group. Benny was to enter the village from one side and cut the telephone and telegraph wires. My group would approach from the opposite side. The two groups, each going its separate way, reached the camp at the same time. The attack was not expected. We surprised the Germans, who were busy putting out fires; they didn't even have time to grab their weapons.

In the beginning we shot with great care, to avoid hitting the Ukrainians who were carrying water to put out the fire. But at our first shot, the Ukrainians dropped their pails and ran for cover. Our plan was to annihilate the German garrison.

The Partisan Benny—Lunka was his name—was the first to break through. He led his group through the gate that had been rent by the first bomb. The Germans ran in terror, and they were easily picked off as they tried to run away. In a few minutes the yard was covered with Hitler's supermen, as they lay dead and wounded. Several of them were afraid of falling into Jewish Partisan hands, and they jumped into the flames. All the buildings burned to the ground except the officers' club and the canteen—they were at the other end of the drill yard. The Germans who were not killed barricaded themselves in those two buildings and shot at us from the windows.

While Lunka was pursuing escaping Germans, I and my group attacked the club-house; but we had to retreat a bit because of the hail of bullets. We tried to storm it a second time. This time also we did not succeed. In this second attack, three of our comrades were wounded. We retreated to the rear of the yard. There we found two trucks. Using them as a blind, we held a short consultation. There, we were quite far from the club, probably 20 meters away.

"I will run over and throw several bombs and hand grenades in at the windows," Sasha said.

At that very instant a rain of bullets showered us, and Sasha fell flat, like a piece of wood, in the middle of the yard. Grenades started to burst around us one after the other. The cries of the wounded Germans pierced the air. We jumped over to the wall of the club-house and we found some Germans hiding there shivering with fear.

Till then, my comrades, the Partisans, had never been so enthused. Like wolves we stormed the Germans with cries of revenge! We destroyed the club-house and then we burned up all the books and magazines. In a few minutes the whole building went up in flames. As we were leaving the club we saw that Benny and several other Partisans were loading sacks of sugar and flour on a large German wagon, and two Belgian horses were in harness ready to pull it away.

We took with us two dead comrades and the five who had been slightly wounded, among them Sasha, who had suffered wounds in both feet.

On our way back to the forest we passed through the village, and we took along the elder of the village, who was notorious for appeasing the Germans. We left a letter with his wife. It was addressed to the commander of the German garrison, Baron von Helman. After the first mine exploded at the gate, he and his staff had escaped to Avratz, to notify the division commander about the attack. The letter ran: "Baron von Helman: Hitler will not destroy and annihilate the whole Jewish nation, but I and a very few other Jews destroyed the entire camp of the German garrison in Alexandrovka." I signed it "The Commander of the Jewish Partisan Group, the Jew Deida Mischa" (Uncle Mischa).

M. GILDENMAN

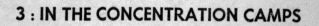

3 : IN THE CONCENTRATION CAMPS

UPRISING IN THE CAMPS

The Nazi concentration camp in all its various forms was the backbone of the whole Nazi regime, the most important instrument in the extermination of the regime's enemies and opponents and the means of enslaving and annihilating peoples and races in whole or in part. Without the concentration camp the continued existence of Nazism would have been impossible.

Immediately after Hitler came to power, large concentration camps were set up in Oranienburg, Dachau and Buchenwald. These were established mainly as places to detain political opponents.

The wave of riots against the Jews, in November, 1938, brought the population of the concentration camps to 600,000. The roster of inmates included not only Jews from Germany but also from Austria.

At the outbreak of the war, there were 21,400 prisoners in concentration camps in Germany and Austria (Dachau, Justenhausen, Buchenwald, Matthausen, Lassenburg and Ravensbruck); but by April of 1942, this figure had increased to 44,700, excluding the many thousands who had died from torture and starvation, and those who had been murdered.

In time, new camps were added. The most important among them were Auschwitz, Noreimgama, Gossens, Neutsvaller, Grossrosen, Maidanek near Lublin, and Stutholz—valleys of death for millions of people from almost all the countries overrun by the Nazis. The camps can be divided into the following groups:

1: Concentration camps that were set up in the beginning to incarcerate Hitler's political opponents, and that were afterwards used to imprison social criminals and Jews. In some camps there were also large numbers of workers employed in secret munitions factories; the claim was that the workers were held there for security reasons. In the beginning, such workers enjoyed a little more freedom than other inmates; but toward the end of the war, they had as few privileges as the rest of the *Katzetniks* (detainees in concentration camps).

2: *Zünderlagern,* or special camps. These were set up especially for German citizens, or German residents of other countries, who refused to work for Hitler or who had been accused of sabotage.

3: Labor and training camps. These harbored either workmen who had failed to comply with regulations, or prisoners who had completed their terms in concentration camps and prisons, and were being held, ostensibly, for continued training. Conditions in these labor camps and other special camps were better, and life was a little easier, than in the concentration camps.

4: Security camps. People imprisoned in these were those who were being investigated or who were awaiting trial. After they were sentenced they were removed to other prisons or to concentration camps. Some of those held in the security camps were in a similar category to those in the labor and training camps: people who already had completed their terms in prison but who had not been given their freedom.

5: Penal camps, or punishment camps for prisoners of war. Life in these was on the same pattern as in the concentration camps, the difference being only formal. However, penal camps were not run by S.S. personnel but by the regular administrative staffs for institutions of justice.

6: Labor camps or forced labor camps. To these were sent all those whom the Nazis had sentenced to forced labor. The law providing for forced labor was extended to cover all the countries the Nazis had overrun.

7: Camps for non-German workmen who had been mobilized as volunteers. Such men were not under guard.

8: Prison camps for special classifications of prisoners.

9: In addition to all the general camps, there were special camps for Jews: Jewish camps and Jewish labor camps, deportation camps for Jews, and others. In this category should be included the special camps for the destruction and extermination of Jews. No special name appears in the official documents for these camps, but among themselves the S.S. troopers used the term Jewish camp, etc. As an example, Chelmno was known as a deportation camp for Jews. Then there were Treblinka, Sobivor and Belsen.

These are just general classifications. They do not describe all the types of Nazi camps, for the Germans created a world of camps of various grades and kinds; in that world they tortured millions of human beings, and in that world millions met their death.

From 1942 on, the concentration camps changed in political significance and in the types of punishment they conducted: they became instruments of forced and slave labor, supplying a giant army of workmen to carry out the objectives of the German war effort. Especially, they strengthened the cartels and the power of the S.S., both of which extended their power and became richer day by day. The agricultural and industrial undertakings of the S.S. depended mainly on the manpower of the concentration camps. The S.S. therefore set up their undertakings in the vicinity of the camps.

Paul, head supervisor of all concentration camps, in his letter to Himmler, the Führer of the S.S. and the police within the Reich, ordered that commencing April 30th, 1942, the main purpose of the concentration camps within the Reich was to be the keeping of prisoners for security reasons, for training and education; and that prevention of crime should no longer be of the first importance, and that the greatest emphasis should be given to colonization. In accordance with this, the character of the concentration camps changed. The commanders announced on April 30th, 1942, that the time of work would no longer be limited, and that it would thenceforth be set by decree of the commander of each camp. No recess was allowed from then on; not even an eating period.

The Nazis organized a network of camps of assorted kinds, within Germany and in the conquered countries, the number of which reached to the thousands. The number of labor camps was especially large. Near every construction project, factory, workshop, road junction, ground fill, and estate there were wooden huts where twentieth century slaves were housed and tortured. Hundreds of thousands spent years draining swamps, rechanneling rivers, laying railway tracks, constructing highways, paving streets, building houses and raising food and cattle. Those hundreds of thousands of nameless slaves gave to the Nazis their knowledge and their strength, their very life's blood, until they were brought low by fatigue and mistreatment, and fell dead or were killed in gas chambers. Their remains were disposed of in crematoria, as ashes for which there was no more use.

The Jews had a special place in these camps, both in the general camps and in the specifically Jewish camps. In fact all the camps had but one goal and aim as far as Jews were concerned: physical destruction. In this no fundamental difference existed between the concentration camp and the forced labor and extermination camp. It was only a matter of time and tempo. In all camps the condition of Jews differed from that of non-Jews, and the question as to whether a person was to be treated as a prisoner or as a forced laborer (indicated by a special paragraph as to the reason for the sentence) did not apply to the Jew. For the Jew, that paragraph contained only one word: *Jude*. For being a Jew was a political crime, and its punishment was deportation to a concentration camp.

Probably, in regard to non-Jews, the labor camps were planned as a means of oppression, as a tool to break the spirit of rebellious political opponents, and of the intelligentsia; and it was perhaps coincidence that they grew so fast and became so productively useful. But in regard to Jews, the camps were planned from the very beginning as annihilation and extermination centers; and only by a real miracle did a few Jews actually survive.

Even the problem of recruiting labor, previously referred to, which changed the character of the camps and brought about the speedy imposition of a reign of terror from the necessity of finding new sources of manpower, didn't bring any relief to Jews. The Nazi attitude toward the Jews remained the same till the end of the war: physical destruction under any circumstances.

In the mixed camps, Jews suffered from the most brutal

196

and terrible tyranny. They were always the lowest in rank, and they were the objects of disgraceful and sadistic torture—not only at the hands of S.S. beasts, but from anti-Semitic prisoners who took advantage of the helplessness of the Jews. Anti-Semitism was rife in all the camps, even among the political prisoners. And although they had for years suffered together with the Jews, the non-Jewish prisoners often identified with, and adapted themselves to, the attitude of the S.S. toward the Jews. Each camp was to some extent self-governing; and Jewish prisoners, when not receiving the most brutal treatment by anti-Semitic fellow prisoners, found themselves under the supervision of criminals and members of the underworld, who satisfied their sadistic impulses by torturing Jews. The camp leaders, the orderlies, the trusties, the detail guards, were chosen mostly from among the penal criminals, who saw in the Jewish prisoner a helpless creature to be used for satisfying dirty instincts and bestial desires.

The extermination camps, as we have said, had their special status in the gradations of Nazi camps. The duties performed there by the Jewish prisoners were either directly connected with death—grave digging, furnace tending for the crematoria—or consisted of farming the vegetable gardens and tending the cattle (which provided food for the camp and the garrisons of the S.S and their Ukrainian assistants), building barracks, cobbling, tailoring, etc.

The condition of Jewish prisoners at every camp was most tragic and difficult; but seven times more bitter and tragic was the condition of Jews in the extermination camps, where the people of the S.S. let them live for a little while, and trained them to do the work of killing and slaughtering their own people. A more fearful thing than this the devil could not create. Day after day, the Jews not only saw with their own eyes how their brethren were murdered in cold blood, but they were forced to help the murderers in this fiendish slaughter.

They even had to pursue the victims into the gas chambers, take out the bodies of those who had been killed and bring them to the open doors of the crematoria.

Then later they had to bury them in mass graves. Sometimes this procedure was reversed, and they had to take them out of their graves and burn them.

Further, they had to number the personal belongings of those who had been killed.

In the death camp of Chelmno people were held in chains in the cellar of a bunker. Only when they were working were their chains taken off. They remained alive only briefly. After a few days, the grave-diggers would be found stretched out on the ground, lying on their faces on top of the piles of dead bodies, with bullets in their backs. So would end their accursed lives. The food given the grave-diggers was no more than a portion of hunger. Mostly they existed on the food that the victims had brought from their former work camps. The workers in the gangs of these death details changed constantly. When a transport arrived, the supervisors would choose the strongest, healthiest-looking prisoners as the new grave-diggers; and the previous ones, shattered and broken in spirit and physically, would be shot. Even the new ones had to be changed day by day and hour by hour, for they could not last, seeing nothing but death all day long. But their fate was entirely pre-planned anyway. The Nazis knew they dared not leave alive any witnesses to testify to their horrible crimes. They also were afraid of a sudden outbreak of desperation, that might bring on mass suicide attempts.

Those who were not brought up and trained in moral resistance had to be doped up so that they would carry out this work as automatons; they were frequently doing things mechanically, without any will. A few of them even acquired Nazi morality, and, as though carrying a torch, they led others into lawlessness and degradation. Those who were stronger of spirit sought ways to inform the outside world about the filthy crimes that were being quietly carried out, so that revenge could be taken. They were desperate people and ready to do anything and everything. They knew that one day, any day, when the Germans had no more use for them, their fate would be the same as the others whom they had watched die and about whom they had to keep silent.

The mental suffering of a tortured prisoner who had to help the hangman to destroy and exterminate his relatives and his brothers and the people of his own race, brought a wave of hatred against the hangman and a consuming desire for revenge; but it brought also terror, a feeling of desperate helplessness, and mental deterioration and degeneration. These people were under constant nervous tension between these two contradictory emotions. The possibility of open revolt and aggressive resistance against the murderers depended upon which of the two emotions was the more dominant. Immeasurable emotional strength was needed—as well as certain abilities—in order to exercise even the initiative to organize, much less carry out, a revolt under the conditions existing in the death camps. A very strict watch was kept on the death-camp prisoners; the eyes of the bloodthirsty enemy were alert to note every move. Besides, there was a need to watch for traitors. The Kapo was the S.S. unit in charge of a camp and fear of it paralyzed the prisoners; its members had authority to change regulations on the spot, so it was very easy for them to make an end of every plan of escape. And also to speed up the total destruction of a camp.

Let us remember that there was, nevertheless, revolt and resistance within the camps—and that it was more or less successful. Groups, large and small, of Jews who dared these actions have brought the German crimes to light and informed the whole world about them. We must therefore assume that many others tried to resist and revolt, that their efforts were choked in their infancy, and that the participants were murdered so that no echo of their efforts should come to us.

The following incident that took place in a labor camp at Konim proves this assumption:

In August, 1943, when the Jews of the camp realized that the time of annihilation was near, a group of five people decided to start a revolt. They planned to set a wooden building afire and run away during the confusion. Their plans were not successful and the whole group committed suicide. Only one participant in the plan was saved, and thanks to him we have today all the particulars about a revolt that failed in the camp at Konim. To evaluate and appraise the heroism of those who died in the Jewish extermination camps, one must realize that so far as we know there never was a collective revolt in a general concentration camp. In these camps there were thousands of prisoners of all nationalities from the countries conquered by Hitler. In some of these countries there had existed organized underground groups. Political prisoners were frequently kept at Dachau; and objectively, one must admit that conditions for revolt were much better there than in the Jewish death camps. The only known revolt in a concentration camp was the plot of the Zonderkomando of Auschwitz; and it was carried through ably by the Jewish underground.

Revolt in the death camps, Jewish participation in the Partisan movement, uprisings in the Ghettos, and the phenomenal revolt in the Warsaw Ghetto—all these are definite proof that Jews did not just yield to the Nazis, but actively resisted and fought to the death the German Juggernaut.

ISAIAH TRUNK

THE REVOLT IN TREBLINKA

The date of the uprising was set at last, for the 2nd of August. There could be no more delays. As the fatal day approached we checked each detail to be sure that everything was ready and that everyone knew his task. Only one problem remained: contact had to be made with the people in Camp A. Until now I had been working in Camp B and had been completely cut off from the other group. As the time for the uprising neared, contact still had not been made and I began to fear the worst.

Finally the day arrived for our date with destiny. What a day it was!!! As the early morning sunrays filtered through the small openings in our barracks, one could already feel the heat of a scorching day. The night had been a sleepless one and all of us were wide awake, stimulated with nervous energy as we realized the importance of the occasion. Everything around us was rotten and disgusting . . . our only escape until now had been in the dreams of freedom and revenge. We yearned to rest our weary bodies somewhere in the forest. The only answer was to escape from the concentration camp; and today, August 2nd, we were seeking the realization of our dreams.

Escape seemed to be suicide. The camp was surrounded by ditches and barbed wire. Guards stood on watchtowers at every corner, while armed Germans and Ukrainians were on constant patrol. To add to our problems, time was short, because we were to be locked up again in our cells at noon. My mind was made up; I had to escape. My goal was simple: to escape and record the Nazi crimes in writing so that the whole world would know what was happening. With this as my aim, I could not fail. It gave me an incentive to fight these sons of the devil, and I had a feeling that fate was with me and that I would succeed in my mission.

It was quiet—the lull before the storm. Every movement we made was tense but deliberate. The Ukrainians and Germans did not suspect a thing. Why should they worry? Were they not in an ideal position? They carried arms and were seasoned killers, while we were, in their eyes, nothing more than weak, helpless, miserable wretches. I began scurrying from place to place like a madman, seeking a way to make contact with Camp A. Suddenly an idea flashed through my mind. The German work supervisor, Leffler, wasn't around; and his substitute, whose name nobody seemed to know, was on duty. This substitute, whom we had named The Brown Shirt, was rather lenient with us. I approached him and told him that we needed lumber to continue our work. The wood was stored in the other camp, and this would give me a chance to make contact with leaders of the rebellion there. For a moment my plan seemed doomed to failure. The Brown Shirt decided that I was too valuable a worker, and elected to send several other people to bring back the lumber. Those he chose were useless as messengers. I had to act quickly. Shaking my head and making motions as though the task before me was very distasteful, I told him that I was the only one who knew exactly what we needed and that, although I hated to have to go, there did not seem to be any alternative. I held my breath for a moment and waited for his reply. Luck was with me; his answer was affirmative.

This was my chance. I had to make contact with the leaders in Camp A. If I failed now all would be lost. We reached the lumber storage room, where we found a German officer and the lumber foreman, a middle-aged Jew. I did not know the latter, but soon learned that he was involved in the plans for the rebellion. I begin to pick out lumber, working my way into the position near the Jew. When the German was temporarily distracted by some other workmen, we quickly exchanged information. The time for the uprising was set for exactly five-thirty.

With feverish haste, I selected the necessary lumber and hurried back to camp. My only fear was that my nervousness would betray me to the Germans. Luckily I was not detected and, as noontime arrived, we were all led to our cells. Once we were inside, the committee planning the rebellion met and I gave them the information that I had obtained on my trip to the other camp. I cautioned them to be patient and quiet. Everybody was assigned his task. We had to provide the Germans with two groups of workers for the afternoon. The weakest men were sent to the first shift. They returned at three o'clock and my group replaced them. Unknown to the Germans, this second group contained thirty hand-picked men who were to serve, two and a half hours later, as the vanguard of the rebellion.

Before departing, we selected another group of people who were to go out late every afternoon. Little did the enemy suspect that, instead of bringing back water, these men would serve as a supporting unit for the thirty leaders of the uprising. All wore regular clothes under their prison work uniforms. Once outside the camp, they would strip their uniforms and attempt to lose themselves in the general population.

The minutes passed; everybody was tense. Zero hour was approaching. We were soon to leave this hell which was full of memories of torture, suffering and death. Before us were rows and rows of dead bodies . . . our friends . . . our families. The dead demanded revenge. We could not fail them—we, the only witnesses to this horrible crime against humanity. As we walked in silence past the ashes of our people, we were confident that we would avenge their innocent blood. Suddenly the silence was shattered: a shot rang out. A tingle of fear ran up and down the spines of those of us who were now leading the revolt. Our task was most difficult . . . we had to get the guards down from the watchtowers which were located at every corner. If the Ukrainians who manned them opened fire, none of us would escape alive. We gambled on one known weakness of the guards: we knew that they had a lust for gold and, on several occasions, prisoners had engaged in illegal trade with them. So, as the first shot was fired, one of our men walked past a watchtower flashing a gold ring. He fell into an ambush and was put to death. We took his weapons and, with the uprising only minutes old, we were already in possession of a strategic position. Slowly, but methodically, we captured tower after tower.

Every guard was killed on the spot. The men at the water well likewise overpowered the guard, stole his gun and broke into the ammunition storeroom. Everybody loaded himself with as many weapons as he could carry and the escape was well under way. Before the enemy knew what was happening, we had taken over the camp. Suddenly, according to schedule, fire broke out all over the camp. As soon as I saw the flames, I began my escape and took with me an axe and a steel rod.

For a few moments the escaping prisoners were in control of the situation, but soon the Germans struck back. Attracted by the gunfire and the sight of the burning camp, German patrols converged on us from three directions. Our goal was to reach the nearest forest and we ran as we had never run before. Five miles remained to be covered . . . five miles between the hell of the death camp and the freedom of the forest. We fled through the fields with bullets flying all around us. Exhausted as we were, we kept on; to stop meant death.

I ran until I was completely out of breath. With freedom in sight, I heard a voice shout at me to halt. I had very little strength left but the desire to live drove me on. A shot was fired and my left arm began to sting. I glanced back and saw a guard chasing me with his automatic pistol aimed in my direction. Fortunately, I was a weapons expert and could tell that his pistol was jammed. Taking advantage of the situation, I let him catch up to me and then I suddenly turned and threw the axe at him. The blade caught him in the chest and he fell to the ground. I was free; I had conquered the last obstacle. I hurried into the security of the dense forest and fell exhausted midst the green bushes and trees.

From the distance was heard the sound of shooting. Now for the first time I looked at my left arm. The shirt had been torn by a bullet and my skin scratched, but otherwise I was unhurt. What a miracle!!!

Now I stood in the forest . . . alone.

YANKEL VYERNIK

THE OUTBREAK IN SOBIVOR

In groups of two thousand they were dragged from the Ghetto and herded into the camp on Siroka Street. From there they were sent further.

The nine hundred permanent residents of the S.S. labor camp on Siroka Street included 500 Jews, who were professional people and had been picked up some time before in the Ghetto of Minsk, and classified; about 100 Jewish prisoners-of-war; and 300 non-Jews who had been arrested for minor offenses. They rose at five in the morning and stopped work at eight in the evening. They received 150 grams of bread per person twice a day. They had potato soup for lunch—and nothing more.

In addition to this tyrannical routine, the commander of the camp from time to time put on shows for the further harassment of his prisoners. For instance, in the evening, when food was being given out, the assistant commander would order the people to stand one behind the other and face forward. Then, holding his cocked revolver, he would rest his hand on the shoulder of the first person in line. He'd shoot the length of the line at those who arrived late, or at anyone who failed to keep the line straight. If he missed his target, the bullet sometimes found its mark among those who had continued to lie on their boards and had not tried to line up for food.

Sometimes the overseer would come in with his two vicious dogs. He would urge the dogs to snap at those prisoners who were not following the order to lie quietly. The dogs would bite and tear the prisoners' covers and clothes, and if a prisoner protested, he would be shot instead of the dog.

One of the prisoners of the camp was accused of stealing 200 grams of bread. He was tied to a barrel and one after the other 20 Nazis beat him, each for a full minute, with the heel of a hatchet or anything that came to hand; they struck the alleged thief, who finally fainted. They revived him with cold water so they could continue to beat him.

On September 18th the Jews were ordered to assemble in the courtyard. It was about four in the morning, and still dark. In the darkness, the prisoners with their bundles in their hands were made to stand in line, and each was given 300 grams of bread. Though the courtyard was full of people, no one spoke; children clung to their mothers, and the silence was louder than shouting would have been. No one was hit or beaten, there was no pouring of hot water on anyone, they didn't order the dogs to snap at anyone. The commander, twirling his horsewhip, announced: "Shortly you will be led to the railroad station. You are going to Germany. There you will be allowed to work. Hitler has seen fit to have mercy on Jews who honestly want to work for Germany. You will go together as families and you may take with you your best belongings."

The women and children were brought to the station in cars; the men walked. On our way we passed the Ghetto. The people in the Ghetto saw us and they threw bread and provisions to us over the barbed wire. They called words of parting and we knew they were crying. All knew what we were in for.

We were locked up in empty boxcars, 70 people in each —men, women and children together. There wasn't a piece of board, or a bench; and to lie down was impossible. With great difficulty, one person at a time could sit down for several seconds. Each stood pressed one against the next. The doors were never opened, and the windows were barred with metal and wire. No food or water was given us. No one could leave the car to attend to necessities. This inhuman confinement continued for four days. The cars were in motion almost constantly, but we did not know where we were or where we were going.

On the fifth day, toward evening, we reached an isolated station. On a white sign was written in large gothic letters: Sobivor. On one side of the station was a forest. On the other side was a triple barbed wire fence three meters high.

The train was moved onto a siding and they brought us

water. It was the first time in five days. We were offered no food. We were locked inside the cars again for the night. On September 23rd, at nine in the morning, the diesel engine backed our train to a gate in the barbed wire fence. On it was the sign: Zonderkomando.

The train was backed in and the gate closed. Hungry, exhausted and demoralized, we started climbing down from the cars. A group of German officers emerged from a white building. They walked toward us with horsewhips in their hands. Leading them was a tall, husky, very fat German, Oberscharführer Gomersky, who had been a boxer in Berlin. He faced us, his feet wide apart, and looked us over. Then he called out, "Carpenters and construction builders without families, forward!"

About 80 people stepped forward, most of them prisoners of war; I was among them. We were sent to a second inner court which had its own inner barbed wire fence. We were led inside a long hut in which were piled boards, one atop the other. They ordered us each to find a board and choose a place. The rest of the people from the train remained on the other side of our barbed wire enclosure. We never saw them again.

It was a sunny, hot day. A few of us went out into the courtyard. We sat down on some wood that was piled there and started to converse. Each spoke of home, relatives, all those who were dear to him. I was from Rostov. I had received no news or information from my family but I was sure that they had been turned out of their home.

Shlomo Leitman was from Warsaw. When the Germans attacked Soviet Russia, his wife and children were in Minsk. They had not been able to escape and had been killed in the Ghetto. He came over and sat near us. He was a husky Jew, of middle height, about 40 years old. He had returned from his work in the outer court.

"Where are you from?" he said to me, speaking in Yiddish.

Shlomo explained that I didn't understand Yiddish, because I had grown up in a non-Jewish neighborhood. Our conversation continued, but Shlomo had to help me understand. I happened to look up and saw pillars of gray

207

smoke curling up northwest of us. The pillars finally drifted into large clouds toward the horizon. The smell of burning filled the air.

"Where is the fire?" I asked.

"Turn your face away," a Jew answered. "They are burning the bodies of your colleagues, your friends and brothers, who came here today with you."

My eyes became wet.

He continued, "They are not the first and they will not be the last. No less than three times a week, long trains like yours bring thousands of people here. This camp has been here about a year and a half. Figure it out for yourself: Jews have been brought here from Poland, from Czechoslovakia, from France, from Holland. Up until now there had been none from Soviet Russia."

The man had been at the camp a long time. His work was to number the belongings of those who were killed. He knew many things. From him we heard where our traveling companions had gone after we left them, and the pattern of the camp's activities. He spoke simply and without emotion. Though he had only just met us, he could see that we had had a great deal of experience. But as we listened, we shivered and trembled.

"After you were chosen and classified, you were sent away. The rest were brought over to another court. Generally speaking, all are brought there. Everyone without exception. There they are ordered to set aside their bundles and undress themselves, in readiness to go to the baths. They cut the women's hair off first.

"Everything is done quietly and in a great hurry. Baldheaded and naked except for a shirt, their children clinging to them, the women are pushed into the next room. A hundred steps behind them walk the men, entirely naked, accompanied by a large guard. There, ahead of them, is the bath house, not far from the place that smoke is coming from.

"There are two buildings there, one for women and children, one for men. I haven't been inside them, but those who have have told me the way they are set up— very orderly and neat. They look like bath stalls, with faucets for cold water and faucets for hot water and sinks to wash in. The people come in, and immediately all the doors are locked and from overhead dark, heavy streams of liquid pour down.

"At this time there is a lot of screaming, but it doesn't last long. Soon the voices turn burned leather and one hears sounds of strangulation and suffocation and convulsions. They say that mothers cover their infants with their bare bodies. The master of the bath watches all that goes on from a little window in the ceiling.

"Fifteen seconds later everything is finished and ended. The floor opens and the bodies drop into cars, which are standing ready and prepared on the floor below, in the cellar of the so-called baths. The cars are packed full of bodies and they roll away fast.

"Everything is organized and the best German techniques are used. The bodies are arranged in piles according to a certain order. They pour gasoline and benzine over them and set them afire. What you see is these bodies going up in flames. We too will go up in flames. If not tomorrow, then after a week, or a month . . ."

That night we didn't sleep, in spite of our tiredness and exhaustion.

September 27th. We worked as usual in the square of the northern camp. About ten in the morning, Kalemali, one of our group, came over to me. He was a young fellow from Bakow; the real name of his family was Shubayev.

He asked, "Sasha, tell me, what is the meaning of this?" Because all the Germans had walked away, and only the Kapo remained near us. "What do you think?"

"I don't know," I said. "But since they are away, let's check with everyone and find out where the guards are stationed and when the guard is changed."

My heart shrank within me. "Where is the bath house?"

"Behind the huts, about 100 meters from here. There is a tall, barbed wire fence, covered with branches. At its corners there are sentinel boxes. That's where the bath house is."

The mattocks and saws were still in our hands, and we

looked across to the other area. We could see no movement, nor was there any sound. We watched and waited.

Suddenly the shriek of a woman split the air, and then we heard many people screaming, and children weeping, and yells of, "Mother! Mother!"

The voices sounded like those you hear in nightmares and delirium when you want to wake and you can't. Soon the women's and children's voices were mixed with men's voices, and then they all merged into a loud moaning like that of scared and confused wild beasts.

Later we found out that 300 victims had been rounded up in the courtyard like a flock of geese, and that while the bath house was being operated for an earlier group, the Germans pursued them, just as geese are driven into a pen, with shouts and a lot of noise, to drown out the dying people's cries.

I was stunned with fear. Not fear of death—what scared me was the realization of my helplessness. I had to do something. My fear dictated my decision.

Shlomo Leitman and Boris Zibulsky came over to me. Both were pale and shocked. Zibulsky said, "Sasha, we must escape from here. Outside is the forest; it's about 200 meters beyond the fence. The Germans are busy now. We'll overpower the guards near the fence, we'll use our mattocks and saws."

"Perhaps we could escape," I said, "but what of the others? All of them will be exterminated immediately. If we can escape and run away, it is only right that all of us should escape, and not one of us should be left here. It's true that some will be killed, but those who escape can take revenge afterwards."

"You are right," Zibulsky said. "But we haven't any time to wait. Winter is almost here, and snow will preserve our footprints. Anyhow, living in the forest in wintertime is difficult."

"Have faith in me," I said. "Wait for me and keep quiet, don't say anything to anybody. When the time comes I will let you know what to do."

On September 29th, at six in the morning, all 600 men and women in the camp were arranged in columns and

210

taken to the railway station inside the grounds. Eight large cars stood on the siding, loaded with bricks. An order was given to unload the bricks. Each person took between six and eight bricks and walked rapidly the 200 meters to where they told us to place them; then he returned as fast as possible.

Near the car and along the road, Germans stood, directing the work. For a mis-step or the slightest pause, the Germans applied the horsewhip. All the work was done in a rush. It took a great deal of shouting and urging. Many people, 70 or 75, were working inside the cars so closely they stepped on each other's feet. If you didn't catch the bricks thrown to you or handed to you, and they fell on the ground, you received 25 lashes of the horsewhip. If you stopped for a second, you received only a beating.

The constant hiss and whistle of the descending horse-whips was almost all one could hear. Everyone breathed heavily and we were covered with perspiration. It trickled into our eyes. We actually ran as we carried the bricks.

In 50 minutes the eight carloads of bricks had been piled to one side; and the next minute we were lined up in columns and returned to camp. The Germans rushed outside the fence to where a train waited, full of new victims.

Eighty of us were brought to the northern camp. There we were divided into two groups. Forty chopped wood, and the rest, including Shlomo and myself, worked in the huts. After only a few minutes, someone came into the hut and announced, "Sasha, we are running away right now."

"How can you do that? Who says so?"

"We decided among ourselves. There are only five guards. We will attack them and break through to the forest."

"Doing something idiotic like that may cause only damage." I tried to convince the fellow that we must not do anything rash. "It's easy for you to talk. The guards are not all in one group. If you attack one, the second one will shoot you. What will you use to cut the barbed wire? How will you pass the minefields? In less time than it takes to tell, the Germans will take counteraction.

"Perhaps someone will succeed in breaking through and

get away, but what will happen to those who are working in the huts? They don't know anything about it and they will be stopped entirely, and we haven't time to tell them. They won't have a chance ever. You say right now it is easy to escape. Well, I doubt it.

"But I think that with the proper preparation, sometimes it's possible to succeed even under the most difficult conditions; even easier than when conditions are good, but there is no judgment and deliberation. You do whatever you think best, I won't stop you; but I will not go with you."

I succeeded in convincing them, and it looked as though everyone had returned to work.

October 11th. Suddenly, in the morning, horrifying screams reached our ears. Right afterwards there was the sound of machinegun fire. Word came immediately that we might not enter the blacksmith shop. The gates of the first camp were locked up; guards were doubled everywhere. We could hear a lot of yelling and shots.

"What happened? What do you think?" Shlomo asked.

"I think that the shooting is coming from the north camp. Perhaps the fellows couldn't control themselves, and started to run?"

"No, not from there. The shooting is much closer, probably in the second camp. I hear women's voices. Surely a train has come in. But why are they shooting?"

It was a long while before things became quiet again.

It was not until five in the evening that we found out the particulars.

A train had come in. When the men were ordered to undress it seems they knew where they were being led, and in their fright they had started to run around naked. But they didn't know which way to run. They knew they were already inside the camp, and the camp had a fence all around. In their dash they reached a fence, and there they were mowed down by machineguns. Many were killed by the bullets; the rest were taken to the gas chambers.

That night the fires burned very late. A storm came up and the flames, reflecting against the cold dark sky, spread a fearful sadness over the camp. Tongue-tied with horror, we watched the fire glow, showing us where the bodies of our tortured brethren and sisters were being cremated.

October 12th. I will always remember this day. Eighteen people in our camp had been sick for several days. In the morning a group of Germans, headed by Franz, came into the hut. Franz ordered the sick to stand up. It was clear that they were being taken away to be killed. Among the sick was one young fellow from Holland who could hardly stand. His wife heard where her husband was being taken, and she rushed after the unit, calling: "Murderers! I know where you are taking my husband. Take me with him. Do you hear? I don't want to live without him. Murderers. Dirty, mean people!" She took hold of her husband's hand and she supported him as they marched together—to death.

At lunchtime, Shlomo and I agreed to gather a small group of people together for consultation, at nine that evening.

We were to meet in the carpenter shop. There were present Baruch; Shlomo; the leader of the carpenters' unit, Yanek; the head of the tailors, Yuzef; the tailor, Jacob; Monyek; Leo Feldhendler; and another man; and myself. In the court, near the gate of the first camp, people stood guard to watch every movement and let us know if anything happened, so we could spread out.

First I told them about my conversation with B'zetsky, and asked each of them to state their opinion as to whether it was right to bring him into our group. Everyone thought that it might be, and that it was right to do it. Monyek went out and returned quickly, accompanied by B'zetsky.

"B'zetsky," I said, "we decided to invite you to consult with us. I think you understand the responsibility you are taking upon yourself in coming here. If we should fail, you will be among the first to be taken out to be killed."

"I understand," B'zetsky answered. "Don't be afraid."

"So, comrades, my plan is first of all to annihilate the officers now in charge of the camp. We shall kill them one by one, without any excitement or noise, and quickly. I think within one hour, no more. We should finish up in a

213

shorter period than this. Delay is dangerous. The Germans may find out that one of them is missing, and cause a commotion.

"The duty of annihilating the officers will be given to people chosen from among the Soviet prisoners of war. I know them and I'm sure that they can be depended on. It's clear that in an action like this brave men are needed, brave and tough. One moment of hesitation, the failure of any one of them, can bring destruction upon all of us. At three-thirty in the afternoon, B'zetsky will leave with three people whom I will choose, on some excuse, and go to the second camp.

"These three will finish off the four Hitler men working there. This will bring the officers in, one by one, to the hall, and it will be possible to annihilate them. So we must watch, to be sure that from the time the annihilation of the Hitler men starts, no person goes outside the camp. Everyone who tries to make noise we must silence immediately or finish him off.

"We have until four o'clock to finish the action in the second camp. At four o'clock those appointed will cut the telephone wires that go from the second camp to the guard towers. The wires must be cut close to the poles to hide where they are cut and to prevent the connections from being restored quickly. At the very same time we will commence the annihilation of the camp officers. One by one, they will be invited to the blacksmith shop. Two people will be ready and prepared for their destruction in each shop. We have only until four-thirty to finish everything.

"At four-thirty B'zetsky and Genyek will line up all the people of the camp as though leading them to work, and the line will move toward the exit. In the first rows will be our people, and those in the front will storm the ammunition magazine. The rest will cover the attack. When those at the ammunition depot have obtained it, they will return to the column, at the head of it, remove the guard at the gate, and attack the gendarmes.

"It's possible that the guard will find out what's going on, contrary, of course, to our expectation and plans, and

214

that they will cut us off from the road to the gate. They may open fire on us with their two machineguns. Well, if we succeed in getting the ammunition, we will battle them. But if we don't succeed, then we must be prepared with another way out.

"Not far from the carpenter's shop, near the barbed wire fence, is the house of some of the officers. We have to assume that even if the field nearby is mined, those are only signal mines and not dangerous. Behind the officers' house we must cut the barbed wire. Those ahead will have to throw stones ahead of them so that the stones will fall on the mines and set them off. Then the road ahead of them will be at least partly clear.

"This plan Shlomo and I have weighed and thought over again and again. There couldn't be a better plan. Now everyone must consult himself and decide in his heart whether he will be able to carry through everything that he has been appointed to do and do it in the right way. Tomorrow, in the evening, we will meet again. Remember, comrades, that you are not allowed to reveal any of this to anyone, not to a brother, not to a wife, and not to a friend. Not one word of what has been said here can be repeated."

There was no time for discussion. One by one, the people left. In the last few days I had noticed that the guards on their way to stand watch were getting bullets, each of them five rounds, and at the time the guard changed they gave the bullets to the men relieving them. So, at the time when the guards are not on duty, it followed they had no bullets. I wanted to check on this, and it was agreed between me and B'zetsky that the following day he would send me to clean the guards' hut.

On October 13th, at ten in the morning, a request was received in the carpenter shop to send a person to the guards' hut to fix some doors. Yanek sent me. First I walked through all the rooms of the hut and checked all the doors. The first room I entered was empty. I closed the door immediately, as though I were checking it. Quickly I opened up one of the closets. In a corner stood a rifle. I had a look into the magazine of the rifle and it was empty.

The bullet clip that was lying on the shelf was also empty. The contents of the second closet were exactly the same.

When I returned to the carpenter shop I went up on the roof. From there the whole area on the other side of the fence could be seen well. On the left side of the camp gates were the railroad tracks, and behind them was the station. Further on was the forest. On the right side, at a distance of 500 meters, was also a forest. Wooden poles lay spread out on the road. Opposite us, Poles worked carrying wood. It was clear that we would have to run toward the right.

That same evening it was decided that the next day, October 14th, we would escape from the camp.

October 14th was a bright sunny day. During the night we distributed the knives. Also we had a couple of dozen hatchets, not large ones, that the blacksmiths had sharpened to our specifications; they were easy to hide under our clothes. Those who needed them most received some warm clothes. When and how we would make the break they didn't know; only the leaders knew.

I worked in one of the carpenter shops. From the windows I could see the courtyard of the first camp from one end to the other. In a nearby hut, Shlomo worked with a group of 20 men, who were especially chosen. They were making shelves for the office.

At four o'clock, the Unterscharführer Berg was to come to the tailor shop to have his suit fitted. At four-fifteen the head of the camp guard was coming for the same reason. The leader of the third camp, Gettsinger, and Oberscharführer Greishut were due at four o'clock in the shoemaker's. Franz had to come over to my hut to check the closets. Unterscharführer Friedrich Gultshtich checked Shlomo's group at the same time.

Baruch was to annihilate four officers in the second camp. The rest were to be invited on different excuses to the blacksmith shop. All the comrades who were to carry out this part of the annihilation were working that day with Shlomo. He was to send them one by one to me so I could explain to each person his mission.

The first to come was Kalemali. His real family name

was Shubayev. In the year 1940, he had finished his studies in communication engineering in a university in Rostov. He was only about 25, tall, steady, with black, curly hair. He talked little. Simple and strong, he was a good comrade and friend.

"With you, I don't have to talk much," I said to him. "You and Monyek are going to the tailor shop. Take with you a wood carver, a plane and a hatchet. Remember, everything must be done so there is no sound."

"It's understood."

"Go, and I wish you success."

Silently we shook each other's hand. He walked away. I asked him to send me Zibulsky.

Zilbulsky was a man from the Don Valley of Russia, a coachman. A husky person, tall, about 35, good-hearted, cheerful, and talkative. He was to be given many things to do; but every mission that he had ever undertaken he had fulfilled.

"Boris," I said as we sat together in the cellar, "I know you better than all the others. You have the most difficult mission. Michael and Beno are to go with you. B'zetsky will come for you and take you over to the second camp."

To Baruch, I said, "Take your hatchets with you."

Boyar I told to "Make up your mind to hit first. You must inspire bravery in the others. If the heart of one person working with you should soften, get someone else to help—in this kind of work we don't have to force anyone."

"You don't have to worry, Sasha. We are only waiting for the signal."

"Don't forget to take their revolvers from those who are killed. Go, and be successful. You must succeed."

At twenty minutes after three Genyek came into Shlomo's hut. I saw through the window that he and Zibulsky and two others were going out to the second camp.

The Unterscharführer Ernest Berg came to the tailor shop on horseback earlier than expected. He got down from his horse, slipped the reins over a post, and walked inside.

What happened inside, as it was told to me afterwards,

was this: when the Unterscharführer walked in, all rose to their feet as usual, and Shubayev went over close to the table. At the foot of the table, in a corner, Yanek was lying, covered with a shirt. The German took off his gun belt, the revolver still in its holster, and laid it on the table. He took off his outer jacket. Immediately Shubayev, the tailor, went toward him; in his hands he held the suit as though ready to measure it. Genyek came close to the table, so he would be able to grab the revolver in his right hand. Yuzef turned the German so his back was to Shubayev, toward Shubayev's right. At the same moment Shubayev came down on the head of the Hitlerite with the hatchet. The German gave a terrible cry, and his horse standing outside was startled and looked toward the shop, turning his ears. A second blow silenced the Hitlerite forever.

The body was hidden under the bench, and covered up with clothing. They also wiped up and covered the blood stains that were on the floor.

Immediately after that, Shubayev came running to my hut.

"Here, this is what you wanted!" He gave me the German's revolver.

"From now on, even if we want to, we can't retreat. Thank God, Kalemali," I said. We embraced each other and kissed one another. He had to hurry back to his hut. The second one to be taken was due shortly at the tailor shop.

"Quick!" I said. "How did the other fellows conduct themselves?"

"Wonderful!"

Shubayev returned to his place. Ten minutes later the Oberscharführer Oberhelm came into the tailor shop; from which, of course, he never emerged. Monyek knocked him out the minute he walked in.

Exactly at four o'clock, as anticipated, the Commander of the third camp, Gettsinger, came to the shoemaker shop. Arkadi Weispapir was at that time busy fixing a footstool, and Grisha stood at the door. Gettsinger was in a

218

hearty mood. It was a sunny day, warm and pleasant, and he was talkative.

"Are the boots prepared?"

"Please—" Jacob handed him the boots. "Try them on."

"Hey, Jacob," the Nazi said while he was measuring the boots. "In another five days I am going to Germany. You must make a pair of nice shoes, for my wife. Remember!"

"I hope that my work will satisfy your wife," Jacob answered.

At this moment, Arkadi brought the hatchet down on him. The body was pushed into one of the corners, where they covered it with rags. They poured sand on the blood spots.

We saw Oberscharführer Greishut coming, walking toward the shoemaker's shop to get his order. At a quarter after four Zibulsky was supposed to return from the second camp. He was excited and trying to control himself. All four Germans had been killed. We had word that the telephone communications had been cut off exactly as planned. No person was allowed to leave the second camp. Baruch was on watch there with those instructions. He asked that we notify him in time when he must take the people out.

"Where are the revolvers?" he asked.

"There are two so far; I have one, and one Michael has. Return meanwhile to the hut to Shlomo. That's an order."

At four-thirty in the afternoon, B'zetsky and his group returned from the northern camp. Just then Unterscharführer Gultshtich appeared in the courtyard.

Shlomo ran out to him. "The putty, commander. I don't know what next to do to fix the shelves. I need your opinion; I need your directions." The people stood quietly with folded hands.

The German started to walk toward the hut, and Kapo Schmidt followed him. When I saw Schmidt, I rushed over to B'zetsky. "Take Schmidt away from here. He must not go into the hut."

B'zetsky took told of Schmidt's hand. "Don't go there."

"Why not?"

"If you want to remain alive, don't interfere. Almost all the officers are dead. The people are watching what you do. Don't interfere, do you hear?"

As Schmidt listened to B'zetsky, he was so frightened he began to tremble from head to foot, and he wouldn't say a word. Meanwhile the Nazi was annihilated inside. Shlomo knocked him out by himself. Shlomo was short and skinny, but one stroke with the hatchet on the Nazi's neck settled everything, and he didn't have to do anything else.

The time had come to give the signal. But Franz was still alive. He hadn't come to check the closets, as we had expected. He was talking to someone in the courtyard, but he didn't go into the blacksmith shop. He, the manager in charge of the camp, hadn't been annihilated yet.

Our tinsmiths came and they brought thin pipes in their hands. In the pipes they had six rifles and bullets. One of the girls brought bullets for the revolvers from the apartment of the dead officers.

News reached us that Engel, a blacksmith from Lodz, had killed two he had worked with that day: the Unterscharführer Walter Reba, and the German who was with him. The German had walked into the shop with a submachinegun. Engel had become suspicious and he killed them while they were still near the door. It was clear that what had happened at the blacksmith shop would be known very soon, and we should not wait any longer. But what about Franz?

"The devil take him," Shlomo said, "sooner or later they will give his ration of lead, for it's coming to him. It's time to get out of here. It's a pity to waste a minute."

For a moment we stood listening. In the camp there was dead silence. I ordered B'zetsky to give the signal. A sharp whistle split the silence. Shlomo sent one fellow to the second camp to notify them that the time had come to run for it. People started to stream into the court from all sides.

In the beginning we had appointed 78 people, almost all of them Soviet prisoners of war, to storm the ammunition magazine. So they took their places in the column in the first rows. But the crowd, most of whom had just suspected something would happen and didn't know when and how, started to push forward and press against one another; and then at the last minute it occurred to them what was going on.

Everyone was afraid he might be left behind, so each one pushed forward and we reached the gate of the first camp all mixed up. Here the commander of the guard came toward us; he was a German from the vicinity of Volga.

"Hey, the devil take your mothers! Did you hear the whistle? Why are you pushing like horses? Straighten out your lines!"

A few hatchets came into view as though there had been a command; they had been concealed underneath clothing, and now they came down on his head.

The attack on the ammunition magazine did not succeed. The rapid fire from a machinegun blocked the way before us. Most of the people stormed toward the central exit, smashed the gates while shooting with their rifles, threw stones at any Fascists who got in their way, and threw sand in their eyes. They were able to get through the gate, and go towards the forest.

One group turned left. I saw them through the barbed wire. But from here on they had to go through minefields 15 meters wide; so many of them were probably killed. I and a few others turned toward the officers' house, and there we broke through to the other side of the barbed wire fence. I assumed that the field behind the officers' house was not mined, and that proved to be true. Not far from the fence, three men were killed; but it's possible they were not killed by the mines but by bullets, because from all sides shots rained on us.

We were already on the other side of the fence, that is the other side of the minefields, and had already gone about a hundred meters. Another hundred meters . . . We must hurry, hurry, to get past the open space where we would be in plain view of our pursuers, a perfect target for their bullets.

"Hurry, hurry! To the forest! Find shelter in the woods! . . ." And behold I was in the shadow of the forest. I stood a second to catch my breath and turned to look back. Men and women were stumbling, weak from running. They came nearer behind me, trying to get to the forest.

It's hard to say exactly how many people lost their lives at the time of the break. Most escaped from the camp; but many fell in the wide-open stretch of land between the camp and the forest.

It was decided not to tarry in the forest, but to spread ourselves out in small groups on all different sides, and continue to run.

The Polish Jews turned westward toward Chelm. They could understand the language of the people there, and they knew all the roads. We, the people from Soviet Russia, turned eastward. Many were helpless: the Jews from Holland, the French, and the Germans—none could speak to each other and there was gigantic space all around us.

The sound of rifles and machinegun fire continued behind us for a long time. It gave us our sense of direction. We knew where the camp was, and we knew telephone communications had been cut off, so Franz couldn't bring military trains. Little by little the shooting was farther away; and at last we couldn't hear it any more.

The day ended, and darkness came. During the night, shooting was heard repeatedly, but it was from afar, and we could hear the echoes. It seemed to us that they probably had pursued us. I stopped for a second, and Boris Zibulsky and Arkadi Weispapir came over to me.

I suggested we continue to walk all night. In a line, close behind each other, I at the head and Zibulsky behind me. We trailed in a long line, with Arkadi at the very end. No smoking, no talking, no lagging, and nobody was to run ahead. When the one who went ahead hurried, the rest must hurry; when the one ahead flattened himself on the ground, so must the next one. If someone saw the spark of a flashlight, he must lie down immediately. We must maintain order and have no confusion, under any circumstances.

We came out of the forest. We crossed an open field about three kilometers wide. Here the road was blocked by a canal, five or six meters wide and very deep. It was impossible to cross it on foot, so we walked alongside. Suddenly I saw, about 5 meters ahead, a group of people. We stretched out on the ground immediately, and Arkadi was ordered to check and find out who the people were. He crept along on his belly until he was quite close to them, then quickly got up and rushed to them. After several moments, he returned.

"Sasha, those are our people. They found wooden poles, and they're floating down the canal. Kalemali is with them."

Supported by the wooden poles, we swam the canal.

Shlomo had been wounded before he got into the forest. Although he ran about three kilometers, he couldn't stand on his feet any longer. He asked me to shoot him, but the Poles didn't want to leave him behind.

How bitter was this news, how great the sorrow! He had escaped from the camp, and on his way to freedom he had reeled and fallen helplessly. We were like brothers. What hadn't we talked about in our cell, as we lay near each other. His straight mind, his calmness, his bravery, his trustworthiness, had encouraged me and given me strength in the most difficult hours. We had planned and prepared the revolt together. We had consulted one another on everything, however little, however important. What would his end be? Would we one day receive regards from him?

Now we were a group of 57. We had walked another five kilometers when we heard the noise of a passing train. Before us stretched a tremendous open space with only small trees and bushes. We stopped walking. Night would come to an end very soon, and it was clear that when dawn broke they would certainly go out after us. The woods around there were not dense, and it would be possible to comb them easily. Zibulsky and Shubayev and I consulted together. It was decided we should lie down where we were; but we must cover ourselves properly and lie there without moving or making a sound or saying a word.

First, I sent a few people to check the woods carefully

on every side for quite a distance. Afterwards, all of us lay down close together.

In the morning, a light rain was falling. Now, in daylight, we could see the vicinity very well. Arkadi and Boris Zibulsky took one side; I and Shubayev the other. We walked about 500 meters and reached an empty field. On the horizon, at a distance of several kilometers, there was a forest. We returned and lay down to rest.

Half an hour later, Zibulsky and Arkadi appeared and told us that about 100 meters away there were railway tracks, and about one kilometer to the right there was a station. Closer to us than that, Polish people were working without a guard. That was all they had seen.

Near the railroad station, two of us, properly camouflaged, were left to check on what was going on in the vicinity. Every three hours we changed the guard.

All day airplanes flew overhead. Two of them flew low over the woods. From where we lay we could hear the voices of Polish people working near the railway tracks. Our people lay close to the ground, covered with branches, and they didn't move from their places until it was dark again. So passed the first day of our freedom and liberation, and that was October 15th, 1943.

Finally evening came. We had just gotten up from our places when two people came towards us, moving very quickly. We understood they were some of our people. They had found the river Bug and were just then returning from it.

"Why didn't you swim across?"

They told us that not far from the river there was an estate. There, they had found out that during the night many soldiers had arrived, and they were closely guarding the riverbanks.

We continued on our way in a row, in the same order as the day before. Zibulsky and I walked at the head of the column, Shubayev and Arkadi at the end. We had walked about five kilometers when we came to the forest. Here we stopped walking. There was no sense continuing to walk in a large group like this. We were too conspicuous, and it was impossible to provide food for so many people at one

224

time. So we divided ourselves into small groups, and every group turned to a different side.

My group included nine people, among them Shubayev, Boris Zibulsky, Arkadi Weispapir, Michael Itskovitz and Simeon Mazurkevitz.

Our aim was to get further to the east. The polestar was our guide. The nights were full of stars. Our first mission was to cut through and swim across the river. To do this, it was necessary to find the right place and set the proper hour. From isolated and quiet estates we were receiving food and getting news and directions. We were being warned which places we should pass by and go around, and where it was better to wait; the country people had learned that prisoners had escaped from the camp at Sobivor, the camp where the gas chambers were, and that the Germans were searching every inch of the vicinity.

I finally reached the estate of Stavky, about a kilometer and a half down the river Bug. The whole day we stayed in the forest. Toward evening three of us walked into one of the estates, the rest remaining outside to keep watch and give the alarm if we had to run for it.

In the house a candle was burning. Near the table, a man of perhaps 28 stood; he was blonde and tall, and his fair hair fell down on his white forehead. His shirt was unbuttoned, he wore no jacket, and he was in his bare feet. He was chopping tobacco leaves. Near the oven sat an elderly man, and in the corner far to the right, near the wall, a crib swung. A young woman sat near the crib quietly reading, the crib rope across her instep, rhythmically rocking the crib.

"Good evening. May we come in?"

"Come in," answered the young man in pure Russian.

"Hostess, cover up the windows."

"Surely," she answered and got up from her place.

"Sit down," the old man said.

We sat down. The people of the house said nothing.

"Perhaps you know where it is possible to swim across the Bug river?" Shubayev asked.

"No, I don't," the young man answered.

"You, father," I turned to the old man. "You are an old

225

timer here. Surely you know. They say that near Stavky the water is not so deep and it's possible to swim it."

"If they told you that, go on and swim. We don't know. We are not going to the Bug river, and we are not allowed to go there. Sit down and rest. We are not chasing you out, but we don't know anything."

The conversation went on for about an hour. We told them that we had escaped from captivity and we wanted to get back home, some to the valley of Don, some to Rostov: and that there was no reason to be afraid of us.

"Listen, please, comrades," the young fellow started to say after a long silence, "I will show you the place. I won't bring you to the river, but I will show you the road. You have to know how to get by a lot of guards on the banks. Some prisoners escaped from a camp not far from here, a camp where they made soap from human bodies. Now the Germans are turning the vicinity upside down. Go, and if luck is with you, you will pass on your way in peace. I wish you success from the bottom of my heart. But if you fail, don't blame me."

"You can put your mind at ease, you are a good man and our friend. We won't give you away. But how can we thank you? Just to say 'thank you' doesn't seem anything. There aren't enough words to express our gratitude. Come on, let's go, come before the moon comes up."

"Wait," said the young woman, "I will give you food for your journey."

We thanked the hostess and we parted from the old man. He blessed us by making the sign of the cross.

This happened early on the night of October 20th, 1943. Our feet were again on the ground of Soviet Russia; and although the Germans were still there, it seemed to us that even the air was different, purer. The roads, the trees, even the heavens were more beautiful, for they were closer to our hearts, and they were friendly to us.

On October 22nd, in the vicinity of Brest, we met Partisans for the first time. They were from a unit named after Comrade Voroshilov.

A. PETZORSKY

226

THE BURNING OF
THE KONIN CAMP

At one time the number of prisoners at the Konin Camp amounted to close on 1,100, of whom 868 came from the Gostynin and Gombin districts. In the course of time, and particularly during 1943, many selections were carried out, and entire groups of forced workers were sent to be exterminated at Chelmno and other camps.

With the increase in extermination activities, and the filtering through of reports about the absolute liquidation of labor camps in the vicinity, all belief in the lying promises of the Germans' work directors began to evaporate. The prisoners, and particularly those among them with responsibilities, became certain that they were doomed. Rabbi Aaronson had considerable influence in directing the despairing thoughts into the channel of action against the enemy. Basing himself on express prohibition in the traditional Jewish law, Rabbi Aaronson combated the idea of suicide. Indeed, as long as this camp was in existence, there was only one case of suicide there. When Rabbi Aaronson learned that the responsible Jews had decided to end their lives in order not to serve any longer as a rod for the oppression of their remaining brethren, he began to call on them to sell their lives at a high price. To smite at the foe, to slay as many as possible and to fall in that unequal struggle, would be a death that would hallow the name of God and honor the Jewish nation. Such a death could help to avenge the blood of our people that had been shed so cruelly, and would accord with the Talmudic council, "If anyone comes to kill you, kill him first." What would be the point, the rabbi wanted to know, in destroying our souls without avenging the shed blood?

The small group who had official tasks began, in the words of the rabbi, to "feel penitent." Together with a handful of expert craftsmen, they prepared plans for revolt. The rabbi participated in all this. Plans for action, whose objective, in the words of Feivish Kamlazh, was "to behave like Samson," were speeded up when the responsible persons found out that in the near future they would also be required to liquidate the last Jew in the camp. Philip Zielonka, who acted as camp policeman for the Germans, was constantly afraid that because of his size and strength the Gestapo would require him to bury the remaining camp prisoners alive. This neither he nor his comrades were prepared to do, no matter what might befall.

A detailed plan, simple yet daring, was prepared. Its main points were: the poisoning of all who ate in the German canteen; the destruction of the railway tracks near the camp; and setting the camp on fire. Duties were allocated. Passwords and signs by which the plan would be acted on were decided on. The group of plotters who first agreed to revolt and take vengeance, as early as the summer of 1942, numbered 15 men. By the end of July, 1943, there were only about eight left. Rabbi Aaronson relates that upon completing the plans, a bottle of liquor stolen from the Gestapo was taken from its hiding place, and the group drank "lechayim" (to life). Feivish Kamlazh and Abraham Seif, in their parting letters, report this decision of the responsible Jews to rise up and revolt.

The leading plotters had neither the strength nor the endurance to carry out the plan. The camp commandant was summoned to the Gestapo offices in town, and believed that the end had come. Only the final stage of the plan then actually was carried out: they set the camp huts on fire and hanged themselves, each at his post and in his working place. That was the end of the "revolt of the responsible Jews"; and in this way Kamlazh, Zielonka, Seif, Getzel Kleinot (the gardener), Kamlazh's father-in-law (Abraham Neudorf), Dr. Hans Knopf of Berlin, and Zalman Nusenowicz, all met their deaths. The latter did not know about the matter at all; but when he saw how things were going, he also hanged himself in his shoemaking shop. Rabbi Aaronson cut two of them down while they were still breathing. They remained alive and in due course came to Israel. To the remainder he carried out the last kindness and buried what was left of their scorched bodies. Several of the camp huts were burned.

The Germans became confused and alarmed. Reinforcements were summoned. The fire brigade and many committees of inquiry arrived from Poznan, the district capital. The rabbi was the first person questioned. Those questioned did not conceal the real reason for the act of revolt, which had been only a desperate protest against the German murderers, and the gloomy and assured prospect that the Konin Camp would end like so many others in the neighborhood. The inhabitants of the region discussed this revolt a great deal. After the inquiries were over, the camp was liquidated and the prisoners were transferred to other camps. The camp's survivors related that during the fortnight of the inquiry they were treated far better and lived under far more humane conditions than at any other time in the history of the camp.

RABBI YEHOSHUA MOSHE AARONSON

RESISTANCE IN
PONYATOV AND TRABNIK*

The representatives of the Jewish National Committee were sent to the district of Lublin because of frightening news that had been brought back from the concentration camps there. It had been reported that 10,000 people had been slaughtered in Trabnik, and 15,000 in Ponyatov.

The slaughter in Trabnik took place on November 3rd, 1943. It started at six in the morning, and by four in the afternoon not one of the 10,000 people who had been imprisoned in the camp remained alive.

On Friday, November 5th, the extermination was carried out in Lublin. All the Jews in the Lublin camps were brought together in the camp at Maidanek and there they were shot to death. About 18,000 people met their end there.

On Monday, November 8th, the extermination took place in Ponyatov.

Early in the morning many motor cars of the Stormtroopers and the Z.D., full of gendarmes, came to the place. They encircled the camp like a linked chain. When the Jews saw that the hour of their death was near, the local Jewish Fighting Organization members set fire to all the storehouses, magazines and workshops, which contained large quantities of clothes for the army. The Jews tried to resist. A horrifying slaughter started that lasted for three days.

On Wednesday, November 10th, 1943, everything was over. Fifteen thousand men had been murdered. They burned the bodies right there; and many were burned alive. The shooting, the cries and the moans of the dying were heard constantly. The smell of the burning filled the air for miles around for more than a week.

In Trabnik, as in Ponyatov, the Jews tried to take up

* (The text of a special announcement of the National Jewish Committee that was sent from Warsaw on November 15th, 1943, to the representative of the Polish Jews in London.)

230

arms against their enemy. The Germans knew that in the vicinity of the two camps there were groups of the Jewish Fighting Organization, so they used a new strategy: they brought into the camps large contingents of the S.S. and many gendarmes—both in Trabnik and also in Ponyatov. Thousands upon thousands of Germans were used to carry out the slaughter.

Signed: THE NATIONAL JEWISH COMMITTEE

THE DEATH BRIGADE

On November 19th, 1943, toward evening, I was ordered by Herches to assemble all those up to 20 years of age, and all the older husky men in the workshop. He ordered some of the older men to surround a wooden building and to let us know if anyone should come close. The rest of the people gathered in the tents, and we played music and sang.

The meeting was held in the workshop. Herches opened it as chairman and what he said was, "Brothers and comrades, the hour of decision has come. We must choose life or death. Tomorrow we will be burned alive or we will leave this slavery and be free. I mention the fire first, then freedom, because a person must always anticipate the worst, in order to be sure that everything will end up well.

"We are not afraid of the fire, for we will face death in the next few hours. Isn't it better to be dead than abused and dishonored? Isn't it better to die an honorable death for freedom, than to go like sheep to the slaughter, to walk in groups of five to the crematoria? In addition, do we want to serve them faithfully all of our lives until our very last breath, helping them blot out the evidence of their murderous acts?"

Little by little Herches came to the point of what part each of us would play. Before he revealed the general plan and gave everyone his assignment, he pointed out that if anyone chosen hadn't enough strength and willpower to comply with the mission given him, he should confess immediately; because the missions and the duties were very important and dangerous.

He divided the people into groups of four, and this was the plan of action: the first group of four was to annihilate the two German guards always stationed near our camp. They were to be exterminated before they could say a word; if not we would be defeated at the outset. To accomplish this mission, two of the four would approach the gate carrying wood. At the very same moment, the second pair would approach the other guard and offer to sell him some shoes. When the second German turned his back to pay for the shoes, one of our two men would choke him. Afterwards they were to take the guards' weapons, throwing the guards' bodies into a tent.

The role of the next four men was to equip themselves with sub-machineguns and grenades. The first two guards being out of the way, this second group would surround the tent of the guardsmen. One of our people would have stopped by the tent and let us know what the Germans inside were doing. Two of the second four were to go inside. The guards would, at that time, be lying on their beds, unarmed. Their ammunition would probably be a short distance from them near the wall. All the guards in this tent would have to be killed outright with one press on a trigger for each; and if that didn't succeed, then one hand grenade would finish off the lot.

While this was going on, the third group of four would move forward and take positions alongside the Germans' canteen on the main roadway. They would have knives in their hands, so that if they met a guard on the way, they could finish him. This group's job shouldn't be difficult, because not once has a guard accompanied any of our people to the kitchen to fetch beer or to do any other errand; there would be nothing suspicious about Jews walking around.

Six of our people were given the duty of seeing that nothing looked suspicious, and that there would be no mention around the camp that there was something unusual going on; because there was always a guard on duty, and far be it from us to arouse his curiosity. If anything unplanned happened, or if there was any slight change in carrying out our plan, no one would have a chance to escape.

Then it was planned that all would be prepared so that at a certain signal, everyone would gather in the area of the tent of the guards who had been killed. Should anyone find any ammunition, they were to take it and arm themselves. Any who could, should also dress themselves in German uniforms and disappear. Those so armed and dressed would have enough time to get several kilometers away before the other guards would have discovered that all the guards on duty had been killed. This was our plan.

While all this was being said, the orchestra played, several people sang, and there were some group songs. Some people brought wood to bank the fires in the ovens. One of our guards ordered an armful of wood and commanded that it be brought to him at a certain place, so it would be ready to be taken at eleven into the bunker, where the oven was to remain heated all night. Everything went properly. From then on we had only to act and pray that we would carry our plan out to the letter.

I was to be contact man in the courtyard. I stood near the kitchen, making myself busy and following with one eye everything that the Germans were doing. Suddenly I saw one of the guards coming over; he wanted to enter. He looked as though he were going to open the gate. The two who were to annihilate him went up close to him, one holding in his hand a few pieces of wood. The second one had a pair of shoes hidden in his shirt. They had already notified the guard that they had a nice pair of shoes for him which they would bring over to him immediately, and the guard was pleased. At the same time, the second pair had to go out after another guard, so I hurried up to the second entrance. They came close to the entrance, which the second guard had to open for them. But there was no sign of the second guard. He must have been delayed.

Meanwhile the orchestra in the hut continued to play. A few men sang casually and their faces showed no excitement. The German cried out and I hurried over to the second entrance. I myself did not hear the outcry, but several men who were sitting in the tents immediately came into the court.

The second pair, who were ready to go out, came closer to the entrance when I told them that the guard had been annihilated. Nearby stood the guard, waiting for them to bring what they had promised. He casually opened the entrance. We knew we must not delay, not even for a mo-

234

ment; so we attacked him. At the same moment we heard shooting behind us.

It seemed that some Germans who slept in another tent also had heard the outcry of the guard, and they had reached for their ammunition and run outside. When they found out something was going on, they opened fire. One of the two men appointed to annihilate the second guard had a plowshare in his hand, with torches attached to it for setting fires. When the guard opened the entrance, he hit him in the face with the plowshare, and I knocked him down and knocked him out with a kick in the head with my hobnail shoes. He had time to call out, *Meine Herren, lasst mich leben!*" (My lords, let me live.) He lay stretched out near the entrance, and every one of the escapees who passed stepped on his face.

The first pair now turned their attention to the guard who stood between our tents and theirs. They came close to the guards' hut. One of the fellows threw the wood on the ground, and the other started to take the shoes from under his shirt. The guard started to take them away as though he were going to hide them in his hut. He was probably afraid someone would pass by and see how he allowed one of the prisoners to come too close to him. It was very strictly forbidden to allow a prisoner within arm's length.

Wood for the oven always had to be thrown behind the barbed wire, and not brought over to the oven. When the guard bent down to pick up his shoes, the fellow who carried the wood jumped on him and started to choke him but he had bad luck and didn't succeed in getting hold of his neck properly. The German started to yell. Both of them attacked him and he became silent immediately.

All of us escaped. First we turned toward the forest. But how could we find our colleagues? And shooting was going on behind us. I was sure that the road to the forest was blocked by the guards, so I turned in another direction, to the road going up to the mountains.

But anyone who thinks everyone tried to escape is mistaken. One Yehuda Goldenberg, previously a Polish soldier, didn't want to participate in this escape at all. After the meeting he undressed himself as usual and lay down to sleep. The others went over to him and asked, "Don't you know what is expected and what will happen?"

He answered, "I know, and God help you to have success in your escape. I hope you are privileged to see the end of all this so you can tell the world how our nation was exterminated. But I, where shall I go? To the city, to a bunker? Who will take me in? I haven't any friends or Aryan acquaintances who will receive me. Even to the forests, I cannot go. It would be useless. I'm not as young as you. I wouldn't be able to hold out. Besides, if I should join you I would hinder you, and you would fail because of me. I'm not so nimble on my feet any more, and because of me you would have to move slowly and you wouldn't leave me on the road. It's true that after you escape the guards will kill me, but it's better for me to be killed here tonight than to be caught on the road. Between ourselves, what have I to live for? My wife and my seven dear children were exterminated; and I, too, prepare to die." He added, "Good night to you! And a successful journey! I hope that God will keep you alive so you may see the end of this war. And I—I ask the favor of an easy death!" He turned his face away and closed his eyes.

I ran toward the mountain. It was dark, very dark. One person couldn't see the next. Behind us was the thunder of shots, and the sound of many exploding hand grenades. After a few steps I stumbled on some barbed wire hidden in the bushes. I fell, got up again and jumped over the blockade of barbed wire. I knew it well—for our own hands had built it. I was running when suddenly I heard some footsteps. I asked, "Who is there?" I was sure this wasn't a guard. A guard wouldn't use a flashlight.

From the bushes came the well-known voice of a colleague, Bok. He had been a waiter. He said, "It's I!"

I called him so he could come closer, so we could run together, because it's better if there are two. Suddenly a third joined us, Moshe Koren.

Now the three of us were running. From time to time we stumbled. At every step there was a hill or a hole. In the darkness we would fall on our faces, then help one another to get up and continue running. On the way we lost Koren. We went up the mountain, and lo, we were standing on a main road. Before us was a junction. One road led to Litzakovska and the other toward Winek.

We stood for a moment weighing which way to turn. I said, "We must go toward the forest."

But Bok argued and said, "We have to go toward the city, to where the Ghetto previously was. There, under the debris of the buildings, we can hide ourselves for a day; and toward evening we will start out for the forest."

But to go to the city one should know the road; and we didn't know which way to turn, to the right or to the left, forward or backward. We were sorry that we had lost Moshe Koren, because he knew the vicinity. In the end, we turned to the right toward Winek.

We had walked a little distance when we heard the echo of steps. My companion wanted to go back up the road, but I felt we must not; so we walked forward toward the sound. We could hear there was more than one person walking. And there was Moshe Koren, and with him Leizer Sandburg, who had been a driver.

So all four of us went on together, Koren leading because he knew the road. We were walking single file, toe to heel, and no one asked where we were going. Willingly we followed, and we were satisfied that we had a guide. We stumbled but we helped each other and held on to one another, walking in a row one behind the other, directing ourselves by sound in the darkness. We held our knives in our hands, ready to fight. Death to anyone who should try to hurt us. We would die but so would he.

Slowly we made our way to the outskirts of the village; and soon we were in the village. Whenever we heard footsteps, we lay down and waited until they moved away; afterwards we got up and continued. Soon we reached the suburb of Nashenya, opposite the Brocker factory. We walked on the side near the railway station, then along the railroad tracks to the stockyard.

Suddenly out of a booth came the manager. He asked, "Who is there?"

Koren answered. The manager called out, "Don't you know that it's forbidden to walk here? Turn around!"

"We are going back, "Koren said, and we retreated several steps.

"Who are you? Halt! Stop," he called out after a few moments.

"We," answered Koren.

"Who do you mean 'we'? Stop! I'm shooting!"

"Don't shoot! Because it's 'we'!" Koren repeated.

The manager of the railway station, when he saw that we were not stopping, started shooting; and we ran away. Koren and I jumped to the right, and the other two ran in the opposite direction the length of the railroad tracks. They were shot; they fell and they didn't get up.

I saw Koren turn to the right. I ran as far as the refinery fence. There I heard the guard calling because he had heard me running and I had stumbled against the barbed wire fence.

"Who is there?"

I stretched myself out on the ground, trying to make up my mind what to do. Where should I go? To the forest? By myself? If I went to the city and walked around in its streets, the first policeman would grab me, because upon my back was attached a big horn, a Jewish badge. Then I heard a whisper. Joyfully I called the name of my companion and after a moment, Koren came nearer. "Shall we proceed?" Koren asked.

"No," I answered. "Let's get our strength and wait for things to quiet down and until the guard of the railroad tracks calms down. Then we can go on our way." We sat and talked about our two unfortunate colleagues. Surely they were lost. Where should we go now, we asked each other.

We returned to the tracks and that time we turned towards Nashenya. Before us was the road. On one side it led to the city, on the other side to some villages. Koren suggested we should go by a certain direction to the city. "But how? This is the main road. Cars are always on the road, German military cars go back and forth constantly. Perhaps they have already telephoned from the camp to

Diehnstellar S.D., and already there may be guards at the entrance to the villages. But what other alternative do we have? Dead or alive!"

We were walking on the road. It was deserted and all was quiet. The waning moon lighted our way. Suddenly all the road was flooded with bright light. The headlights of a car came closer. Koren whispered. "We are lost!" He was cursing me because I had encouraged him to turn toward this side of the road.

"Don't pay any attention to the car. March with faith," I answered.

The car came closer. We took good hold of our knives, prepared to fight for our lives. We thought that our end had come. The car stopped for a moment, turned and disappeared.

We breathed freely. We hid ourselves behind some buildings and waited until the car had moved a way up the road. After a few minutes I went out to check on how far away the car was. Fear froze me. It was returning! Perhaps its passengers would want to check our documents? I retreated behind the building. I was sure that the car was coming closer, because its headlights were lighting up the road again. In the end it passed us by. We came out of our hideout and continued on our way.

It was a clear moonlit night, the moon mirrored in the puddles at the side of the road. Through the cracks of the curtained windows came little slits of light.

Inhabited buildings! How happy were those who lived there! They didn't know how lucky they were. If they knew about these two tired people, walking here in the street with bent heads, dirty, wet through, before them only death, not knowing where to turn! It would have been pure joy to us if we had been allowed to stay even in a dark cellar, if only for one night.

The barking of dogs reached our ears. Watchdogs for their sleeping owners. The whole city was fast asleep and the village clock rang twelve midnight. We were, we felt, walking into space, picking our feet up and setting them down in the same place. Meanwhile we were approaching Sultovia Bridge on Zamustinovska Street. Here we stood and looked for a long time. The prisoners had said to each other that we would meet here; but no one had come. Perhaps all had fallen on the way! Or perhaps they had already gathered here, and when they saw that we were delayed, they had gone on their way without us. We were alone, we two.

LEON VELITZKER